I'll Be Your Blue Sky

ALSO BY MARISA DE LOS SANTOS

The Precious One

Falling Together

Belong to Me

Love Walked In

By Marisa de los Santos and David Teague

Connect the Stars

Saving Lucas Biggs

I'll Be Your Blue Sky

Marisa de los Santos

HARPER LUXE
An Imprint of HarperCollins*Publishers*

FIRST HARPERLUXE EDITION

ISBN: 978-0-06-279143-6

Library of Congress Cataloging-in-Publication Data is available upon request.

18 19 20 21 22 ID/LSC 10 9 8 7 6 5 4 3 2 1

For Jennifer Carlson,
friend and agent,
who loved Clare Hobbes
from the very beginning

I'll Be Your Blue Sky

Chapter One
Edith

June 1950

It was what she would remember always: how the second she stepped inside, before she'd so much as taken her first full breath of new air, she was struck by the feeling—the understanding, the *certainty*—however improbable, that the house was Joseph. Not merely that it felt like something he would choose or that she saw his handiwork everywhere—fresh paint, thick as cream; refinished pine floors; green apples in a glass bowl—but that it *was* him, sturdy and open, light swooping in through every window, forthright and decent and kind. She would not have supposed that a house could be kind, but this one was.

It smelled like sawdust and lemon oil and reckless salt wind. The tile countertop was pale green edged in black. In the next room, two chairs—modern ones made of curved rosewood and with square gold cushions—faced the fireplace. Three tall windows ran along the back wall, each a lambent rectangle of outside world: emerald yard, iris sky, and a platinum flash that Joseph said was a canal leading out into the bay.

Edith stood still and straight in her going-away suit (even though they'd gone only a few miles down the road) and let herself be held by the house, like a firefly cupped between two careful hands. She felt Joseph waiting behind her, halfway inside the door, one foot on the smooth floor, one on the gray-painted boards of the front porch. He had not carried her over the threshold, knowing she would prefer to walk in and to see the place, for just this first time, alone.

They'd been married two hours earlier in a centuries-old, tiny country church with a clear Palladian window overlooking a bean field, a view Edith would not have expected to be beautiful but was, the breeze threading like fingers through the low rows of ruffled leaves. Edith would have married Joseph in the middle of that field or barefoot on the sand dunes or on a street corner with taxis honking their horns. She would have married him in her oldest dress. But as she'd stood in that church, she had been grateful to be in white lace, her skirt belled like the *Campanula carpatica* flowers from her childhood backyard. The dress; the window; the chapel's vaulted ceiling; the quiet voice of the rector; and Joseph's mother, radiant in her pew, smiling and weeping at the same time: all of it kindled the moment into something bright and splendid. All Edith needed was him, of course, but Joseph deserved splendor.

His mother, Anne, was the only wedding guest, although Joseph's friends could have filled the church and spilled out into the churchyard, into the old cemetery with its tilted stones, into the bean field. But he'd known that she would have no one, her father gone, her few close friends scattered far and wide. He hadn't even wanted his mother there for fear his bride, though long accustomed to motherlessness, would feel her father's absence—he'd been dead ten months—even more keenly. But Edith had insisted on his mother. Anne had loved Joseph unflaggingly his whole life, had written him a letter every day he'd been in Europe photographing the war and even after, when he'd stayed to, as he put it, tidy up. It seemed only just that she bear witness. More than just; the thing was impossible without her.

Edith explored the house, which was larger than she'd expected, bigger than most of the surrounding bayside cottages in this Delaware seaside town, a place

Joseph had visited for a week as a child the summer before his father died and had never forgotten. On the first floor, in addition to the kitchen and living room, there was a small bedroom and bath and a large closet that Joseph, with the help of a plumber, had converted into a darkroom. Upstairs, there were two more bedrooms, one big enough to serve double duty as an office, another bathroom, this one with an enormous claw-foot tub, and a small sitting room with a sofa and a squatty black woodstove polished to a shine.

Up a narrow flight of stairs was Joseph and Edith's bedroom: sun sifting drowsily through windows hung with rose-bouquet-printed barkcloth, a bed taking up most of the room, an oval braided rag rug on the wide plank floor at its foot. And everywhere hydrangeas, enough to make Edith gasp, great bunches billowing from vases on every surface: deep pink on one dresser, luna moth green on the other; light blue and mauve lacecap on the antique writing desk; a single, heavy purple pom-pom nodding from the sink in the bathroom; and next to the bed, a bouquet of bridal white. Edith smiled at the memory of Joseph early that morning, marching into the hotel restaurant with his shirt sleeves rolled up, gardening gloves stuffed into the pocket of his pants, and a sly smile. He had refused to explain his whereabouts, but now she imagined him at daybreak, clipping blooms, maybe even purloining them from people's yards, striding around town with armfuls of flowers, loading up his car with every shade of sunrise to decorate this room at the top of their house.

The house had been part of the proposal.

"I've found us a home, Edie, and now you really have to marry me so we can go live in it."

"We could live in it anyway," she'd said, tracing the outline of his lips with her forefinger. "We could be a tremendous scandal."

He had laughed and kissed her and told her all about it. About the house but also the canals—a network of them, like streets made of water—tranquil except for the occasional leaping fish or tiny, pulsing, gossamer sea nettle, barely there, a scrap of living creature like a floating whisper. About the salt marshes and inland bays, and, of course, the ocean.

"You and I have seen too much these past few years, Edie. You with losing your dad; me with the war and the tidying up afterward. We need fresh air, open water, sun rising out of the ocean every evening. We need the *ocean,* Edie. Can you imagine it?"

She just about could, but she had to ask, "I can see being there most of the year, but what about winter?

A beach town might be especially dreary in winter, with freezing wind coming off the water and gray, gray skies. What will we do then?"

Edith shut her eyes, dropped backward onto the bed, and remembered Joseph's face when she'd asked that question, surprised and bemused, his brow furrowed, as if the answer were obvious.

"Why, I'll be your blue sky," he'd said.

What could she do, what could anyone do with a man like that but marry him and live in his house near the ocean?

For a moment, her eyes still shut, Edith lay on her back in the center of her marriage bed inside the house that was Joseph—down to the banisters and the light switches and the fat stove and the writing desk slender legged as a cat—listening to the house, breathing in the clean perfume of it, and then she opened her eyes and, for the first time, saw that the ceiling was painted sky blue with here and there a wisp of white cloud, and she was certain that there had never been so much gratitude in the history of the world.

From down below, she heard a faint whine, which she knew must be the back door opening, so she jumped up off the bed to look out the center window. Joseph stood on the back lawn at the edge of the canal, his hands in his pockets, his wedding jacket slung over one arm. Edith tugged open the window and called out, "Joseph!"

He spun around and stared up at her, his face breaking into a broad smile.

"Hey!" he shouted.

"Oh, my darling Joseph. Thank you." It came out hoarse, too hushed for him to hear, so she cleared her throat and sang it, "Thank you!"

He opened out his arms and said, "Look at all this. Ours. Can you believe it?"

"Yes," she said, laughing. "Yes, I can!"

"Come down, Edie. Come down and see the rest!"

"Oh, my darling," she whispered once more before she wiped her eyes, kicked off her shoes, shimmied out of her stockings, and ran down to where he waited.

Chapter Two
Clare

Until Cornelia piped up with, "You know what? I never liked that iris, either. I mean, it was pretty enough—but bad, a truly bad, bad, low-down, dirty, and despicable iris," I was so busy composing a mental list of ten reasons to marry Zach that I hadn't even noticed I was shredding the poor thing to bits. Shredding the iris, I mean, not Zach, although I suppose you could argue that while frantically racking my brain for reasons to marry a man I was promised and slated to marry within thirty hours wasn't exactly ripping him to pieces, it wasn't exactly nice, either. In fact, I was fairly positive that it would break his heart if he knew. Especially since I got stuck after reason nine.

We—my mother, Viviana; my almost-mother, Cornelia Brown; and I—were making centerpieces at an outdoor table at the resort Zach had found for our wedding, a pearly, columned, historic dreamboat of a hotel sailing atop an oak-and-pine-studded crest of Blue Ridge. Purple mophead hydrangeas and lithe white irises listed in buckets at our feet. A swimming pool stretched out graciously before us—a fountain like a great hibiscus blossom sprouting from its center—and a swimming-pool-colored sky smiled dotingly down.

Zach had texted the weather forecast to me the night before: three straight days of seventy-two-degree highs, cloudless skies, and zero humidity. Nice weather by any standard; by June in southwestern Virginia standards, a minor meteorological miracle. Perfect wedding weather, which should have made me perfectly giddy. Instead, I found it unsettling, even creepy.

"What is this? Stepford, Connecticut? Brigadoon? Camazotz?" I'd grumbled to myself during my postbreakfast (French toast decorated with edible flowers) walk around the grounds. "Where's the humidity? Where are the damned mosquitoes?"

I dropped the rags of iris onto the tabletop, stared down at my hands, which were sticky as a murderer's, and sighed. It wasn't that it was hard to think up reasons why anyone would want to marry Zach. He was so generally, generically marriageable it was almost funny. Handsome, smart, hardworking. A law school star from a wealthy family. No criminal record. Good manners. Naturally curly hair. A golden boy if ever I'd seen one: wheat-colored curls, tawny brows and lashes, eyes the color of India pale ale. Even his car was gold. The man was a bona fide catch. Give him a chaise and four, an estate, and ten thousand pounds a year, and any Austen heroine would go stumbling over the countryside in her Regency heels to get to him.

No, if my task had been to list reasons why *anyone* should marry Zach, I could have reeled them off, lickety-split, and mangled no flowers in the process. But here at what was surely the eleventh hour—God, eleventh and a *half*—I was hell-bent on coming up with reasons why *I* should, a different matter entirely.

My mother dunked a paper towel into one of the flower buckets and handed it to me. I scrubbed zealously at my palms, as Cornelia and my mother looked on.

"Something on your mind, Lady Macbeth?" Cornelia said. She reached out and tugged on the paper towel until I relinquished it.

I shrugged. "Guess I'm just a little nervous."

"Completely normal," said my mother, briskly.

"Oh, yes," Cornelia said, nodding. "Classic, even. Prewedding jitters. Cold feet. Absolutely everyone gets them."

"Did you?" I asked.

Cornelia suddenly became occupied with poking a single iris into a hillock of hydrangea, narrowing her eyes, positioning the flower just so.

"You didn't, did you?" I asked.

"Oh. Well. Gosh. I . . ."

"Cornelia."

She gave me an apologetic smile and shook her head. "Nope. I was actually even a little impatient."

"A little?" said my mother, with a snort. "I know it was over a decade ago, but I seem to remember your trying to browbeat Teo into eloping with you even after you two had set a date *and* signed the catering contract."

I laughed. For my professional party-planner mother, the catering contract marked the point of no return.

"I may have done that. Once or twice." Cornelia laughed. "Per day, every day leading up to our wedding, including at our rehearsal dinner. But I'd known him since I was four years old. It was time to get that show on the road."

"What about you, Mom? Jitters?"

"Oh, not with Gordon, but remember, I was twenty years older than you are now. With my marriage to your father, though, God, yes. Jitters upon jitters."

"Your marriage to my father lasted all of three years," I pointed out.

"Three years and nine months, actually. I just kicked him out after three."

"Oh, much better. Very reassuring."

Simultaneously, my mother's and Cornelia's faces softened into looks of concern. Oh, those two women. Suddenly, all I wanted in the world was to sit there with them, blessed by the beam of their gaze, watching the sun glance off their glossy heads of hair, and tucking flowers into other flowers, all day. Or for the next three days. Or for a lifetime. Sit, bless, beam, glance, tuck. Yes, a lifetime would be good.

"Darling," said my mother, quietly, "do you need reassuring?" just as Cornelia reached across the table and pressed her hand over mine.

"Of course not," I said, my eyes filling with tears. "It's just—" A sob snagged in my throat.

"It's all right," said my mother. "Whatever it is it's all right."

"Of course it is, sweetheart," said Cornelia. "Never fear."

I planted my elbows on the picnic table and covered my face with my hands.

"Please," I said from behind my hands. "Just—"

"What?" said Cornelia. "We'll do anything."

I flapped my hand in their direction. "Talk!" I squeaked.

"About what?" asked my mother.

"Anything!"

We sat, tinsel threads of birdsong drifting and tangling in the air around us. Finally, Cornelia said, "I'm calling it. Time of death 9:41 A.M."

Through a gap in my fingers I saw her holding the remains of the iris. She lifted it to her nose.

"Well, that's interesting, Viviana," she said.

"What?" asked my mother.

"This flower has been lacerated, mutilated, has suffered devastating internal injuries . . ."

"And external," supplied my mother.

"*Profound* external injuries," agreed Cornelia.

"She was twisting it," observed my mother, "in addition to ripping it."

"I saw," said Cornelia. "The thing is horribly injured and irreversibly dead. And yet it still smells lovely."

"Like jellyfish."

"Precisely," said Cornelia.

"Even when they're dead and washed up on the beach, they'd sting you as soon as look at you."

"They would."

"Oh, and what about that mad dog in *To Kill a Mockingbird*?" said my mother. "The one Atticus shoots and then says is—"

"Just as dangerous dead as alive," finished Cornelia, grimly. Through my fingers, I watched her nod. "Actually, I looked that up once."

"I thought maybe you had."

"And what I discovered is that the rabies virus can live on for months in the body of a dead animal in freezing temperatures."

"But it never gets that cold in Alabama," said my mother, skeptically.

Cornelia smacked the tabletop. "Exactly what I said to myself! Alabama is such a warm state that it isn't even that cold in February, which is when Atticus shot the dog. However, even in warm temperatures, the virus can live for hours and can be transmitted as long as the saliva is still wet!"

"Saliva is such an unappealing word. And I wouldn't say that that accounts for the statement that the dog was as dangerous dead as it had been when it was alive and staggering toward them down the street."

"No. But I suspect Atticus exaggerated in the interest of protecting his children."

"That would be just like him," said my mother. "Oh! And then there's the praying mantis."

"Ah, yes," said Cornelia, with relish, shifting into a nature show narrator's voice. "During the mating act, the female savagely bites the head off the male, and, undaunted by his headless state, he continues to thrust—"

"Okay!" I said. I took my hands away from my face. Cornelia handed me a paper towel, and I dabbed at my eyes.

"Was that possibly *not* the best example to bring up at the moment?" asked my mother.

I smiled. "I'm physically incapable of laughing right now, but I do appreciate the effort."

We sat together in the lemony morning light, not speaking, my mother and Cornelia with their hands clasped on the tabletop, the centerpiece making temporarily suspended, and for one lovely, breathing moment, *everything* felt suspended, as if we three, the birdsong, the crisp, weightless air, and the wealth of flowers hung outside of time, so that it wasn't the day before my wedding or any day. No irrevocable catering contracts, no hordes of guests arriving in waves over the next twenty-four hours, no gifts amassing like tires in a junkyard.

A tall, thin elderly woman in a loose chambray dress and green gardening clogs walked by. Leaning on a cane, with a book tucked under her free arm, she navigated carefully across the grass, her eyes on the ground, and then just as she got to where we sat, she raised her head—her white hair starry as dandelion fluff in the morning sun—and smiled at me.

"Courage, dear heart," she said in a ringing, surprisingly young-sounding voice, then dropped her eyes, and walked on. We all watched her go, patient step after patient step.

"Thank you!" I called out to her. She paused, shifted her book to her other arm, and raised her fist in solidarity.

Once she'd disappeared, my mother and Cornelia stared at me, questioningly.

"*The Voyage of the Dawn Treader*," I said.

"What?" said my mother.

"Oh!" said Cornelia. "Aslan!"

"When he comes to Lucy in the form of an albatross," I said. "'Courage, dear heart' is what he tells her."

"Good grief, how you loved those books," said my mother.

The gardening clog woman's voice came back to me, silver as a tossed coin: *Courage, dear heart.* Courage. *Courage.* Fine. Who was I to disobey Aslan?

"I was making a list," I explained, and once I'd eked out those first five words, the rest came tumbling faster and faster.

"I'm not proud of it. But I honestly thought it would be easy. That's why I started it because if it were as easy as I thought it was going to be, I'd know we'd be okay. I guess it was kind of a test. God, that sounds awful. Not like a math test or a trial. More like, what's it called? Litmus. Still bad, I know. The point is I expected the reasons to just stack up neatly—*click, click, click*. But then I got stuck, and even some of the items I was dead sure about seemed, I don't know, flimsy? But the worst part is that the more I worked on the list, the more I realized how terribly, awfully much was riding on it. Which is so wrong and stupid. The whole thing reeks of betrayal, not only making the list, not only not being able to finish it, but being *desperate* to finish it. Because I've already said yes, and this ship is smack in the middle of the ocean, no getting off, and Zach's a good person; he deserves better than a stupid list or than a-a-a fiancée who would make one. And listen to me: I can hardly even get my mouth around the word *fiancée*! What in God's name will I do with *wife*?"

I stopped, panting and hot faced, panic charging at me from every direction. I braced myself for the bone-shaking impact of it, but before it arrived, my mother and Cornelia exchanged one glance—blue eyes locked on brown—the tiniest movement, but you could almost hear the thunderclap of it, feel the earth shift on its axis: their forces joining. On my behalf.

"You're a natural list maker, Clare. As soon as you

could write, lists, lists, lists," said my mother, calmly. "It's who you are."

"But this is different," I said.

"Would you like to share the list with us?" said Cornelia.

"Now?" As if another time would be more fitting.

"You don't have to, but it might help to haul that puppy out of your head and into the world. We can swear to reserve all judgment, if you like." Cornelia lifted her right hand and slapped the left onto an imaginary bible. My mother did the same.

"Maybe I want judgment," I said, twisting my hair. "I can't tell. I've lost perspective."

"We can play the judgment by ear," said my mother. "Judgment as needed."

"The items are in no particular order," I warned.

"So much the better," said Cornelia.

"Wait," said my mother. "Just to clarify: What is this a list of, exactly?"

"It's a list of ten reasons why I, specifically—not just anyone but specifically I, Clare Hobbes—should marry Zach."

"Got it," said my mother. "Shoot."

"Let 'em rip," said Cornelia.

I cleared my throat.

"One: he makes a perfect egg over easy." A goofy flutter of a laugh escaped me. "I told you they were in no particular order."

"Oh, I don't know about that. Over easy *is* your favorite," said my mother.

"And he stripes them with sriracha!" I said.

"Stripes!" said Cornelia. "How incredibly thoughtful."

"Two: he really, really wants me to. Zach wants me to marry him more than anyone has ever wanted anything from me in my life."

"Are you sure?" asked Cornelia, solemnly and as if she had someone specific in mind. I could guess who the someone might be, and for a second, I faltered.

"Zach says he will never have a happy day for the rest of his life if we aren't together. Not 'I can't imagine having a happy day,' but 'I will never have a happy day,' with this total assurance. No one has ever said that to me."

"Ah," said Cornelia. "Yes, I can see how maybe no one would have."

"Three: anytime he goes to someone's house or apartment, he takes a gift. And I'm not just talking about to fancy dinners, but on any occasion. Baseball-watching parties. Study sessions. Board game nights. Drop-by-for-a-beer kind of occasions. And not just flowers or a bottle of wine. But action figures. A funny T-shirt. A copy of the *New Yorker* with a Post-it marking an especially good article. A giant bag of gumballs. A garden gnome."

"How completely adorable!" said my mother, and Cornelia clapped her hands.

What I did not add was that I knew what all the gifts were because, about a month after we'd begun dating, Zach had mostly stopped going places without me. If he were invited over to a friend's house, he would ask me to come, and if I declined, he'd smile, shrug, and stay with me. And if I were invited somewhere, he would ask to come along, so charmingly that I would forget how to say no. Eventually, because it was just easier, I accepted it all, asking people ahead of time he if could come, saying yes to him even when I was tired or had too much homework or loathed watching baseball (I always loathed watching baseball). My friend Hildy declared it hideously dysfunctional and took to kidnapping me, sneaking up on me at the library or as I was coming out of a class and whisking me off to a restaurant or a bar or to her apartment. I felt bad about not telling Zach, worse about outright lying to him, but time alone with Hildy was far beyond a guilty pleasure. It ranked up there with food and sunlight and books.

"Four: he sincerely tries to reduce his carbon footprint. He has a low-emission car but rides his bike or walks whenever possible, even in the freezing cold;

checks his tire inflation obsessively; drives no more than five miles over the speed limit, ever, even on the highway; never eats beef; consumes only locally produced food. He actually taught himself how to *can*."

"Amazing," said my mother.

"Impressive," said Cornelia. "Although I do worry about botulism."

I didn't say that no matter how a conversation with Zach about climate change began (fracking, Hummers, a documentary on polar bears [there being no sadder sight on Earth than a starving polar bear, all baggy skin, huge paws, and haunted eyes]), it would end with an exhortation to save the world for our future children and their children and their children's children, my stomach backflipping harder with each generation. Zach with his long line of offspring conga dancing relentlessly into the future, while I could not for the life of me—not after an extraordinarily good day with him or a few glasses of wine—envision even a single baby.

"Five: if we're in a fight, he won't walk away or go to bed or hang up until it's resolved."

"Oh, that's a good one," said my mother. "Going to bed mad is wretched, like trying to sleep with sand in your sheets or with a possible gas leak in your boiler."

I had to laugh at this; only my mother would equate

the risk of death by carbon monoxide with the discomfort of sand.

"I agree," I said. "Who could ever marry someone who would let a fight just dangle there overnight?"

Cornelia raised her hand. "I did."

"You're kidding," I said. "Teo? But he's the best person in the world." It was the God's honest truth.

"Yes, but he believes in the restorative power of silence, walking away for a while, calming down, looking inward," Cornelia said, "which is obviously incredibly annoying."

"Someone should smack him," growled my mother.

"Don't think I haven't come close. More than that, though, he's got this *faith*."

"In God?" I ask.

"In us—which seems to amount to the same thing for him." Cornelia rolled her eyes. "He trusts in our ability to weather any storm so much that sometimes he actually forgets we're fighting. He'll just walk into a room where I'm fuming and start telling me a story about how it's so windy that he just watched our neighbor chase his trash can lid all the way down the street. And I start laughing and forget that I loathe him and everything he stands for."

"The rat bastard," said my mother.

"Poor Cornelia," I said. "Number six: Zach never tailgates, ever, no matter how slowly the car in front of him is going."

"Because the driver in front of you could be anyone—an organ donor, a war hero, a man who's just lost his best friend, a kid with a new license doing her best," said Cornelia. "Not tailgating acknowledges the mystery and humanity of strangers. It's one of those small habits that speaks volumes."

"Like how someone treats waiters," said my mother.

"That was number seven," I said.

"Well, bravo, Zach," said my mother.

"Eight: he laughs at my jokes."

"Huge," said Cornelia. "Colossal. Immeasurable."

"Nine: he sings all the time, even though he has a horrific voice."

"Lovely," my mother pronounced.

"Really?" I said. "Not a little—flimsy?"

"He's at home in his own skin," said my mother. "Nothing flimsy about that."

I knew what she meant, but I also knew if I were honest with myself—and when it came to Zach it seemed I could be somewhat less than absolutely honest—including his singing on my list mostly qualified as wishful thinking. I might have declared it the exception that proved the rule, although I've never been sure enough about the meaning of that phrase to employ it with confidence. In any case, despite his goodness and goldenness and aforementioned obvious marriageability, Zach had never struck me as comfortable being Zach. Taut, edgy, a man of fidgeting hands and rustling energy, he was the kind of person who said something and then watched for your reaction, ready to revise, rephrase, backtrack, but so deftly that you might not even notice.

"And that's where I got stuck," I said. "Hence the iris."

"A good, solid list nonetheless," declared my mother.

"I know," I said. And good and solid was, well, good. Also solid. What it wasn't was luminous. Or transcendent. But I didn't say this out loud.

"It's true that nine isn't ten," observed Cornelia, "but it almost is."

"Oh!" My mother pointed at me with both fingers. "The book thing!"

A shiver crept over my arms. I knew exactly what she meant.

"The thing he does with the books!" expanded my mother. "The thing you told me about."

"Zach does something with books, and you forgot to put it on your list?" said Cornelia. "That's doesn't sound like you, Clare."

"I didn't forget," I said.

"No?" My mother tipped her blond head to the side and eyed me.

"Whenever he sees me reading a book," I said, slowly, "he buys it and reads it, too."

"So you can talk about it together!" said my mother. "Share in the experience."

But one glance at Cornelia's face told me she understood.

"Every book?" she asked, quietly. "When you don't ask him to?"

I nodded and watched the same shiver that had crawled up my arms ripple over her scalp. She slid her fingers through her boy-cropped hair.

"What?" said my mother.

"I don't know," I said. "It's hard to explain."

"The inside of a book is a private space," said Cornelia. "Someone barging in uninvited is—" She shivered again. "Every book? Really?"

"Sometimes, I hide them from him," I confessed. "I stick them in the trunk of my car, in the spare tire compartment, and go get them only when he's not around."

"Of course you do," she said, waggling the ruined iris contemplatively. "And he wants to talk to you about them afterward? All of them?"

"I don't have the heart to tell him no," I said. "He's just so, um, eager." Dogged is what I'd almost said. Obsessive. "Not so much to tell me what he thinks or to argue but to know what I think. In detail. He asks question after question. Sometimes—"

"Sometimes, what?" asked my mother.

"Sometimes, I think he won't be satisfied until he climbs inside my head and lives there." My laugh after I said it sounded limping and fake even to me, and when I got my nerve up to look at Cornelia and my mother, I could tell they weren't fooled, either. Worry bracketed my mother's eyes and mouth, while Cornelia's expression bordered on horrified.

"You know what, though?" my mother said at last. "I'll bet he has no idea that he's barging into your inner life and leaving his footprints all over it. I'll bet he's just trying to be nice. Trying too hard, obviously, or going about it the wrong way, but still truly trying."

And—*whoosh*—there it was. Number ten, bursting out of the darkness. Hallelujah.

"That's it!" I cried and threw my arms into the air in a V for Victory.

"Number ten?" said my mother.

"It's an essential fact of Zach," I said. "Which is maybe why I overlooked it the first time around; it's too obvious. I mean, I'd never claim to know what the *central* essential fact of another person was because that's overstepping, but if I ever *did* decide to make a claim like that, I'd say his is this: he tries so hard to be good."

A tiny pause riddled with birdsong. Then:

"Ah!" said my mother. "Well, there you go!"

"Good is good!" said Cornelia. "List complete!"

They were the very picture of cheerful supportiveness, their inflection, the corners of Cornelia's twinkling cat's eyes and of my mother's crescent moon smile all tipping appropriately upward. But I knew their faces. If I had a list of faces I knew best in the world, theirs would make the top five. And what I read in them now was concern.

"Okay," I said, sighing. "Just say it."

"It's only that, well—" said Cornelia. "Does he have to try *very* hard?"

"Yes!" I said. "But that's what makes it so beautiful! It's hard and he does it anyway. I told you how his mother died when he was a baby, and he grew up with that horrible father (sorry to speak ill of the dead but the man was a nightmare) and that mean older brother. Even his uncles and cousins are awful. All those cold, stone-faced, judgmental men. Can you even imagine growing up like that?"

"It sounds difficult," said my mother.

"Beyond difficult," I said. "It warps you. Wait, that

sounds bad. Zach isn't warped, but goodness has to be something he chooses. It's not a knee-jerk no-brainer for him the way it is for people who grew up loved every second of their lives."

I heard the note of contempt in my voice, contempt for the consistently loved, the thoughtlessly thoughtful, and even in my worked-up state, I knew I couldn't let that stand. My voice went tender. "And yes, I'm one of those people, and I'm grateful. To both of you especially and to Teo and Gordon and everyone else. All I mean is that goodness might not always be Zach's first impulse, and sometimes he gets it wrong, but he always feels terrible afterward and scrambles to make up for his mistakes."

"Does he often get it wrong?" asked my mother, evenly.

I flashed on his face, still and shadow-carved, his eyes flat as glass. A "shut up" like a slap. Mean laugh scything toward me out of nowhere.

"Not often at all," I said. "And he's so sorry afterward."

"All right. But about his having to try so hard . . . Now, don't get mad," began Cornelia. "I just want to understand. Wouldn't it be easier—"

"To be with someone effortlessly kind and good?" I said.

"Even naturally kind people struggle with it sometimes," said Cornelia. "But yes."

"Don't you see, though? I love how much he wants to be different from the rest of his family. He could so easily have gone down the same road as the others, but he refused. He refuses all the time, every day, as best he can. That takes courage, I think, to fight what comes easiest to you. And he says I make him want to try even more."

Cornelia stood up, walked around behind me, looped her scrawny arms around me, and held on hard. "Oh, darling Clare, girl made of sunshine, of course you do."

I held on back. Cornelia was a tiny person, with a little angled face and child's wrists. One of my hands covered both of hers. But when she held you, you felt instantly stronger and also like a bird in a nest.

"His sister disappearing the way she did," said my mother, shaking her head. "That kind of loss changes a family forever."

When Zach was ten, on a summer night, his tempest-haired, shimmering, rebellious eighteen-year-old sister, Rosalie-called-Ro, who had been his only mother for most of his life, vanished from their family's house in Northern Michigan. No note. No good-byes. Not even a fight with her father to explain her disappearance, even though there had been many, many fights before that. Just her car parked at the lip of the inland lake near their summerhouse, the water lapping the front tires, the keys still in the ignition. Local police investigated, dredging the lake while Zach looked on, a fact I had been horrified to learn. But they never found Ro. Everyone assumed she had run away to California (a place she'd never visited but worshipped, plastering the walls of her room with photos of beaches and deserts, the Hollywood sign, the Golden Gate Bridge) or else had gotten drunk and drowned in some other body of water of which there were many nearby.

And once the authorities had given up the search, despite his virtually unlimited resources, financial and otherwise, Zach's father had refused to look for her or to allow anyone else to look for her. "She'll come home when she's hungry," he said. But she never did, and Zach's older brother, Ian, their father, and the rest of the family simply erased her, until eventually no one even said her name, not in front of their father or anywhere else. Zach's father wrote her out of his will, paid a stranger to box up and give away her belongings, disappeared her as surely as if he'd lit a match and burned her right out of the family picture. I'd immediately assumed it was because he was heartbroken at the loss of her, but Zach said no, that was giving the man credit for heart he didn't have. She was the bad, ungrateful child;

the family was better off, his father said. Still, I understood that her absence, that smoking, black-edged, wild-child-shaped hole, was at the center of all their lives.

"His father was pretty gruesome even before, but Zach thinks there might have been hope for his brother, Ian, if she'd stayed. Now, there's only hope for him," I said, then added, "A lot of hope, though. At least, I think so."

"I'll bet you're right, sweetheart," said my mother.

"So?" said Cornelia. "List complete?"

I nodded.

My mother waggled my poor broken-down iris. "Pay your last respects, and let's get back to these everlasting centerpieces."

"Adios, iris!" I said, and my mother tossed it over her shoulder.

"Now then," she said, taking up a centerpiece-in-progress. "Just to refresh your memories: you put a few spikes of iris into each hydrangea bouquet, placing the irises so that they stick up a bit from the hydrangeas, as if the white flowers are butterflies that have just landed on the purple. If you stick the irises too deeply into the hydrangeas, all will be lost."

"All?" I asked, smiling.

"All," said my mother, sternly. "So remember: *butterfly effect.*"

And—boom—there he was with his sudden white smile and careless hair, casting his rangy shadow across the picnic table: Deveroux Tremain. Cornelia's science-loving stepson. My friend for the past four years; my boyfriend for the five years before that, although *boyfriend* had always felt like too fluffy a word for what Dev had been to me. Starting at the age of thirteen, I had loved him so truly and easily and thoroughly that for five years, "in love with Dev" was my ordinary state, and it was only later, when we shifted—jarringly, painfully—to friendship, that I recognized it as a state of grace.

We were fifteen the first time he tried to explain chaos theory to me. It was late June of the first entire summer I spent at Cornelia and Teo's house in Wilmington, Delaware. I'd spent chunks of summers at their house before, along with some spring and fall breaks, and at Christmastime, they would drive to Virginia where I lived with my mother in the same neighborhood as Cornelia's and Teo's parents.

Cornelia had come into my life when I was eleven, although it's far more accurate to say that I came into hers. Fell. Plummeted. A stunned, reeling, heartbroken child plunging headlong and out of nowhere into her urban, single-woman life of coffee shops and black-and-white movies and late nights whirling with witty conversation, and whom, without questioning or even stopping to think, she had reached out and caught. In the space of a few days my bipolar mother had had a breakdown and my estranged father had died, and, reflexively, Cornelia pulled love around me like a coat, tugged it shut, and did up the buttons, as if I belonged to her. And so I did.

Dev did, too, to her and to Teo, the father he'd discovered when he was thirteen. Between Dev and his mother, Lake, Cornelia and Teo, Cornelia's and Teo's parents, their brothers and sisters, my mother and me, we were a family, a sprawling, messy, glorious one, expanding like a galaxy over the years to include my stepfather, Gordon; Lake's boyfriend, Bruno; Cornelia's brother Toby's wife, Ella; Cornelia's brother Cam's husband, Niall; and all manner of scrumptious children, including Toby's son, Jasper; Cornelia's sister Ollie's son, Charlie; and Cornelia and Teo's children, Rose and Simon, whom I loved beyond description.

That first full summer at Cornelia's house returns to me in sparkling scraps, sensory flashes: backyard nights needle-pricked with fireflies; *clonk* of a basketball; my hands sliding under Dev's T-shirt and up his back; *chit-chit-chit* of a sprinkler; the fragrance of sunscreen, citronella, chlorine on Dev's skin; slap of playing cards on porch boards; the little matching valleys above Dev's collarbones; shaving of moon resting on a rooftop; Dev's slate-blue eyes; lumpy ground under my shoulder blades, my hand in Dev's while the Perseid streaked the sky; and Dev at Cornelia's kitchen table explaining chaos theory, the butterfly effect, his hands tracing "the sensitive dependence on initial conditions" in the air, his face the most alive thing I'd ever seen. It's why I'd ask him about it, to see his face do that, but after a while, I fell hard for the idea itself, and for weeks afterward saw large and distant consequences in every slight motion: butterfly wings, yes, but also the flick of a squirrel's tail, the snap of a branch under my foot, Dev's quick over-the-shoulder glance at me when we rode our bikes. That Dev could brush my bare shoulder with his mouth and kick up wild weather years and miles away felt equal parts amazing and inevitable.

We weren't in love anymore, but the thought of my friend Dev worked its own miniature butterfly effect, took the tension out of my backbone, and the day was suddenly not creepily picture-perfect but exactly the right amount of nice. I shut my eyes and felt the whole of the blue sky unfurling like a sheet under my breastbone. When I opened my eyes, Cornelia was smiling at me.

"The sensitive dependence on initial conditions," she said. "He always lost me at the math. But until then, I was right there with him."

"So was I," I said.

Chapter Three
Edith

October 1949

It wasn't the presence of dead, beautiful things that broke her; nor was it those glass eyes, pair after lightless pair. It wasn't even the fact that her father would have worshipped this place, would have stood in the octagonal rotunda, hat pressed to heart, shy and devout as a pilgrim; she had only to close her eyes to see him there, sun—swirled with galaxies of dust—falling like snow through the domed ceiling's oculus. No, what did it, knocked the breath from her body, were the labels, humble white rectangles in glass display cases, each offering its tiny, hard-won piece of truth: the common and binomial names of the bit of life next to it—iridescent beetle; dried fern; moth, fat bodied, wings decked with eyes—and the date and location of its finding.

It was October. In March, her father had suffered his first stroke. His neighbor, Gladys Polk, had found him lying on his side on the shore, his sketchbook ruined, his slack right cheek pressed into the spring thaw mud, and Edith had left her nursing job in Pittsburgh to move back into the little house in Connecticut, near Long Island Sound. He'd had the second stroke in June, more ravaging than the first. In mid-August, he had died, not peacefully. And yes, it was the end of suffering, the end of weakness, drooling, spoon feedings, and—so much worse than all the rest—his wild-eyed, fruitless clawing after words and memories, but, to her shock, the end of all this brought Edith nothing but intractable pain. She imagined she felt like a person struck by lightning. Worse than the grief was her shame that she couldn't even be relieved for him, a state of affairs that didn't last only because, eventually, nothing was worse than the grief. It became everything, every waking minute (if she could be said to be awake) of every day, an arid, tearless, terrible mourning.

She never left the house, slogging from room to room through the thick fog of quiet. Sometimes, it choked her, physically, the absolute lack of her father's footsteps, his voice, although really the house was hardly quieter than during all the years they had lived in it, just the two of them. A slow-moving, deliberate, soft-spoken man with a hungry mind. A child who shadowed him, asking questions.

He had been a high school biology teacher, a good one, but she'd always known his heart wasn't in the classroom. It was in the marshes and woods surrounding their house, in mosses and skeletons, nests and tracks, calls and songs. They could spend an hour watching dragonflies, the hovering and darting, the sudden exquisite hairpin turns, her father explaining in a near whisper how each of the four wings is controlled by separate muscles. He taught her how to use the net, the killing jar, how to spread and pin and label. Schmitt boxes with hinged lids were stacked in every room, meticulously organized.

Every bit of it felt holy, but it was the labeling she most cherished. She stayed still while he wrote, her breath held in a prayer that his hand would be steady, the tiny printing clean and clear. She recognized these moments for what they were: love, what else but love. Love in the painstaking handwriting. Love in his recitation of the Latin names and her solemn echoing of them, their own private call-and-response. Love, too, in walking through the woods, squatting side by side at a tidal pool. Love—oh, so much—in his teaching her how to put together a crow's skeleton, the reverent naming of the parts, her fingers handling the precious, hollow bones.

One day in September, a month after she'd buried him, Edith failed for an hour to inflate her lungs properly, as if she'd used up all the air in the house, so she tore open the front door and reeled out into the daylight, heart banging, chest burning, thoughts unspooled. An hour's walk along the shoreline—every stone and reed and bird track an affront, the sheen on the water brutal as a punch—and she knew without doubt that it was possible to die of grief.

Acting on pure instinct, she ran back to the house and cleaned it from top to bottom, a task that took a week. She organized and packed away her father's papers without reading them, her father's clothes without so much as pressing a shirt to her cheek. The refrigerator alone—ripe with rotting food—took hours. Scrubbing left her hands raw and cramped, her knees black and blue, but it reminded her that she was a body instead of just a ransacked heart and a flailing brain, and if she did not exactly want to live, she at least wanted to stay alive, to walk upright, keep the blood fanning its steady current through her veins. Not to be dead just yet was as far as her hope could reach. But it was something.

That night, Edith called Doris Cole, a nurse she knew

who had taken a job at a hospital in Washington. Edith did not particularly want Washington or Doris, but all that mattered was getting away. She didn't want a job, either, at least not immediately. She would sell her father's house, her only inheritance, and everything in it. She would donate to her father's school the Schmitt boxes with their carefully labeled specimens. If she could share rent with Doris and if she lived as frugally as she usually did, she calculated that her money could tide her over for at least six months. She imagined walking streets with names she'd never heard; she imagined anonymous edifices, monuments, milky stone and plate glass. No coppery water's-edge smell, no cordgrass or cattails or cormorants. Despite her indifference to Doris, when Edith heard her familiar chirpy voice on the phone saying, yes, good gracious, come, affection for the woman seized her so that she could barely eke out a thank-you.

Once there, Edith avoided the Potomac as best she could, glad that the famous cherry trees wouldn't tempt her, having relinquished their clouds of blossom to the Tidal Basin mud months earlier. Skirting the monuments, which struck her as forbidding, she immersed herself in art, something her father had never cared for, some days wandering distractedly through the galleries, catching mere color and shape with her peripheral vision, other days standing before a single painting for so long she seemed to enter it, the world around her dimming, the conversation blurring to hum. Although her father had never taken her to church, she felt most moved by the religious paintings: Mary's deep blue robes and whisper-frail hands in Van Eyck's *Annunciation;* the peacock perched like an angel on the stable roof, a kneeling man touching, with heartbreaking gentleness, the tiny foot of Christ in the *Adoration of the Magi* tondo.

But after two weeks, despite her better judgment, the Natural History building drew her irresistibly. Even so, she scrupulously kept to the unfamiliar. Stegosaurus skeleton like a giant puzzle. Lions and giraffes, looking startlingly alive, that Teddy Roosevelt had brought back from his African expedition. The great fossil whale, *Basilosaurus,* suspended from the ceiling in the Hall of Extinct Monsters.

And then, despite all her carefulness, to be undone by little white rectangles in glass cases.

When her knees buckled, he caught her. It was no cinematic swoon; she did not arch like a willow branch or rest lightly in his arms like a bouquet of lilies. She went down hard and sudden, and he hooked her under the armpits—so roughly it left bruises—just before she hit the floor. If she had had the capacity for anything but sorrow, she would have been mortified by the sounds she'd made, primitive and raw and racking, as if every pent-up sob from the last month had torn itself free from the center of her body. He half carried, half dragged her to a bench, and she turned toward him and shuddered against his chest, her fists gripping and ungripping the fabric of his shirt. His arms went around her as automatically as a mother's, but he didn't stroke or pat or press her to him. He simply held, until her weeping stammered, guttered, and went out, finally, all at once, like a flame; then, he let go.

She drew away, leaned backward against the bench, and laid the backs of her hands against her closed eyes. When she could speak, she meant to apologize, but what came out instead was, "What a way to begin," a fact that would only mortify her later that evening and that she would chalk up to being shaken and confused. Joseph would always insist that she *knew*, somehow, on some gut level, and she would argue that, with all her vast inexperience, she was the last person to instinctively recognize love. Still, it was odd.

But there in the museum, Joseph didn't point out the oddness or tell her not to think twice about falling into his arms like a sack of rocks. He handed her his handkerchief and said, "I think we should go see the Lincoln Memorial," and maybe because she was too exhausted or too startled or maybe—as Joseph forever believed—it was because she acknowledged—without knowing why or how—the inevitability of *them,* she said, "Well, yes, all right. I haven't seen it yet."

In the cool, pale, columned space, with Lincoln watching over them, noble as God, but still touchingly human with his crooked tie and open coat, like a man resting for a moment on a park bench or in an armchair, she found her grief rearranging itself, moving to the edges of her mind enough for her to begin to speak, more calmly than she could have imagined possible even an hour ago. She talked about her father, his life and death, and Joseph listened.

Chapter Four
Clare

Almost before I knew it was Zach, I knew he was stressed. It was there in his bouncing half jog, the way he brandished a giant bouquet like a sword over his head; it flickered around him like an aura. And even though *stressed* was much too mild a word for what Zach was, for the state that could overtake him like a fever, it was the one we always used. As the child of a bipolar parent, even one as successfully medicated as my mother, I sometimes wondered whether Zach's moodiness was something more than moodiness. The one time I'd tried to gently broach the subject, he'd snapped at me and then deflated to a blank sadness that lasted so long, I'd finally apologized—almost entirely sincerely—and taken back what I'd said—much less sincerely—and I never mentioned it again.

But the way he'd pull vivacity over the surface of his anxiety like a crazily colored tarp never quite stopped freaking me out. For instance, I knew that when he got near enough for me to see him in detail, his cheeks would be fuchsia, his eyes bright, his hands restless, his laugh full of blazing sunshine; he would possibly make an extravagant gesture, like dropping to one knee to present me with the flowers. He would almost definitely call me "gorgeous." And I'd be torn, as always, between wanting to run far, far away and wanting to wrap him in my arms and keep him safe forever.

Zach didn't drop to one knee. Instead, he caught me up in a hug that lifted me clean off the ground and spun me around, no easy feat, since at five foot nine, I'm a mere two inches shorter than he is. The spinning made me feel ridiculous, like an actress in a gum commercial, but, once I was back on the ground, to make up for not appreciating his romantic gesture, I nestled my face into his neck and kissed it.

"Hey, gorgeous," he said, pulling back a couple of inches and grinning so hard a muscle twitched in his cheek. With one finger, I touched the twitching spot.

"Hello, you," I said.

He handed me the bouquet. "I realize giving you flowers right now is like bringing coals to Newcastle, but I wanted you to have your favorite."

Favorite. Before I even glanced down into the heavy, brown paper, ribbon-tied cone, I knew what I would find, and sure enough, there they were: twenty-four waxy blooms, splayed open like hands, freckled, edged in white, and as pink as the flush flooding Zach's neck. Stargazer lilies.

Months ago, Zach had asked me what my favorite flower was. The question had been part of one of Zach's I-want-to-know-everything-about-you-Clare sprees and had come sandwiched between "What was your field hockey number in high school?" and "What is your earliest memory?" I'd answered those two honestly (eleven and my mother singing to me while bathing my fingers in ice water after I'd grabbed a bee when I was three years old), but I'd lied about the flower. It wasn't the first time I'd done that: coolly slid an arbitrary untruth into one of Zach's mini-interrogation sessions. The exact circumstances of this particular lie were blurry in my mind, but I clearly recalled the surge of satisfaction telling it brought. Still, if I'd foreseen how that one tiny lie would blossom into bouquet after bouquet of stargazer lilies, God help me, I never would have told it. Not only am I, heart and soul, a white tulip girl from way back, I actually detest stargazers, which look fake to me even when they're real, and the fragrance of which makes me instantly, overwhelmingly queasy.

Now, even in the open air, their cleaning-fluid smell was making my nasal passages want to scream. But when I looked up to see the nervous, hopeful expression in Zach's eyes, I not only smiled in thanks but, as punishment for lying to him in the first place, lifted the bouquet to my face and took a long, hard inhale. He smiled back, and for a second or two, relaxed, but then, as if they had a mind of their own, his fingers began to flutter like a keyboardist's against his thighs, and he said, "Remind me never to ride in a car for two hours with my brother again, okay?"

"Let me guess. Late Coltrane. No, wait. Ornette Coleman." Like his father before him, Ian listened almost exclusively to jazz, the more beboppy and experimental the better. Zach avowed that, also like his father, Ian only did it to demonstrate his esoteric taste, not because he actually liked the music. "No evidence of pleasure whatsoever. Zero. No head nodding or toe tapping. It's like he's listening to white noise." Whatever the effect on Ian, the wild, asymmetrical dissonance never failed to run like a razor blade over Zach's nerves.

"Worse," said Zach. "He snapped off the music. And lectured, *declaimed.* About marriage."

"But Ian's never been married."

"Yeah, as if not knowing shit about a subject ever stopped him. Like the clone of my father he is."

"So what did he say?"

"No idea. I blocked him out completely. All I heard was blah, blah, blah, and whenever he pointed at me or banged his palm on the steering wheel, I nodded. Worked pretty well, actually. God, at least Uncle Lloyd and the bad seeds were in the car behind us. If they'd been there, I might have had to slit my wrists."

"Or theirs," I said, cheerfully. The bad seeds were Uncle Lloyd's horrible twin sons, Jerome-called-Jeb and Ralph-called-Rally.

"Good idea, but I don't think you can bleed to death when you're bloodless."

By now, his finger thrumming had reached such a crazy tempo that it was probably leaving bruises. I took one of his hands in mine.

"Just try to relax and forget about them," I said, softly.

Zach's gaze went blank then flared; he yanked his hand away as if he'd touched something rotten. "Don't tell me to relax!" he almost shouted.

I took five or six quick, backward steps away from him. I may even have skittered, like a frightened mouse. The movement had to be entirely reflexive, some left-over, evolutionary fight-or-flight thing, since I knew—of course I knew—that Zach would never hurt me. And the bongo drumming of my heartbeat in my ears, that was reflexive, too. For a moment, we stood like statues, before Zach's taut face slackened and paled and he shut his eyes.

"God, I'm sorry," he said, and he opened his eyes and reached his arms out to me, and even though I knew he really was sorry, I didn't walk into them. Instead—another reflex—I tossed him the flowers.

"Oh, stargazer lilies!" said a voice. "You know, I've always admired them. Their total refusal to be self-effacing or shy. I've always thought the stargazer was an audacious kind of flower."

It struck me as such an unexpected and wondrous thing for someone to say that for a moment, I forgot to worry about whether or not she'd witnessed my and Zach's argument. She stood on the path a few feet away, beaming at the bouquet and leaning on her cane, looking oddly glorious, with her green shoes and blue dress and silver hair, as if she'd been spun together out of the land and sky that surrounded her: the old lady from this morning. I saw that she wasn't holding the book anymore, and, flustered, I wondered if she'd finished it. Her eyes met mine and held. She smiled. Nothing in the smile said she'd overheard our conversation, but, even though we all stood about the same distance from each other, right then, the points of our triangle seemed to shift—equilateral to isosceles—with the old woman next to me and Zach far away, alone.

"They're Clare's favorite," he said, brightly.

I turned and saw him standing there, gripping the bouquet in both hands, his fingers crumpling the brown paper, exhaustion and tension sapping him of his usual glow and making his handsome face look old. And because I knew he loved me to the absolute best of his ability and, more important, because no one should ever look that way the day before his wedding, I walked over to him and took the flowers back.

"Yes, they are," I said.

In a book I loved as a kid, a girl named Randy plays a game in which she wanders around the wide yard of her family's big, quirky, wonderful house and pretends that she is a traveler, far from home and alone in the world. It's nighttime, so, through the windows, she can see the family—brothers, sister, father, housekeeper, dogs—moving around in their warm, interior light, going about their evening rituals, while Randy, outside in the cooling air, can hear bathwater running, a dog's bark, a radio, the father's typewriter, all the blessed and ordinary music of a happy family, and she stands in the grass, getting sadder by the second, aching with longing and loneliness. And then—*whoosh*—she allows herself to suddenly remember that the house is hers, the family is hers, and flooded with the sweetest relief, she runs inside.

Maybe because from the time I was a baby until I turned eleven, in what I still think of as the BC (Before Cornelia) era, it was just me and my mom, a dyad that felt whole but fragile, I never played this game. But after that, once I had at least four different houses that felt like home, I played it a lot. A lot, a lot and for way longer than I'd admitted to anyone, except for Dev, and even he didn't know that, occasionally, I still played it. It was a way to remind me of my own luck, I think, and I guess I got a little addicted to it all: how thoroughly my imagination could fool me, the stinging loneliness, the rush of joy.

But on the day before my wedding, as I walked out of a side door of the hotel in my rehearsal dinner dress to see most of my family—blood relatives and otherwise—coming toward me, instead of me playing the game, the game played me. They were moving in my direction in pairs or threes, rising like suns over a gentle green-furred slope, clear as day, but it was as if I saw them through a thick pane of glass. My mother and Gordon; Cornelia and Teo and Dev's mother, Lake; Teo's parents; Cornelia's parents; Teo's sister,

Estrella-called-Star; Cornelia's brother Toby and his son, Jasper; Cornelia's other brother, Cam, and his husband, Niall; Hildy with Dev's and my friend Aidan; and finally Dev with Cornelia and Teo's children, Rose and Simon. All in summer dresses or pastel-colored shirts open at the neck, clean and gleaming and tidy haired, with seven-year-old Simon barefoot in the soft grass, Dev carrying his shoes.

I stood in the sun in my rehearsal dinner dress, shivering, besieged by the loneliest thoughts in the world. *They aren't mine; they will never be mine again; they'll go on being together and happy and a family without me because I'll be gone. I have lost them.*

It didn't make sense. It wasn't true. People got married all the time without losing their families. Marriage was addition, not subtraction. But everything about their casual togetherness hurt me: a tan arm draped over a shoulder, a hand in a pocket, smiles, and eye rolls, and headshakes, a light, teasing slap, their voices all in a jumble.

Teo saw me first. He stopped in his tracks, pressed his long brown hands to his heart, and then broke into a jog.

When he got to me, he kissed my cheek and gave me a smile. Half Swedish, half Filipino, Cornelia's husband, Teo, is a toffee-colored, green-eyed genetic miracle with a smile that could melt a glacier. The fact that it didn't quite melt the thick glass between me and everyone I loved scared me so much that, for the second time that day, I started crying. Luckily, this time there was no sobbing, just cold in my throat, and heat in my eyes, and a few meandering tears.

"Hey," said Teo. "You okay?"

I pressed my lips together and nodded.

"Really? Because I think you're crying."

I brushed at my damp cheeks and swallowed hard. "Nope. I'm fine. It's just that—well, you just—smell really good."

It was true, like honey and limes and barbershop powder.

Teo laughed. "I get that a lot."

And then they were upon us, a hugging, kissing, joking, fragrant flock of family. First Aidan and Hildy, arm in arm. They kissed me. Same time, different cheeks.

"Hold on. Synchronized kissing?" I pushed them both to arm's length and eyed them. Aidan and Hildy had a long-standing if sporadic "thing" between them, one that they both enjoyed but that neither ever quite followed through with. "You can't be flirting again already. You just got here!"

"I'm irresistible is why," explained Aidan.

Hildy shrugged. "It's true."

She leaned in and whispered into my ear. "How're you holding up?"

"Medium," I whispered back.

"Are you lying?"

"No fair asking."

"Sorry. I love you, and Aidan and I can have the getaway car ready at a moment's notice."

"It's been all of, what? Fifteen minutes? And you two are already at the joint-getaway-car stage. Sheesh, you move fast."

Hildy winked. "You know it, girly."

Toby caught Hildy in a headlock from behind.

Hildy grimaced. "Guess it's Toby's turn."

Toby gave me a bear hug, like the big teddy bear he was. "So what happened to the plan that you'd marry me when you grew up?"

"Who says I'm grown up?" I said.

They came to me, one by one. Gorgeous Rose-never-called-Rosie, nine years old and already Grace Kelly elegant, turning up her cheek for me to kiss before throwing herself into my arms. Cornelia's mother, Ellie, pressing a pair of antique blue topaz earrings into my palm ("My grandmother's. Your something blue."). Cam bowing low over my hand and kissing it, duke-like, then chucking me under the chin. My stepfather, holding my shoulders, saying, "Best girl in the world. The best, best one," his eyes full of tears. And so, little by little, touch by touch, word by word, they drew me back to them. There was no rush of relief, no sudden reentry into the world of my family, but by the time my mother was tucking a stray lock of hair behind my ear, the glass barrier between us had grown so flimsy I almost—*almost*—didn't notice it was there at all.

Last came Dev in a blue-checked shirt, holding Simon's white sneakers, his face still like a story I'd read so many times I could recite it—slate-blue eyes, black lashes that went all the way around like a ruffle, a thin scar cutting a straight line through the outer tip of his right eyebrow (bike accident, age sixteen), another under his chin that I couldn't see right then but knew was there (swing-jumping-off accident, age six). And now, here, his smile, guileless as a little kid's, sudden as a lit match. Back when we were in love, even after we'd been together for years, that smile never stopped taking me by surprise. It was found money, an arrowhead, a shooting star, a great, shiny stroke of luck every single time. Dev flipped one of Simon's shoes into the air, caught it with his usual unconscious grace, and, still smiling, said, "Hey, Clare."

I should have answered right away, but I didn't because—and I guess this is the downside of knowing someone by heart—right then, without meaning to, I noticed what *wasn't* there: no pink flush down the center of his cheeks ("like Hawaiian Punch stains," I'd once told him); no shifting from foot to foot; no slight lift of his shoulders; no faint abstraction in his eyes, as if he were silently reciting the multiplication or periodic table, a trick he used to steady himself. Not one of Dev's telltale signs of discomfort or sadness. And if he wasn't uncomfortable or sad, he must have been comfortable and happy, and, as someone who cared about him, this should have made *me* happy—obviously it should have—but all I could think was that on the eve of Dev's wedding, teetering on the very edge of his future with another woman, I could never have greeted him, tan and bright eyed and grinning like a ten-year-old, without even a trace of regret, a wisp of wistfulness. I could not have *flipped shoes*, for God's sake. Honestly, despite the fact that the two of us had broken up years ago, I probably would not even have come at all.

"You came." The words just fell out—*clunk, clunk*—but because there were only two of them, even in my annoyed state, I hoped Dev had missed the note of accusation in my tone, and an outside observer, even one who knew him pretty well, probably would have sworn he had. His smile held steady for sure. But there was the pink flush, two streaks about an inch and a half wide, running down the exact center of each cheek, and if the rush of satisfaction I felt upon seeing them made me a bad person, I didn't care. Our five-year romance aside, Dev and I had been best friends for years, although to be perfectly honest, for the past few months, our once rock-solid best-friend status had felt shaky. Even so, the thought of my marriage as being barely a blip on Dev's emotional radar screen was just too much to bear.

But there they were: two pink streaks. Blip. Blip. I was so busy rejoicing in those blips that I neglected what was clearly my duty at that moment: to bail us both out of our awkward silence with a joke.

Finally, Dev said, "Hey, how could I not be here? I sent back the RSVP card with the *yes* box checked, which basically amounts to a blood vow in your mom's world, right?"

"You renege on the *yes* box and you're blacklisted for eternity. The party planner code of conduct is pretty clear on that point."

Two semidecent jokes. And still the air fizzed with tension.

"Which is why," said Dev, gamely, "you shouldn't tell her that I considered, and I mean *strongly* considered heading to Reverend Wiley's Salvation Nation instead."

On our drive here, my mom, Cornelia, and I had passed six billboards advertising Reverend Wiley's fundamentalist megachurch, each bearing a different antiscience message, and every one had made me think of Dev.

Now, I said to Dev, "Big Bang Equals Big Bust."

"Christians Are the Real Endangered Species," said Dev.

"Adam and Eve Weren't Swinging from the Tree of Life."

"Jesus Didn't Have a Tail."

"Except." I stabbed my finger into the air. "The photo with that one was actually a chimp crossed out with a big red X, not a monkey. And chimps don't even actually have tails."

Dev shook his head sadly. "After that, I'm not gonna lie, doubt crept in."

"You lost faith in Reverend Wiley?"

"By the time we got to the Salvation Nation exit, I thought, hey, he might even have been wrong about God's wrath instead of climate change melting the ice caps."

I laughed, and, just like that, we were normal again.

"So you kept driving," I said, smiling. "And came here."

"Plus, I figured you'd want to see my haircut." He ran a hand over his uncharacteristically cropped head.

"I was dying to see your haircut. How did you know?"

Dev shrugged and grinned. "I know everything."

I am a person who usually pays attention. While strikingly un-Zen in most ways, I spend most of my time being fully present, watchful, so tuned in to the people and things around me that it can get exhausting. Maybe it comes from having spent most of my childhood alone with my mother, who even before her breakdown and subsequent bipolar diagnosis, was all quicksilver, mutable brilliance, and so necessary to me that I kept track of her with what could only be called vigilance, half worried she'd disappear in a puff of colored smoke and sparkles. Or maybe it's just that I am one of those people who believes that at least half of love is simply paying attention. In any case, I don't drift in and out. I don't float. Life doesn't go by in a blur.

Except that on the eve of my wedding day, at my rehearsal and rehearsal dinner, that's exactly what life did. The practice ceremony itself was an almost total loss, memory-wise, less like something I experienced than like something I caught out of the corner of my eye. Faint music; people moving around; mouths stretching into smiles; the linen-clad crook of my stepfather's arm under my fingers my only certainty.

The edges of the dinner stayed a little more crisp, but even that was mostly impressions. I remember the red, green, and gold of a tomato tart, the miniature lake effect of mist rising from my just-poured champagne, Zach squeezing my hand hard and harder under the table as Ian gave a toast that I swear featured—although how was this possible?—Winston Churchill's quotation about never, never, never giving in. Fairy lights spread out in constellations against the white canopy, the pinch of my new high-heeled sandals, my wistful envy as I watched Hildy and Aidan's playful flirting. The bell of Rose's dress as she whirled, solo and in perfect self-containment, on the dance floor. Cornelia's cheek against mine, her voice whispering, "Courage, dear heart," into my ear.

There was one stark moment of clarity. Near the end of the evening, I headed toward the dessert table, which someone had decorated with Zach's stargazer lilies, now in a towering green glass vase, and at which Dev stood, scarfing chocolate-covered strawberries with the happy oblivion of a six-year-old. Just before I reached the table, Zach materialized at my side. I watched Dev spot us, swallow his berry, and wipe his fingers on a napkin so that he could shake hands with Zach, which he did, firmly. Zach clapped him on the shoulder and thanked him for coming.

"Having a berry or six, are you?" I said.

"Me?" said Dev. "I was just admiring this large and impressive vase of large and impressive flowers."

Zach slipped his arm around my waist. "Can't take credit for the vase, but I brought the lilies this morning. Had to make sure my girl had her favorite flowers."

Confused, Dev pointed to the vase. "These flowers?"

"Yeah," said Zach, kissing my cheek. "Ever since she told me they were her favorite, I made it my personal mission to keep Clare in stargazers."

Dev's eyes met mine for maybe two seconds, but I recognized who looked out at me through that startled gray-blue glance: the boy who had given me white tulip bouquets and prom corsages for years (which often took some finagling and sweet talk, since tulips were not necessarily florists' go-to corsage flower), who had actually spent two fall afternoons planting white tulip bulbs in both his father's and his mother's yards so there would be a little trace of me there every spring, the boy who didn't personally care about flowers enough to loathe stargazers but who had habitually fake-gagged at the mere mention of them just to keep me company. That boy and the man he'd become knew I had lied to Zach as surely as he knew my name, and even after his baffled gaze flicked away, the lie stayed.

As this lie ping-ponged invisibly between me and Dev and the oblivious Zach, I flashed back to another one. Last Christmas at my parents' house in Virginia, the first time I'd brought Zach home. Dev, Cornelia, Teo, and their extended families had come for dinner, a crowd so big and bustling with storytelling and goofing off and children wound up on candy and pie that Dev and Zach scarcely talked until the evening was almost over.

Zach and I were washing dishes—a weirdness in itself, since washing dishes was a holiday job Dev and I had tackled together for so many years it was almost a religious ritual—and Dev came in, per Cornelia's instructions, to pick the bones of the turkey clean and cook down the carcass for stock. Because, at Dev's entrance, I could feel Zach starting to simmer right along with the water in the stockpot, I commenced to talk. And talk and talk, I guess hoping to somehow stave off his full-boil stressed state with an onslaught of words. I can't even remember what I said, but at some point, I must have reminisced about a bygone holiday because Dev, who looked a little bewildered but was good-naturedly trying to squeeze in appropriate responses to my breathless, frantic, tumbling stories, said something like, "Oh, yeah, that was the same Christmas Toby's dog Wilbur ate an entire pecan pie and threw up on the opened presents under the tree. Totally demolished that scarf you knitted for my dad."

"I took it personally," I said. "I mean, it was an unholy, holey, dropped-stitch wreck of a scarf, but I'd worked on that sucker for weeks."

Dev smiled. "Hey, it was your first effort! I thought it was pretty good, actually. And you know he would've worn it no matter what."

"True. He probably would've been wearing it when he got here today," I said. "Nice of Wilbur to spare Teo seven years of mortifying neckwear."

Until Zach burst out laughing—a throaty, cut-loose, tension-fraught string of hahahahas—I'd forgotten him and his simmering. My throat tightened at the sound.

"Wow, I guess this is what it's like when people have known each other forever," he said, all grins, his eyes glittering. "You two and your stockpile of stories."

I opened my mouth, but nothing came out. I stared at Dev, asking for help.

With one glance at Zach's face, Dev assessed the situation, laughed, and said, "Pretty exciting stuff, though, right? And the dog vomit/holey scarf story isn't even the top of the stockpile. There's also the time we were studying and I spilled coffee on my SAT prep book."

It cracked my heart a little, Dev's turning traitor to our past, his trying, for Zach's sake and I guess mine, too, to make our relationship sound like boring kids' stuff, like nothing, when, for us, for years, it was nothing short of sacred. And he needn't have bothered. Zach's bubbling, steaming stress didn't cool; instead, as sometimes happened, it did a states-of-matter quick change: from boiling to solid ice. In an instant, his fidgety hands stilled; his voice flattened like a snake under a car tire.

"No, I think it's adorable," Zach said. "Clare told me she's always thought of you as the brother she never had."

Dev's shoulders lifted in an almost imperceptible flinch and he turned his face, but not before I saw the hurt on it. I stared at Zach, stunned at his lie, the ease with which he told it, and, more than anything, the fact that he fully expected me to keep quiet about it. And the sad truth is that I almost did keep quiet. Or maybe not almost, but, for at least five whole seconds, I was definitely tempted. Zach had been at my parents' house for three days, during which he'd met every single member of my family, and all had gone smoothly. But three days of smiling watchfulness, of walking the tightrope of Zach's moods had wrung me out. For the first time in ages, I was glad to see a holiday at home end, and it almost had. We'd come so close. If I had kept quiet about Zach's lie, and then apologized privately, later, to Dev, we could have been home free.

But then, Dev looked up with what I recognized as his peacekeeper smile, and I just knew he was about to play along, to back up Zach's lie—or, more horribly, what he must have thought was *my* lie because no way could he have thought I'd actually meant it—to say something not just totally false but also cosmically wrong, and since only a truly yellow-bellied and empty-hearted monster could have allowed such a thing to happen, I jumped in with the first sentence that popped into my head, "That's just wrong."

"What?" said Zach, blinking with surprise, evidently completely thrown off by my failure to be complicit in his lie.

"I never said that."

I watched Zach regroup, tossing off shock like a hat and replacing it with a regretful, embarrassed face so authentic looking that it probably would have fooled most people, but it didn't fool me. He scratched his head, sheepishly. "Uh, right. My bad. Sorry to bring it up."

Disgusted with him, I turned to Dev. "It? There's no it. Because I never said that," I told him. It suddenly seemed crucial to be as clear as possible. "Not because

I wouldn't say it, but because I wouldn't think it. Ever. How could I? Zach is mistaken."

Without looking up from the stockpot, Dev nodded. "Okay."

Zach mumbled, "Hey, sorry," and backed out of the kitchen, scalding me with a glare and leaving me dreading the conversation I knew we'd have later. But when later came, instead of getting mad, in a not uncharacteristic sharp swerve toward sweetness, near tears, Zach apologized for the lie, for letting his insecurity get the best of him.

Standing in the shadow of those poor, innocent lilies with the memory of that old lie and with this new one snared between the three of us, I hoped against hope that Dev would do what he ended up doing: be complicit in *my* lie, keep quiet, and walk away. But, as I watched him go, even before I could exhale with relief, I saw myself for who I was: a woman who would yank someone else's lie into the light and feel noble about it, but who wanted to keep her own—and wanted help keeping her own—safely tucked away in darkness. I turned to Zach.

"I need to tell you something."

He smiled and touched his nose to mine. "Go for it."

"I lied."

Zach pulled back. "About what?"

I'd been gearing up for full disclosure, for telling him how I'd felt sometimes that he wanted not just my present and future, but all of it, to stamp his name—like a kid going to summer camp—on every important belonging I'd ever had, on my past, my private thoughts, my likes and dislikes, on the books I'd read, until they were his instead of mine. I had thought I'd tell him how lying about the flowers had been an act of self-preservation. But looking into his worried amber eyes, I didn't have the heart.

"Stargazers aren't my favorite flower."

Zach burst out with the laugh of a person who had been holding his breath. "Is that all?"

I refused to be let off that hook so easily. "No, it was awful of me to lie. We just happened so fast. And I had all these years of being myself before I knew you, and that life, well, it was just so full of *details* that had been mine for so long, and, I guess there were just moments when I didn't want to share all of them with you, which I suppose is fair enough, but I should have just said that to you when you asked the flower thing, but I couldn't figure out how, and so I said, 'Stargazers.' And I'm sorry."

Zach nodded. "I get it."

"You do? Really?"

"You wanted to start fresh with me."

I sighed. "Oh, Zach."

"Roses or whatever were part of your old life. Stargazers are part of *our* life. I feel exactly the same."

"That's not actually it."

He lifted my hand and kissed it. "Not to be a jerk, but I think I might see this more clearly than you do."

"Why would you?"

"Because I'm not blinded— No, blinded is the wrong word." He thought for a few seconds. "Distracted. I'm not distracted by loyalty to my past, to my family."

I shook my head in confusion. "What?"

"I *like* knowing that from here on out, we'll be each other's family, something completely new and better than what we had before. But you're more attached to your past and way closer to your family than I am to mine, so leaving them behind probably feels a little like betrayal to you."

"Zach, wait. My family won't stop being my family. I need them."

He smiled an eager, childlike smile. "Of course they won't stop! But everything will change! In a really, really good way."

"Zach—" He cut me off with a kiss.

"Just trust me when I say that we will be okay. Way, way better than okay. I love you so much. You know that, right?"

No simmering. No fluttering fingers or twitch in his

cheek. He was so happy and glowing and trusting and true, this man who had taken the whole of himself—past and future, body and soul—and placed it in my hands.

"Sweet Zach," I said. "Yes. I know you love me. I know. I know. I know."

Chapter Five
Edith

They gave each other gifts.

From him to her: a newly moribund sand dollar clothed in blue velvet spines; a skate egg case, glossy and horned as a beetle; a glass and red plastic hummingbird feeder; an edition of Audubon's *Birds of America.* This last he wrapped with a ribbon and told her to untie it only when she was ready.

One late autumn morning, she sat on the back steps with the book resting on her knees and opened it. The pages offered up heartache, certainly—some of the birds now extinct, their vivid portraits turned to elegy—but the plates of the marsh birds her father had loved didn't bruise her as Joseph had worried they might. Instead, the precision of the drawings, the service to accuracy over romance—all the weird and sharp-eyed grace of the animals intact, so many of the birds in motion, necks snaking, beaks open or with a fish clapped between them—the sensibility alive inside those pages brought the essence of her father, all that had been lost in those last weeks of his slow dying, back to her.

From her to him: a cookbook called *The Home Book of French Cookery* (after he mentioned that during his postwar years in France, he'd developed a love of French food) and the promise to make him a new dish every week; two solo canoes, made in Maine and so fluidly ribbed and curved that they seemed less constructed than grown.

Edith and Joseph would spend hours paddling the inland bay, threading the narrow salt marsh channels that opened out to ponds, Edith carefully collecting flora and fauna, scooping crabs or moon jellies into buckets, hungry for the names of everything, Joseph content just to look and talk about what he saw. They sat in their separate canoes, but Edith felt she had never been so close to anyone, the salt pond waters laid down like a cloth of gold between them.

From him to her: a camera, a compact black-and-silver 35-millimeter. He taught her how to use it, how to develop her photos in the tiny, magical, chemical-smelling darkroom off their kitchen. Edith avowed that the elemental differences between them appeared in their photographs, their souls made manifest in silver gelatin, delineated in black and white and gray: Joseph's all wide views, everything airy, included, and soaked in light, never without a slice of sky; hers close-in, all detail, edges, obliquity. Her photos surprised her. She meant only to capture the small specifics that intrigued her, but the resulting prints riddled and tricked: horseshoe crab tail transformed to a pointed skyscraper, salt marsh hay to a child's tousled hair. She saw her work as shy, elusive but Joseph looked at her photos of him—the landscape of veins on the back of his hand, the nape of his neck after a haircut—and caught his breath at the intimacy. She looked at his of her—silhouetted in her canoe backed by waves of cordgrass, head thrown back, face to the sun or standing at the ocean's edge before a storm, shoes dangling from her fingertips, hair whipped by wind—and felt that she was seeing herself, for the very first time, as she really was.

Chapter Six
Clare

I was only looking for a place to catch my breath.

But the instant I practically fell into the tiny outdoor alcove—surrounded on three sides by high, manicured boxwood, a secret compartment of green containing one white bench—and saw the old woman I'd come to think of as *my* old woman, I felt as if we'd planned it. She wasn't reading or drinking coffee or looking at her phone (if she had one) or doing any of the things people do when they're sitting on a bench alone. Her hands lay one upon the other on her pale yellow cotton skirt, and when I stumbled around the corner and saw her, she turned her face to me serenely and patted the spot on the bench next to her.

"Don't talk," she instructed. "Take a moment," and I

obeyed, sitting, shutting my eyes, and pulling the clean morning air into my chest.

Except for my hyperventilation and desperate, crab-like scuttling away from my bridal brunch, my wedding morning could not have been lovelier: cool and crisp, greens and golds running wildly over the surrounding hills, the forget-me-not sky interrupted only by translucent, wedding-veil clouds. Zach had gone golfing with all his male family members, his severe discomfort with them eclipsed only by his insistence on doing our wedding entirely "by the book," including the mandate that the groom not set eyes on his bride until she walked toward him down the aisle.

With just my people there, the informal brunch should have been easy, but a sleepless night had left me wired and restless. Everything—my relatives' smiles, the bowls of berries, the glass pitchers of juice, the diamond on my finger, my new white-and-green Stan Smith sneakers—looked overbright, garish even, and despite the lofty ceilings, sheer curtains, and delicate chandeliers, the room felt airless and like the walls were closing in. And because, in these ways, the room resembled my own chest cavity, after a few sips of obnoxiously orange apricot nectar, I turned to my mother and, gasping a little, said, "I'm sorry but I just need—"

and, before I could finish, she said, "Do it. Whatever it is, go ahead," so I bolted for a side door and stumbled out into the air.

I don't know how long I sat on that bench with my eyes shut, but eventually, my breathing slowed and my rib cage expanded and the rushing river sound inside my ears went away along with the dark red static on the insides of my eyelids, and only then did I open my eyes and say, "I'm sorry."

"Unless 'Sorry' is your name, there is no reason whatsoever to say it."

"I'm Clare," I said, putting out my hand.

She took it. Her hand was as long and thin as mine but much softer and cooler, her loose skin as silky as talcum powder. "Pleased to meet you, dear Clare. I'm Edith."

"It's my wedding day."

"I thought maybe it was."

I sighed, a deep, stretched-out sigh that seemed to begin at the soles of my feet. "I feel like this is the first chance I've had to catch my breath in months."

"I've always found that phrase funny. 'Catch,' as if it's gotten away and you have to chase it down with a butterfly net."

I smiled. "Butterflies, again. You're right. That's how it feels."

"So tell me. You and your fiancé had a whirlwind romance? A short engagement?"

"Yes. I mean, Zach and I have been together for a year, but since we got engaged in early February, it's been like falling, like one long, breathless fall."

"Like in *Alice in Wonderland*?"

"But faster. I keep looking around and thinking, 'How in the world did I get here?' "

"How *did* you? Would you like to tell me?"

I looked into Edith's dark brown eyes. In her old face, tan and pink-cheeked but crosshatched with wrinkles, her eyes were like her voice, young and crystal clear. Also sharp. Also kind.

"You know what? I would. I haven't told the complete and unedited story to anyone, not even my mother or Cornelia, but I would really like to tell you."

"Good. No editing allowed. Full speed ahead."

"Okay, then. It began with Zach's father's dying. I don't mean it began when his father died, but as he was dying, at his deathbed, I guess it was, although we didn't actually spend much time in his father's room. They had a hospice worker do the true watching over. Zach didn't want to and said his father—who was very much out of it by the time we arrived—would have considered it an intrusion, for us to sit next to his bed and physically watch him die. Since Zach had previously told me that his father also considered hugs and text messages an intrusion, I believed it. So maybe this wasn't technically a deathbed vigil, but it was a vigil. God, was it ever. The entire family was there. Zach. His brother, Ian. Awful Uncle Lloyd and the horrible cousins Zach loathes. I was the only woman, and everyone seemed to expect me to make food, so I did, and I was so grateful to have something to do with myself that I couldn't even resent it properly. We waited. We kept watch, day and night. Mr. Barfield had chosen to die at their family's lake house in Northern Michigan, and even though Zach said it was beautiful there most of the year, in February, it was just plain bleak. Freezing. And not just the weather outside the house, but inside, too. Inside was worse. I expected sadness, maybe regret, because surely the Barfield men are the type to leave the important things unsaid, but instead, everyone seemed angry. Stone-faced and sarcastic and perpetually on the edge of exploding."

"Maybe they resented having to feel emotions they weren't accustomed to," said Edith.

I glanced up at her, startled. "You might be right. That's a more generous take than my own. I thought they just resented not being in control, which doesn't happen to them very often. Ian kept shooting out his arm and glaring at his watch like he was waiting for a train and it was late."

"Death. So inconsiderate."

"Exactly. But I don't think death was the only thing they were waiting for."

"What else?"

I remembered the way they'd all jump when the landline rang or a car drove by—its tires crunching through the gravel of the country road, its headlights sweeping an arc across the oak-paneled walls. The way they would afterward seem angrier than ever.

"Zach's sister, Ro, disappeared from that house when she was eighteen and he was a little boy. As strange as it sounds, I think all of them were each, in his own way, waiting for her to show up."

"She didn't."

"No."

"And Zach? Was he angry, too?"

I hung my head and nodded. "He behaved just like the rest of them. I hardly recognized him. And for the five days we were there, it was like he didn't recognize me, either."

"I've heard that happens with families. You think you've changed and then you go home and fall back into the same old roles. But that must have been hard for you."

"It was terrible. It got so I couldn't stand to touch him. I felt really bad about that. It's awful, isn't it? To shudder at the thought of touching your boyfriend?"

"No."

"I hated every second of being there. Finally, I couldn't stand it anymore. I called the airlines, changed my flight, called a cab to take me to the airport, had my bag packed, all before I told Zach I was going. Which was unfair of me. Thoughtless. I should've told him."

"Changing your plans sounds like an act of self-preservation. Maybe you thought he would say no."

"Usually, he tries so hard to be nice, to be everything the rest of his family isn't. But he wasn't himself up at the lake house."

"What happened next?"

What happened next was the part of the story I had never told, the part I'd tried to stop telling even myself.

The lake house was a big, fancy house pretending, with its log walls and goofy, creepy antler chandeliers, plaid furniture, wood-burning stoves, and floors of worn flagstone or pine boards, to be a humble one. But as big as it was, the Barfield men seemed to fill every room.

Slamming a book shut here, pounding away at a laptop there, arguing about money and politics (even though they all seemed to be in agreement about such topics), cursing the spotty Wi-Fi, the whine of the wind outside, the paucity of channels on the television. They paced the floors with their heavy feet (they never took their shoes off to the point that I wondered if they slept in them). And even though they barely took notice of me, I grew to dread running into them. When I looked up from studying to find one of them in the room, the hair on the back of my neck bristled. When one unexpectedly spoke to me, I flinched.

So after I'd made all the arrangements for my early departure, I didn't have the energy to go out into the house and risk bumping into a Barfield. Instead, I sat on the bed I supposedly shared with Zach—even though when it came to sleeping in it, the most we did was overlap by an hour or two, which was fine by me—with my coat on and my bags at my feet and my heart in my throat, and waited for my ride.

And then Zach walked into the room and saw me there, and in a low, dangerous, gritted-teeth voice said, "What the fuck is this?"

Because I felt small sitting, I stood up, planted my feet. "Look, I'm sorry, but I just can't stay here."

"*What?*"

"Zach, I'm not helping anyone here, not even you. You hardly speak to me. And the atmosphere, the *air* in this house feels poisoned. I'm going home."

Zach snickered, the meanest sound I'd ever heard him make, and shook his head. "Yeah? Well, that's where you're wrong."

"I changed my flight. I'll see you whenever you get back, but I can't be here anymore."

"We'll change it back."

"You're not hearing me. I don't want to be here anymore. I'm leaving."

Without taking my eyes off Zach's face, I leaned down and picked up my carry-on bag.

"Stop saying that you're leaving!" he said, loudly.

And then Zach—sweet, joke-appreciating, tailgating-averse, gift-giving Zach—took one step toward me, his face rigid with rage, jaw clenched, eyes narrowed, and fear started ringing in my ears like a siren. I'd seen Zach angry before, but never this angry, and never at me. I tried to remind myself that he loved me, but the fear just rang louder.

"Please don't tell me what to say. Or do," I said, my voice shaking. "I am leaving."

"Shut up!" he hissed.

Then, he picked up my suitcase, tossed it onto the bed, unzipped it, and threw it against the wall. As the suitcase hit, it opened like a mouth and vomited out my clothes. For a second, I stood frozen, stunned, then some animal part of me kicked in, and I tore open the bedroom door and ran, down the hallway, out the front door, and blindly across the lawn, my teeth chattering, the frozen ground bone-jarring under the soles of my shoes.

I didn't know for sure that he was following me until I heard his voice breaking raggedly through the dark and cold. "I'm sorry, I'm sorry, I'm sorry."

I swung around, brandishing, without really meaning to, my heavy carry-on bag. "Stay back!" I shouted.

But he had already stopped. He stood on the edge of the road, maybe twenty feet from me. When he dropped to his knees, a blade of moonlight lit up the tears on his face. The cold bit into my cheeks, my bare hands. The cloudy sky low as a basement ceiling overhead.

"Clare," said Zach. "I don't know what just happened, but I know I would never hurt you."

He sounded so sad.

"The cab is coming soon," I said, my voice shaking. "And I'm getting in it."

He nodded. "Yes! Definitely, you should go home. I should never have brought you here, and I'm so sorry."

I wrapped myself up in my own arms.

"I love you," he said, starting to cry. "You're the only person I love."

He pressed his hands to his forehead. "I don't love my father, but I can't imagine him being dead or, like, a world without him in it. Isn't that strange? It's messing me up, this place, my family, his dying. I'm not myself."

I could feel my fear ebbing and gentleness opening up inside me, but I didn't let myself give in to it. "I realize that, but you can't keep me here. You can't try to scare me into staying. It's just wrong."

"I know. So wrong. I hate myself right now a lot more than you hate me."

The despair in his voice coaxed the last bit of fear out of me. I walked over to where he sat. "I don't hate you," I said, softly. "I know you're having a hard time."

He didn't look up, just ran a hand lightly down my shinbone, then let it fall onto the ground. "I love you so much. Nothing else matters to me."

"I hear the cab coming," I said. "I need to go. If you could just bring my clothes when you come back?"

He nodded, miserably. "Ugh, of course. I'm so sorry about your clothes and everything. I'm sorry about everything."

As the cab pulled up, I rested my palm on top of his

head, then combed his hair with my fingers. "I'll see you when you get back."

"More than I deserve," he said, bitterly. "Thank you, Clare."

He was still sitting there, eyes on the ground, when the cab drove away.

Just as I finished talking, a bird began fluting complicatedly on a nearby low-hanging tree branch, and since it would have been discourteous not to listen, we listened.

After the last firework trill dissolved against the summer sky, Edith said, "*Turdus polyglottos.*"

"Excuse me?"

"An unfortunate name but the one Linnaeus bestowed on the northern mockingbird, and I do have a soft spot for Carl. However, I think the folks who later changed it to *Mimus polyglottos* made a wise choice."

"I agree."

"I think that particular member of the species must've spent some time listening to Mozart."

Her eyes locked on mine. "Back to how you got here. If you don't mind my saying so, it's difficult to trace a clear path from that lake house story to this wedding day of yours."

I sighed. "After his father died a few days later, he

came straight to my apartment from the airport. He asked me to marry him as soon as possible. He would've eloped right then I think."

"Was it his urgency that persuaded you? Urgency can do that."

"Not only, although I'm sure that was part of it. But also he said I was his bright light, his life raft, his one hope of not being sucked back into the darkness of his family. He swore he could not, under any circumstances, be happy without me, and, as hyperbolic as that sounds, I knew he meant it."

"You're his blue sky. When everything else is darkness."

I started. "Yes! Exactly."

"But is he yours?"

"No one, not one person, has ever needed me like he does." Even I could see how I'd swerved around her question, but in all the weeks leading up to this day, this had been my go-to answer to any question about Zach. Multipurpose, flexible, enough.

"Some may *love* you just as much. Although love's not really the point."

I blinked. "It's not?"

"Usually, love is the point, almost always, but not this time."

"So what is?"

She leaned toward me and took my two hands in hers, her coffee-colored eyes shining and deeply serious.

"No one should live with someone who scares her."

I stopped breathing. And I know Edith's statement might not have burst forth out of nowhere and streamed like a sizzling comet across everyone's psyches. Some people might even have regarded it as too simple and obvious to matter. But it mattered to me. To me, this sentence was a revelation. Because the truth is that long before Zach burned holes in me with his glare and his words and hurled my suitcase against the wall, he had scared me. The anger that would seep like battery acid or flare like a gasoline fire at professors or other drivers or people on the news or (and especially) his father and his brother, Ian—part of me stayed wide awake always, keeping watch for it. Despite his general kindness—a kindness I knew he'd worked hard to achieve—Zach had scared me all along.

"You know what scares me more than his anger, though?" I said, slowly, looking at my lap. "How close he wants to be to me, all the time, every second. I realize closeness sounds like a good thing, but it's like I can't turn around or smile at something or read something or *have an experience* without his popping up, asking questions, relating. And I'm not even that private a person. I mean, here I am pouring out my secrets to someone I just met. But I miss keeping to myself what few things I actually ever kept to myself, without feeling like a traitor. I miss solitude, even though before this, I might have said I didn't especially like being alone. I really miss having light and space around me. What scares me most is the thought that I never will again."

"Oh, dear girl," said Edith, softly.

Suddenly, a tremble went through the hedge to my left, and there stood Dev, in a dove-gray linen shirt so nicely cut and perfectly suited to him that I wondered if a girlfriend had chosen it. He'd been at the brunch, but I'd been so flustered, I hadn't noticed the shirt before now. In one hand, Dev carried a white bowl.

"Stealing china from the hotel, I see," I said.

"Hey," he said, flushing a bit at the sight of Edith. "Sorry to interrupt."

"I'm Edith." She swiped her hand through the air in a windshield wiper wave.

"I'm Dev," said Dev, swiping back and smiling. Then, he turned to me. "A few minutes ago, they put out these tiny cinnamon rolls, and I know how you have a thing for undersized food."

He handed me the bowl, inside of which were nestled four cinnamon rolls the size of half-dollars.

"I figured I should steal you some because they were going like—" He paused, waiting for me to finish the simile.

"Undersized hotcakes?"

"Yup."

"Well, thanks," I said. "They're adorable, like four curled-up baby hedgehogs."

"Exactly what I thought." Dev shook his head. "Weirdo."

"You know, you could've just saved them for when I got back. You didn't have to traipse all the way out here."

"Okay, (a) I did not traipse. Like, at all. And (b)"—he shrugged, sheepishly—"I may have been sent on a mission to check on you."

"My mother?"

"And Cornelia. I told them you were fine, that you'd probably abducted some nice person and dragged her into a hedge to talk her ears off, but they made me come anyway."

I sighed. "I don't know if fine is exactly the word I'd pick."

Dev knitted his brows. "You need anything? Besides tiny pastries, I mean?"

I lifted my chin. "Nah. I'm okay. Go back and tell

them I'm just getting some air and I'll be back in a flash."

Dev gave a thumbs-up. "Nice to meet you, Edith. Make her share." He pointed to the bowl.

"If I have to wrestle her to the ground," said Edith.

A snow-white burst of smile, a rustle of hedge, and Edith and I were alone again.

"Zach needs you," she said. "What do you need?"

I squeaked out a laugh. "You don't mess around, do you?"

Edith smiled. "All right, try this instead. You mentioned wanting light and space. It made me think of a room, an actual, physical place that is all yours. Do you have one?"

"Well, no. I had an apartment, but I gave it up when we got engaged. Anyway, it had stopped feeling like all mine a long time before."

"Sometimes," Edith mused, "in order to hold your own, you need a place of your own. Light and space to move around in safely. A place to breathe easy."

"I used to." I thought for a moment. "Or maybe what I mean is that I used to not need one because, for the last few years at least, I carried my safe place around with me, like a turtle. But now, I don't anymore."

"Oh, Clare. I am so very sorry you don't anymore."

I put the cinnamon roll bowl on the bench next to me, took Edith's hand, and hung on for dear life.

"May I say something else?" she asked, after a long pause.

I nodded, numbly.

"I know the pull of a dark, complicated man, the kind who has trouble loving anyone but you. But let me tell you this: the ones who look like home are home."

"What?" I stared at her, puzzled.

"They're where you go." I shook my head, not understanding, and she slid her gaze to the bowl next to me and then back.

"Oh! You mean Dev."

"I don't know. Do I?"

My body relaxed, and I smiled. "Oh, Dev. Dev is *Dev.* He was my first love, from the time we were thirteen until I graduated from high school. I don't even know if it was love the way other people mean love."

"No? Explain."

I laughed. "We were so young. Sometimes, I think we were like those chicks in biology class. We *imprinted* on each other more than anything else."

"Sounds to me like as good a description of love as any. But what happened? Why did it end?"

Surprised, I said, "People don't usually ask that

question. We were kids, each other's first love. No one expects that to last."

"Including you and Dev?" Her hand held mine as calmly as ever, but the entire rest of her seemed to bristle with skepticism. It occurred to me to wonder if anyone had ever managed to lie to Edith in her entire life.

I shook my head. "No. *We* expected it to last forever. But then he went away for months and months, even though I asked him not to, and I was lost. I know that sounds trite—lost without him—but I was so directionless. I stumbled through my days like some kind of wounded animal. Sometimes, I'd be driving to someplace I'd been lots of times before, and I'd literally get lost."

Suddenly, I had a thought. "Oh, gosh, you know what? He was my safe place."

"Yes, it does sound that way. But you couldn't carry him around like a turtle shell. When he was gone, the safe place went, too?"

"Yes. I've never thought of it that way before, but yes. I hated that I didn't know who I was without him and that I couldn't function. So when he got back, *I* left *him*. I told him I needed to grow up and figure out how to be a full-fledged, happy person without him."

"That makes sense to me."

I groaned. "Except look where it got me. Four years later, and here I am: cold feet on my wedding day, like some idiot cliché." I covered my face with my hands and pressed hard against my eyes. "I've made a total mess of everything."

"Or maybe it worked, the growing up," said Edith, quietly. "Maybe it was all leading up to right now."

I dropped my hands, turned my face to the blue sky, and sat completely still, listening to Edith as hard as I could, even though I knew her words just might upend my life like a table, sending everything crashing, so that I'd have to start over. Or maybe not "even though," maybe "because." With the state I was in, I couldn't say for sure.

She went on, gathering steam. "Maybe this moment is the test. I have been watching you because I'm old and that's what I do: sit outside of things and watch. I see that you're a good person, a loving daughter, a true friend. What if it's time to be your own friend, Clare? If your grown-up self took you by the hand right now, where would she lead you?"

No one should live with someone who scares her.

My heart began to pound, but I sat up as straight as I could. "Could *you* hold my hand again, just for a minute, before I go?"

"Courage, dear heart," said Edith, and she held.

I deserved to remember his face until the day I died. I don't mean his face after, but the way it looked before, when I knocked on his hotel room door, and he said, "Come in," and I did. His face in the tiny, shiny, hope-lit spot of time before I started talking: the trust, the instant openness, like something blooming, and the joy.

I shut the door and leaned against it.

"Hey," he said, grinning, turning off the TV, and standing up. He still wore his golf clothes, a pink-and-white-striped polo shirt and frog-green shorts. "You're totally breaking the rules, you know."

I held up my hand to stop him from walking toward me and forced myself to keep looking at him.

"Zach, I need to say something."

"Anything."

"I am sorrier than I have ever been in my life and than I ever expect to be again, even if I live to be a hundred, but I can't marry you."

He opened his mouth, but no sound came out. Like I'd thrown something heavy at him, he rocked back on his heels and fell into his chair.

"Give me a sec."

He placed his hands on top of his head, fingers drumming, and shut his eyes. When he opened them, he said, "I get it."

"You do?" Heaven help me, I felt relief at the possibility that I'd be let off the hook so easily, even though no one had ever deserved it less.

"You need more time. And, come on, of course you can have it."

The relief flipped over and died.

"Honestly, I've been worried that I rushed you. I almost said something the other day, but I chickened out, which was wrong of me," said Zach. "And screw all this, the big wedding, our families. Bad idea. My family alone is too much. What was I thinking?"

"Don't," I said, my eyes filling with tears. "Don't take the blame."

"We should've run away. But now here's the thing: to hell with them all. We'll wait and do it alone, just the two of us, whenever you're ready. On a moment's notice even." He ran a hand through his hair, excitedly. "How could I not have seen that just the two of us would've been so much better? The whole point of getting married is to be just the two of us, making a new family on our own terms. Forget the rest of them."

"No, it's not them. It's us. It's me. I love so many things about you."

"Well, I like the sound of that," he said, with a shaky smile.

I shook my head. "But I can't spend my life with you. I can't envision it all, and I promise you I've tried."

"But I can fix that! I can change, and you'll change, too. That's what happens in a marriage, you adapt to each other!"

"Zach, please listen to me," I said. "I never feel completely like myself when we're together. I can never quite relax. I've always known this deep down, but I wouldn't admit it. You're a good guy, and I wanted to make you happy. But we aren't home to each other."

"I'm a *good guy*?" Zach winced and slapped a hand to his stomach, as if he'd been punched.

"That came out wrong. You're decent and kind; you try so hard to always do the right thing. That's what I meant."

"You're home to me. You are. I swear."

"But," I said, "you aren't to me. You're a lot of wonderful things, but you're not home."

He opened his hands and with a sweet, almost childlike certainty, said, "I can be."

Very, very gently, I said, "No, you can't."

"What? You mean ever?"

"Ever. I'm sure of it. I'm so sorry."

He seemed to consider this, then shook his head. "You don't mean it. You'll change your mind."

"No."

"It might take time, but once the dust has settled from all this big wedding bullshit, you'll change your mind."

"Please don't—"

Zach cut me off. "Clare, just go now. No wedding right now. I get it. It's fine. But we'll talk soon. I'll be patient; I'll do anything to fix this, which is how I know it's going to be okay. Plus, I love you."

Without a word, feeling every inch a monster, I left.

Chapter Seven
Edith

June 1951

Joseph became a photographer for the local paper, one that served not only the string of beach towns, but the entire southern portion of the state. Before he offered him the job, the editor, Beau Fleeger (cigar chomping, fast talking, bighearted, all of five foot four), warned Joseph that it'd be pretty damned tame stuff after what he'd been doing in Europe, but Edith knew that her husband would delight in it. Holiday parades, high school football games, fireworks, society weddings (as much as there was a society), political rallies, ribbon cuttings, even the occasional funeral or petty crime (trespassing, break-ins, public drunkenness, a gas station attendant robbed at gunpoint): it was what Joseph had missed most during the war, all the small, scattered pieces of the precious and luminous ordinary, evidence that life insists on continuing.

Then, on a summer afternoon, one week shy of Edith and Joseph's first anniversary, the Driver twins, Robbie and Susie, twelve years old, were out in their dinghy checking their crab pots when a storm hit. Except for its sudden and unexpected arrival—bruise-colored clouds materializing along the tree line to the east, then a rush of wind spilling them like ink across the sky—the storm was unremarkable, no hail, no flash floods, no miles of downed power lines. Wild, tree-snapping winds, some stomps of thunder, spatters of lightning. A typical summer squall, short-lived as a tantrum, certainly not the kind of weather event that kills people. Except that the Driver twins never came home, a fact their parents discovered only when they returned from work, hours after the storm had fled the scene, blowing out as spasmodically as it had blown in.

John Blanchard, the town's chief of police, hastily put out a call for a search party, and half the town showed up, men, women, teenagers. Known for his cool head, blond hair, and perpetual air of calm, John was Joseph's friend. The two men ran into each other at crime scenes and town events, and occasionally, John called when he needed photos for a police file. In the case of the search party, he left the role Joseph would play ambiguous, saying only, "Better bring your camera."

"To photograph the happy Driver family reunion," said Joseph.

"Hell, I hope so," replied John.

Because she couldn't bear to be home by the phone, at loose ends, swinging between hope and dread, Edith tugged on a pair of blue jeans and the knee-high rubber boots Joseph had given her for Christmas and went along.

Some of the searchers set out in boats, others combed the woods edging the salt marshes, hoping the kids had put ashore and taken shelter amid the trees. Just before dark, the Drivers' neighbor, eighty-year-old Roger Payne, found the boat, overturned, empty as a husk, and floating farther out in the deep waters of the bay than anyone had dared imagine. Most people went home after that, disheartened, promising to come back at daybreak, hungry less for their dinners than for the lamp-lit rooms and solid floors of their houses, the living faces of their own children. They wanted to watch fireflies hover and flicker above the cut grass of their lawns, to pull tricycles into the safety of backyard sheds.

A few kept searching, including Edith, Joseph, and John in John's skiff. They navigated the maze of channels and inlets and ponds, kept close to the water's edge, raking flashlight beams through the marsh grass and brush, disturbing sleepy birds: black ducks, clapper rails, and willets, and once a blue heron, breath-stoppingly huge, that broke from a clutch of shrubs and, after one prehistoric cackle, winged silken and liquid-necked, noiseless as a paper airplane, low across the water and into the night.

They found them just as the sun slipped above the horizon to simmer in the tall grass and beam pink against the white sides of the houses far to the west. Robbie at the mouth of an inlet, snagged in the talon-like roots of the pine trees that gripped the shore's edge and hung out raggedly over the water. And Susie, not twenty-five yards away, lying facedown in a plot of thickset, feathery plumed phragmite weeds. They were both fully dressed, except for their shoes. Even Susie's hair had stayed braided.

Once the three of them were ashore, John Blanchard took off his glasses and rubbed his eyes. "We'll need to photograph them, Joseph. Just for our records, not the newspaper. God knows, no one wants or needs to see this."

Joseph just nodded, but in the morning light, he looked not merely sad but haunted, his eyes hollow, his mouth trembling. When he raised the camera, his hands were shaking, so without a word, Edith took the camera from him, wiped the tears from her face, and stepped into the tea-colored water, stirring up tempests of silt with her boots. As she photographed first Robbie, then Susie, she tried to put her emotions away, to focus only on the act of taking accurate pictures, but in the end, whatever it took to turn a dead child into any other two-dimensional scrap of light and shadow, she didn't have it. The details pierced her: the exposed strip of pale skin on Robbie's leg where his shorts rode up, the straight line of Susie's carefully parted hair. Edith moved around the children, catching them from a variety of angles. By the end, she heaved with dry-eyed, audible, chest-burning sobs that didn't stop, not when John and Joseph lifted the twins into the boat, not when she covered each with the blankets they'd brought to warm them, if only they had found them alive.

But later, at home, she did stop, and it was Joseph who cracked, shivering and weeping and saying, "Oh, God. Oh, God. Oh, God." Edith understood that it wasn't just the deaths of these children that were shaking him to the core, but also all the deaths from before, during the war. She built a fire, even though it was summer, wrapped her husband in quilts, rocked him in her arms, and wove a cocoon of words, descriptions of every loveliness that crossed her mind, birds and mosses and flowering plants, the sound of a creek rattling through woods, a cluster of cabbage butterflies fluttering, dance-like, on a patch of ground. She gave him morning coming through their bedroom windows and the shapes of leaves. She gave him the names of things.

Because the pain of losing the children hung on hard, Edith would do it for weeks, this whispered comforting, and each time she would lie awake long after he'd fallen asleep, enfolded in two sorrows, Joseph's and her own, but also in a radiant, awestruck gratitude at what she understood was the great honor of her life, not being loved but loving, soothing this good man, making him feel safe.

Chapter Eight
Clare

Even though I didn't have much time to develop expectations in the numb three hours between those two conversations, the first with Edith and the subsequent one with Zach, I *had* expected relief. Maybe not over and above other emotions, but I had expected to walk out of Zach's room and be aware of it, running silvery through my psyche beneath the guilt like an artesian spring. Honestly, I'd expected to have to hide it, to keep every trace of it off my face for Zach's and decorum's sake. And I'd expected hiding it to be hard.

But the relief didn't come. Not as I was walking away from Zach's room. Not when I walked into my own to find my wedding dress, camellia cool and eyeing me from its padded satin hanger. Not when I went into the bathroom and splashed my hot cheeks and then downed the complimentary bottle of fancy water—culled straight from an actual artesian spring in actual Fiji—gulping frantically and loudly, like a person who'd been lost in the desert for a week.

Not even when I witnessed the same sort of relief I'd expected for myself illuminate—sunburst style—the faces of my mother and Cornelia.

Instead, I felt purely horrible, and I don't mean I felt miserable, although I did. I mean I felt that *I* was horrible: transfigured into something heavy and misshapen, mean and core-rotten and cruel, coated so thickly in horribleness it was like I'd been rolling in it. I had been mad at myself before. I had been disappointed in myself. But I had never, until the moment I called off my wedding to Zach, been repulsed by myself. In one ten-minute conversation, I had wiped my name off the list of kind and decent people. By the time I got to the door of Cornelia's room, I had begun to believe—to *know*—that I'd never been on that list in the first place. All those years I'd spent thinking I was a good person—once, a long time ago, Teo had told me I was a good person, made of good materials; "Just being you is being good," he'd said, and I'd believed him—when I had really been hopelessly bad all along.

If I had expected to fling open the door and announce my news—and I think I had expected that, the flinging part definitely—by the time I actually stood outside it, I could barely bring myself to knock. I listened to my mom's and Cornelia's voices, and I knew that they were getting the kids ready for the wedding. I knew that my mother said, "Just a few more, Rose. Gosh, you're being so patient and staying so still!" because she was curling Rose's hair. I knew from Cornelia's singing "High Hopes"—cheerfully but with a note of exasperation and interspersed with commentary like, "Would you look at that perfect loop? I've never seen a more perfect loop in all my life"—that she was trying to inspire Simon to tie his own shoes, a task he loathed. Typical, goofy family stuff, but as I stood outside that door, steeped in my own horribleness, it all struck me as astoundingly beautiful.

You don't even deserve to overhear this, I told myself, *much less to go in and be part of it.* But I had to go in. There was music to be faced, a wedding to be dismantled (oh, God, the wasted money alone made me feel like a criminal), and anyway, deserving or not, even in the smack-dab, ugly middle of my self-loathing, I wanted them, my mother and almost-mother. I wanted just to be near them. No flinging open the door for me, though, just barely more than a brush of knuckles against the frame.

Cornelia called out, "Dev, if that's you, get in here and take this shoeless wolf-boy of a child off my hands!"

I opened the door. "It's not Dev."

Everyone, even Simon the wolf-boy, went still, staring at me.

"I'm not marrying Zach," I said, bleakly. "It's over."

That's when the relief broke like morning across their faces. After one quick glance at each other, they shook it off, composed their features into looks of concern, but I'd seen it. And still I felt only wretched.

"Oh, honey," said my mother. "What happened? Can you tell us?"

"It's just that no one should live with someone who scares her." I blurted it out, but as soon as I had, I hated myself. If I'd sat for hours calculating what explanation would garner me the most sympathy and support from these two particular women, I would have made a beeline for that one. The words sounded overblown, underhanded, manipulative, painting me as the victim when I was the monster; the fact that the words were also true just didn't matter.

"Oh, God," said Cornelia, standing up from her chair.

"No," I said. "It wasn't like that. He never hurt me. I just mean—"

I tipped sideways and leaned against the wall.

"Kids!" said Cornelia, clapping her hands. "Run down to your brother's room. Tell him to take you out on the lawn for—oh, anything. What's your favorite game?"

"Croquet," said Rose. "But in my dress?"

She fanned open her rose-sprigged skirt with her two hands, and love for her squeezed my heart like rubber bands. I would've given anything to go with her, to be a nine-year-old girl in a dress, heading out into the sunshine to play croquet.

"No worries, darling," said Cornelia, smiling. "Tell Dev I said you need to play outside. No shoes necessary."

And in a rush of pastels, clean hair, and gorgeousness, they were gone. My mother and Cornelia turned to me, waiting.

"Okay," I said, holding up my hand like a traffic cop, "but you are not allowed to comfort me. I am a terrible, careless, destructive person for letting things get this far."

"But—" said my mother.

"Promise. No reassuring words. Not even a hug."

"You drive a hard bargain," said Cornelia, narrowing her eyes.

"Promise."

They sighed and nodded.

With as little editorializing and emotional display as possible, I recounted my conversation with Edith.

"She helped you. Maybe she saved you," said my mother, quietly. "A total stranger."

"Don't," I snapped. "I see where you're going, and no one, *no one* is allowed to feel guilty or take responsibility for my mistakes. They're horrendous and all mine."

"We had misgivings," said Cornelia, sadly. "All along."

"But you trusted me," I said. "Because I've always been pretty trustworthy. Just not this time."

"You know," said Cornelia, pointing Simon's shoe at me. "And I'm really not comforting you here or letting you off the hook or whatever it is you don't want me to do, but you know that however terrible you think what you did was, doing the thing you didn't do would have been much, much worse. Unforgivably worse."

"Yes," I said, grimly. "I do know that."

"Go home, sweetheart," said my mother. "Leave everything to us."

I shook my head. "'I won't be gotten out of anything anymore, thanks.'"

It was a quote from Cornelia's favorite movie. She smiled but shook her head.

"The power of *The Philadelphia Story* is nearly limitless, but nope, not this time," she said. "You must let us do this. We command you. You're not the only one who feels guilty here."

I started to protest, but she cut me off with a hand slash to her throat.

"You don't get to tell us how to feel, my girl," said Cornelia. "We watched you around him, always on tenterhooks, constantly poised to jump in and smooth things over. We should have intervened, helped. At least, let us help you now."

"I can't just leave you to deal with the fallout!"

Cornelia said, wryly, "If it makes you feel any better, there's bound to be plenty more fallout later. You can deal with that."

"Go pack," said my mother, pointing to the door. "Everything but your wedding dress. Then, go home. Although you are certainly not getting behind the wheel of a car."

"But I want to be alone." This wasn't true. Being loathsome and cruel, I was actually the very last person I wanted to be alone with, but I didn't want other people, either. What I would've most preferred was to be put in a medically induced coma for at least a week, possibly a year.

"Sorry," said my mother. "Not on those winding country roads, not with those shaking hands."

"They aren't shaking."

I glared at my hands, the little traitors, clenched them to try to stop the trembling, then gave up in disgust.

"We'll ask Dev to drive you back," said my mother.

"Not Dev," I said, quickly.

She glanced up at me, startled.

"Because it might hurt Zach," I said.

Such a sweet and considerate girl, so thoughtful of Zach's feelings, so protective.

God, I made myself want to throw up.

Hildy and Aidan drove me home, and even though the two of them were among my very favorite people to both talk and listen to, I couldn't do either. In the backseat, I hunched my shoulders, pulled my cardigan around me like a straitjacket, and tried to think about nothing at all, while outside the car windows, twilight dwindled, turning the Blue Ridge gray.

At 4:22 A.M., at home in my childhood bed, I woke up panicked, sure in my bones that I'd made a terrible mistake. Zach was right when he'd said marriage meant adapting! Everyone knew that! I should have stood by my word, zipped on my stupidly expensive white dress, and marched down the aisle straight into my beautiful future. Panting, sweating, with my heart stuttering and my sheets twisted around me like a boa constrictor,

I swore to myself that it wasn't too late. I would call him, beg him to take me back. I would fix everything. My scrambling hands groped my bedside table for my phone and yanked out the charger.

On the illuminated screen was a text message from Dev that he had sent after I'd fallen asleep: If this is totally inappropriate and exactly what you don't need, delete immediately. The message accompanied a photo of him and Teo shoving handfuls of wedding cake into their mouths, the pocked and dilapidated cake listing in the background. I didn't laugh, but I almost did, came closer than I ever thought I could, leaning back into my pillow and smiling ear to ear into the dark like an idiot, and not only because the photo was funny, but also because of what had always been true: even when I wasn't with him, just knowing that Dev existed in the world made me happy.

Okay, no, that hadn't *always* been true. Almost always, but there was a year in there—my last year of high school—when it hadn't been true at all, not by a long shot.

When we were a couple, Dev and I didn't live in the same town and would go as long as two months without seeing each other, and there were moments when I missed his physical proximity acutely and in very specific ways: his arm against mine—the slightest whisper of skin on skin—as we lay on our backs on a blanket, staring at the night sky, or his head in my lap as we watched TV, the blue light resting on the side of his face. But, while there were tough days, the missing never hurt that much because we texted constantly, e-mailed, and talked into the night, and I could always see an end point not far away, a date on my calendar, circled with a heart and marked "D-Day."

And then Dev went to Africa. *Africa.* Not Spain or France or Oxford, England, or New York or any other place I'd ever heard of a person spending his gap year. Dev signed on for nine months in South Africa doing HIV/AIDS education and assisting in a rural medical clinic, with an additional three months at an orphanage tacked on for good measure. South Africa, and not even Capetown, but a village so tiny and remote that his phone would be useless.

When he told me he wanted to do it, my whole body went cold, but I gave him my support. Who could argue against helping people who were sick and poor? Who could align herself against *orphans*? Also, the gap year wasn't just for these people; it was for me. Dev had skipped eighth grade, so that even though we were the same age, he'd graduated from high school a year ahead of me. But our plan had always been to start college together. He deferred his acceptance to the University of

Virginia, where I would apply early, and where, as a resident of the state and a crackerjack student besides, I was sure to get in. The one year apart meant we'd spend the four following—and all the years after that—together.

I held up nobly—everybody said so—until Dev's graduation party, a week before his flight to South Africa, when I stood in Cornelia and Teo's pretty, bloom-riddled backyard watching Dev laughing at something Cornelia's brother Toby had said, his head tilted forward, his eyes dancing, and felt the bottom fall out of my world. I didn't settle for just breaking down; no, I exploded like a pipe bomb, barely making it into the house before the jagged pieces went flying. Sobbing hysteria, flailing, unintelligible ranting. When my mother put her arms around me, I threw them off and ran blindly upstairs and into the nearest bedroom, which happened to be Dev's. Confronted with his books, his computer, his sneakers lined up in a row inside his open closet, his Milky Way poster, his basketball signed by Allen Iverson, his old cotton quilt worn to the softness of silk, and picture after picture of a dark-haired girl so glossy and sassy and blithely grinning that she could not possibly be me, I lost my bearings and fell, missing the bed and landing on the rug, completely unhinged. Dev lay down on the floor of his room and held me, clamped on tight and whispered *shh, shh, shh* like a mother to a child until I finally calmed down.

A few hours later, when I'd regained the ability to sit up like a normal person and speak in sentences, I begged him not to go away or at least to go somewhere in the United States, a place with phone service and Internet, a place he could fly home from at Christmas and that I could save up and fly out to once or twice, a place without black mamba snakes, dengue fever, unstable governments, and lions (it would take months for me to flush with shame at my stereotypical depiction of Africa, that's how far gone I was). I expected Dev to agree to change his plans and was stunned when he didn't. He said it was too late to cancel. He said the trip meant a lot to him. He talked about how privileged he was; when he used the phrase "giving back," I covered my ears and considered screaming.

Which is when he took my face between his two hands, and in the most loving voice I'd ever heard, said this: "We're *us,* remember? Even when we're apart, we're together. Quantum locality? Electron entanglement? Remember? We're outside the space-time continuum, Clare, where distance just *isn't.* Wherever I am, I'm yours. We'll be okay. I'd never leave if I weren't sure about that."

They may have been the sweetest words he'd ever spoken to me. They may have been the sweetest—and also nerdiest—words anyone had ever, inside or outside the space-time continuum, spoken to anyone. But I didn't care. All I wanted was for him to stay.

He left.

And I turned into a person I didn't know. Sad. Disorganized. I stopped finishing books. Slept a lot. Got quiet. Lost too much weight. Quit tennis; played the most halfhearted field hockey in the history of the sport. Stopped going out on weekends with my friends. For the first time in my life, my grades slipped; that they didn't fall to wrack and ruin was due to a combination of autopilot studying and sympathetic teachers. I believed what everyone around me believed, that I was in limbo, waiting for Dev to come home so our life together could start back up, but then an odd thing happened. When it came time to apply early action to UVA, I let the deadline pass by, and when I did apply to colleges, without discussing it with anyone or examining my motives, I found myself sending my application there but also to a lot of other, more far-flung places, big midwestern universities, two colleges in California.

Worried about my lackluster, weirdly un-Clare-like letters and the reports of my decline he'd been getting from his parents and Cornelia, Dev skipped the orphanage, came home early, three weeks into April, and drove down to Virginia to see me before he'd even unpacked his bags. Even though I could tell he was shocked by the changes in me—shocked and tender and heartbroken—our reunion was joyful, but when he saw the stack of acceptance letters on my desk, he breathed, "Oh, wow," and looked like he'd just lost his best friend. Still, when I said, "I'm sorry. I don't know why I did that. Of course, I'm going to UVA," he's the one who said, "I really want you to, but I think you probably did this for a reason."

So he went to Virginia, and I went to Michigan to figure out how to be a real person without him. Our plan was to stay together, but after two months, I understood that it wouldn't work. Steady-hearted and ever at home in his own skin, Dev could keep the faith, love me outside of space and time, carry me around like a turtle's shell, same as always, but I still didn't know how, so at Thanksgiving break, on the worst day of my life and probably his, I broke it off for good. Eventually, because we couldn't stand not to be, we became best friends, and Dev became a person who sent me perfectly timed, completely inappropriate wedding cake pictures, a person whose mere existence in the world made me happy.

So I didn't call Zach after all. I walked downstairs, made coffee, took it outside, sat down on a white Adirondack chair under a blooming catalpa tree, tucked my legs under me, sipped, and watched a hummingbird stitch and hover among the columbine, doing some sipping of its own. Relief did not wash over me. I still felt like a low-down, selfish, disgusting scoundrel, but there, in my own backyard, I could envision a time when I might feel slightly less bad, slightly more like the old Clare, deserving of at least a little forgiveness.

The sense of almost-peace lasted all day. I took a long walk, followed by a short run; weeded the flower beds; played chess on my computer; and, in a breathtaking stroke of luck, found a shoeshine kit in the top of the odds-and-ends closet and shined every shinable shoe in the house, a task that will forever rank—even if I live to be a hundred—as one of the most bone-deep satisfying things I've ever done.

After sunset, I walked to a nearby, pocket-square-sized public park, lay down on a bench with a sweatshirt tucked beneath my head, and watched tiny bats careen against a sequined sky. Home again, I took a shower, put on my high school gym shorts and my oldest, softest T-shirt, dug up my set of Narnia books, plopped down on the family room sofa, and submersed myself up to my ears in *The Voyage of the Dawn Treader.*

I'd just gotten to the chapter where Eustace wakes up to discover he's been turned into a dragon, when I heard a car come down the driveway. Or *start* down the driveway; it pulled in and then stopped, sliding a wedge of headlight light between the not-quite-shut curtains and onto the wall. Gordon and my mother weren't due back until the next morning. Fear zipped through me, and I tried to wish the car back down the driveway and into the night, but the wedge stuck, unwavering, to the wall. Thirty seconds later, the back screen door creaked and someone began to bang out a slow, continuous doomsday rhythm with what sounded like the heel of his hand.

"Clare! Are you there? Please tell me you're there."

Zach, either drunk or crying or both.

Thud. Thud. Thud. Thud.

"Clare! Please! I don't need to come in. Just come talk to me!"

Our next-door neighbor's Irish setter, Galway, began barking; Hedwig, the corgi across the street, followed suit. I knew that soon the entire neighborhood would go off like a string of canine firecrackers.

"Coming!" I called and with dread creeping up my spine, I walked into the mudroom, switched on the outside light, and turned the knob. Zach stood on the second step, his elbow propping open the screen door. With his golf cap, T-shirt and shorts, tear-streaked face, anxious eyes, and shaky smile, he looked like a fourteen-year-old, here to confess that he'd broken my car window with his baseball.

"Oh, Zach," I said, sighing.

"Will you come out and talk to me, just for a minute?" His words slid into one another, blurred at their edges.

"God, tell me you didn't drive here."

"No, no. I wouldn't do that." He jerked his head in the direction of the driveway. "Ian. He only agreed to it because I threatened to drive myself. He said, 'All we need is for you to get a DUI and bring more shame and ignominy down upon the dignified heads of your family.'"

"He said that, did he?"

Zach waved his hand aimlessly around in the air. "Something like that. We spent last night at his fancy condo in Baltimore. The natives call it *Bawlmore*, which is pretty appropriate since I've been bawling more these past couple days than I ever have before."

"Ian drove you all the way from Baltimore?"

"He did. You know, you should probably let me in or else you come out and shut the door. Wouldn't want to let bugs into your family abode."

Zach held the screen door open for me and edged away so that I could slip by him, then he let the door shut. We stood a few feet apart, just at the foot of the stairs. He took off his cap and ran his hand through his hair.

"I feel like I should get down on my knees," he said, with a limp chuckle.

"Zach, why are you here?"

He smiled bleakly. "I just needed to check to see if you'd changed your mind yet."

I started to speak, but he reached out and touched a shushing finger to my lips. Reflexively, I jerked my head back like I'd been stung and could have kicked myself afterward.

"And on the off chance that you hadn't changed your mind yet," he went on, "I wanted to ask you to please consider doing it soon because no one will ever, ever love you like I do."

His voice broke at the word *love,* and he pressed his golf cap to his eyes, then took it away. My own eyes burned, and I wanted to hug him so badly that I clasped my hands behind my back to stop myself.

"How could I have caused you so much pain?" I whispered. "I'm so sorry."

"Hey, all you have to do to fix it is come back to me. On any terms you want. We can start all over. God, we can *date,* even. Remember when you took me hiking?"

I swallowed a sob. "A bee stung you. And it rained."

"I loved it."

Behind my back, my two hands gripped each other for dear life.

"Zach, I can't come back to you."

He reached out and rested his hands against my upper arms. I didn't flinch. "You don't have to decide now. I just wanted to check and see if maybe you had, but you don't have to until you're good and ready."

"Please. I've decided already."

He froze and I watched his soft expression clear away like a window defogging. For a split second his hands began to grip my arms, but then he yanked them off, spun around, and frisbeed his hat into the shadowy yard where it snagged on a rosebush.

"*This* is why," he said, his voice rising. "This is fucking why!"

I stepped up onto the first step.

"Your perfect house! Perfect family! I hate my family because they suck, but I hate yours even more!"

I stepped onto the second step and silently slipped my hand through the screen door's handle, my thumb on the button.

Zach whirled around, his teeth flashing in a bitter grin. "Your perfect parents! And Cornelia and Teo, whoever the hell they even are! Not even blood relatives. All those *people*. *They're* why you think you don't need me! Right? Am I right?"

I stood, fear thrumming through me, the yard looking watery and weird, the button under my thumb the only solid and true thing on the entire planet, and then, from deep inside the house next door, on the other side of the row of flame-shaped cypress bushes, Galway began to bark, to send clear, wild sounds flying into the night.

"Shut the hell up, dog!" spat Zach.

Drawing his leg back like a soccer player taking a penalty kick, Zach slammed his foot against the terracotta planter next to the back gate. He probably expected to send it flying, but the planter merely fell over and lay on its side, intact. In the yellow light, I could see a handful of potting soil splash out, but the fern inside didn't budge. In the stillness that followed, Zach stared down at the planter, and I pulled open the door and slipped inside the house.

"The neighbors will be out here any minute," I told him, quickly. "You need to leave."

Without taking his eyes off the planter, Zach nodded. "Okay. Okay. I'm sorry. I'm really sorry. I didn't mean to do that. We'll talk later."

He swiveled his head to catch my eye. "Okay? Later. Soon."

I didn't speak or move, just regarded him blankly, through the screen, then watched as he jogged out of the yard. As I listened to Ian's car pull out fast, tires whining, and blast off through my pretty, sleepy, tree-lined neighborhood, there it was at last, unmistakable, ribboning like a cool, bright stream up through my chest, trickling down my legs and arms: relief.

Chapter Nine
Edith

Edith didn't fit.

She had not fit before, plenty of times, although she was nearly positive that she had never been regarded as odd, not full-blown odd anyway. *Aloof* was what she usually got, even occasionally—ridiculously—*mysterious,* her sort of looks somehow taking the more accurate adjective *shy* out of contention. Although even *shy* wasn't quite right. The truth was that Edith had always done her best within a clearly defined context. School. Nursing school. Work. She could talk—could even be funny or clever—when there was something real to talk about: books, tests, teachers, current events, music, patients, cases. *Concepts.* Edith could get downright voluble about concepts. Evolutionary theory. Communism. Fascism. Ethics.

She could talk to the grocer about vegetables, to the butcher about meat. She had talked to her father about birds, fungi, tides, bees, ants, the phases of the moon, predator and prey, the cycle of life.

When she fell in love with Joseph, she discovered, for the first time, her gift for telling a story, for finagling beauty and humor and weirdness out of the everyday with the right detail, the proper metaphor.

But coffees, cocktail parties, neighborhood barbecues, all these seemed to her like games the rules of which she'd never learned. Conversations reminded her of the time when, as a little girl, she tried to catch tadpoles with her fingers, the subject matter darting and slippery, wriggling away at the last second. Her confusion turned her, not fluttery, but blunt, keeping quiet, then tossing a comment like a stone, sending the tadpoles skittering off. In the ungainly silence that followed, the other women would sip their drinks, bite into a canapé or deviled egg, telegraphing *Poor Joseph, what an odd bird his wife is* to each other with their eyes.

But for Joseph's sake, she kept trying. In truth, Edith would've spent her days with only her husband. To her, his body alone was a world—rippling, bristling, full of weather, flavors, seasons, never the same two days in a row—and their private sphere of house, yard, marshes, bay, ocean, beach was an entire universe. Both were enough to command her rapt attention, to fire her imagination, to bring her joy for a thousand lifetimes. Honestly, the idea of wanting to spend time with people one did not love absolutely mystified her. But Joseph liked company, small talk, sharing food. Magnetic, gregarious, he drew people to him and was drawn in return. And he wanted her with him, so she went.

But she never fit. Even looking like everyone else eluded her. All her life, she had never managed polish or tidiness, never, even as a child, been perky or pretty or cute. She'd understood—because she had been told—that she was a certain kind of beautiful, with her long, angular face, her strong brows, curving mouth, dark, feathery lashed eyes, but, distracted by books and animal tracks, mud, water, insects, and bones, and half in love with loneliness, she had never cared. A gangly girl, now she stood tall, narrow hipped, broad shouldered, leggy as a heron. In an era of things staying in place, of starch and hairspray, she was loosely gathered, pieces of her forever apt to ravel, crease, fly away. In the salt air, her long bob uncurled, tangled in wind. Her lipstick smudged.

At home, she went without makeup, lived in blue jeans and Joseph's shirts, her hair held off her face with a scarf. In the beginning, when they first fell in love, for the first month perhaps, her beauty mattered to her as it never had before. She loved her face because Joseph did, because it was something she could give him, but it was as if once she had handed it over to him, had given it into his keeping for good, she forgot about it. When he photographed her, he laughed because she never posed, never offered the planes of her cheeks to the light, never even remembered to look into the camera. Instead, she watched him, cherishing each piece of him with her attention, his hands holding the camera, his brown hair falling on his forehead, the shell-curve of his ear, the way the collar of his shirt opened to reveal, like a secret, the triangle of skin at the base of his throat.

Chapter Ten
Clare

The morning after Zach's nighttime visit, he texted me a long, sad apology that made me ache for him and that ended: I messed up like I messed up at the lake house. It's like I have this well of anger inside me and I don't know how exactly it got there and I don't know how to cap it so that nothing gets out. But I think I can learn, especially when it comes to getting angry at you. Because god Clare I know you deserve better and I understand why you'd run away from a person like me. But I still wished you'd stayed. I know you could fix me if you were here.

I texted back: I messed up, too, Zach, so badly. But I really believe you don't need me to change the things you want to change about yourself. You're smart and strong and good enough to do it on your own. I hope I am, too.

Even as I tapped out the message, I was dogged by the thought that it might not be true. What if Zach did need me? What if I were his only hope? I understood how arrogant that sounded, but the fact was people *did* need people. People saved each other all the time, every day. What if, in the grand scheme of things, I was supposed to stick around and save Zach?

It would have been so easy to text again, to tell him that he was right, that I would get on the first plane back to him. I could envision myself typing the words. It would make him so happy. Imagining his happiness was almost more than I could bear.

If you went back, you could never leave again, I told myself. *It would be too cruel. If you went back, it would be for forever.*

That *forever* is what sent me backward, reeling away from the edge I'd been standing on. I realized I would probably go back to that edge more than once, but on that day, I turned off my phone, set it down, and ran up the stairs the way I used to when I was a kid, taking them two at a time, clomping like an elephant. I remembered how back then, I hadn't been running away from anything; I had run out of a pure, free-floating urgency, just because if you were going someplace, you might as well get there fast.

For the next week, I threw myself into business matters. Zach and I had been all set to move from his spiffy apartment to an even spiffier one, Zach having insisted that no marriage could thrive outside the presence of granite countertops and a very sparkly, nearly noiseless dishwasher, so my belongings were already boxed up and ready to go. The image of those stacked and neatly labeled boxes patiently waiting to be carried into a future that no longer existed was one of many that haunted me in the days following our breakup, but the boxes made Hildy's shipping my stuff to my parents' house easy enough (easier for me than for Hildy, obviously, who, in typical Hildy fashion, told me to shut the hell up every time I tried to thank her).

I borrowed money from my parents to cover the cost of my half of the apartment security deposit, the moving company's security deposit, and all the other deposits toward a future that had turned out to be the opposite of secure. I wrote a half-charming, half-frantically-desperate letter to the graduate speech pathology program in Boston that I'd bailed out of when I'd agreed to marry Zach, asking them to please consider reinstating me, if not this year, then—pretty please with sugar on top—the next. I returned wedding gifts and penned endless notes of apology to the givers and to all our would-be-turned-would-not-be wedding guests, and if I say that I felt every word of those notes carve themselves into my skin like in that scary Dolores Umbridge detention scene in the fifth Harry Potter, I'm exaggerating, but only a little.

And, through it all, each night, I spent hours texting and talking with Zach, whose moods encompassed every permutation of heartbroken, from grieving to enraged, from bitter to sweet to bittersweet, from pleading to threatening, from repentant to accusatory, from hopeful to hopeless, sometimes all in a single conversation. It was brutal, and maybe the hardest part was realizing—like a plunge into ice water—that I loved him, a fact that had gotten lost in all the prewedding hubbub of his loving me and in the post-nonwedding hubbub of shattering his heart. True fact: Zach was lovable and I loved him. I could not marry him, but I loved the complicated, contradictory, sweet, knotty humanity of him, and it is one thing to crush the heart of a man who loves you unrequitedly and quite another to do it to a man you love back. I cried a lot. I scrolled through old photos on my phone late into the night. At least a dozen times, I came one breath away from asking him to take me back.

For three weeks, I regrouped, introspected, considered my options, although from the outside (and sometimes from the inside, too) this process looked a lot like taking long walks, staying up late watching old movies with my mom, and lying on various items of indoor and outdoor furniture binge-reading the books from my childhood.

And then, one day, Edith gave me a house.

It started with a letter from a Philadelphia law firm, and the letter led to a phone call, to a few more phone calls, to a car trip, to a meeting at a glossy conference table with a robot-like, staccato-voiced, auburn-haired lawyer named Eloisa Dunne, who explained that Edith Herron had died of cancer just two weeks after I'd met her at the hotel in Virginia and had left me a house in a pretty—or so Eloisa Dunne had heard, not being a beach person herself (a fact that did not surprise me)—coastal town called Antioch Beach, Delaware. Eloisa Dunne was not authorized to give any other information regarding the deceased and in fact *knew* no other information but explained that the house had been uninhabited for nearly sixty years. However, it was in remarkably good shape, since a property maintenance company had cared for it since Edith Herron had moved away in the 1950s. The company was paid through an anonymous trust that had been put in place not long after her exiting the property, and as there was still at least five years' worth of money left in the trust, I was obligated neither to live in the house nor to care for it. I need not even go there, although the house was mine to keep or to sell.

"I imagine it would be worth a very tidy sum these days," said Eloisa Dunne. "Anyway, the residence seems to have been a boardinghouse for a few years, and consequently, it has a name: Blue Sky House."

A light dawned.

"Say that again," I said.

"Blue Sky House. Not your typical house name. But quaint, I suppose."

You're his blue sky. When everything else is darkness. But is he yours? Edith's voice, bell-clear and ageless in the morning air.

"I won't sell it," I said, so quickly that my mother gave me a surprised glance, and even Eloisa Dunne's eyes widened briefly and blinked once in her otherwise motionless cameo face.

"'Sometimes, in order to hold your own, you need a place of your own,'" I said. "Oh, Edith."

"Clare?" said my mother, frown lines between her eyes.

"It's what she said to me. Light and space all my

own. A place to breathe easy. I told her I used to carry my safe place around with me like a turtle, but then, when I got involved with Zach, I somehow stopped."

I stared at my mother in wonder.

"So she gave you one," my mother said, softly. "An almost total stranger talked you out of your engagement to the wrong man and then gave you a safe place to go. Unbelievable."

"Yes. It is unbelievable." I thought for a moment. "Or it should be. Somehow, though I didn't expect this at all and I know it's rare and even sort of crazy, it's somehow believable anyway. Because of Edith. Because of how she was."

"How was she?" asked my mother.

"I don't know. Bigger than the rest of us. Overarching. More *part of things* than regular people. And more knowing."

"Maybe because she was dying," said Eloisa Dunne.

I stared at her. With her foggy, faraway eyes and turned-inward expression, she suddenly didn't look like a robot at all.

"My mother did that, in her last days," she went on. "Became intuitive, as if she'd tapped into some cache of understanding the rest of us couldn't get anywhere near. And she was so peaceful. I'm sure she didn't actually glow. But in my memories of her, she's glowing."

The three of us sat there, considering whether death's nearness could transform a person, whether it could maybe turn their personal borders watery and permeable so that more of the world got in. Eloisa was the first to snap back to herself. She slid a manila envelope out from under her stack of legal papers, unfastened it with one quick motion, and handed it to me.

I looked inside. Keys, a lot of them, each one tagged. I turned the envelope over and spilled the keys onto the conference table, then fanned them out with my hands. *Front door. Back door. Cabinet One. Cabinet Two. Fireproof box.* And so forth.

"I wonder," I said, slowly.

"What do you wonder?" asked my mother.

I smiled. "I'm going to sound crazy again, and maybe it's just me projecting all of this stuff onto Edith. Probably. That would make sense. But anyway, I feel as if, in addition to giving me the house, she's giving me herself. I think she wants me to discover who she was."

"And you wonder if one of these keys—?" said my mother.

"Exactly. I wonder if one of them will unlock Edith. I hope so. I had exactly three encounters with her, none of them long, but I hope so. I hope so so much."

Chapter Eleven
Edith

August 1952

It was during what they both knew would be their last canoe trip together that Joseph made her promise to live.

"And by live I mean all the way, with all your heart and soul."

"If there is any of either left," she said, but she canceled out the rueful words with a broad smile because she would not, could not, had sworn not to since he'd first fallen so ill, give him cause to fear for her.

"My precious Edie," he said, "you must promise to give yourself entirely to someone or something because that's who you are. You are a genius at devoting yourself; it's what makes you happiest."

"Not to someone," she said, firmly. "And you may as well not even try to talk me out of that, mister, because you won't, not if you throw every ounce of your charm at me. You are my only someone. I will stay devoted to you and to no one else, ever. That's that."

He eyed her skeptically. "I'm not so sure, but never mind. Something then. Find something. Of course, the world should cherish you in return, but that will take care of itself. Nothing in the wide world is easier than loving you."

"Says you," she teased.

Joseph laughed and she could see his features tighten with pain, watched his right hand grope vaguely at his back, felt the canoe move side to side as he shifted his big, newly angular body in search of the comfortable position she knew he wouldn't find, and there it was: the sensation of spinning on a cliff's edge, the tearing, metallic screech of losing him forever gripping the back of her throat. She looked away from her husband, squinted at a bird flying low above the water until she felt the canoe's wobbling cease.

She pointed. "A shearwater. Not a very elegant bird, really, all that stiff-winged teetering, like a seesaw."

"Unlike you, my elegant bird," said Joseph, reaching for her hand. She set down her oar and clasped his hand, which had grown thinner but was somehow still square and strong and familiar.

It was she—and not the nurse but the lover—who had noticed the first symptoms: the faint yellowing of his eye whites and skin (she saw it earliest on the pale places untouched by sun, like a pollen stain on the smooth skin across his hip bones and the tops of his thighs), and a new articulation of his ribs and cheekbones and spine and wrists. Such slight changes, but she had taken his body apart—focusing on one tiny piece of him at a time—and put it back together so often, with her camera and her eyes, and had mapped the intricate, stretched-out landscape of him with her own bones and muscles and nerve endings so many times and with such absorption that she detected what most people would have missed.

Still, it wasn't early enough, not even close—a fact he'd so vehemently forbidden her to torture herself with that she'd complied. Once he began to go down, he went so fast that she began to have dreams of wildfire racing through dense forests, leaving black and skeletal trees, or of a skyscraper being violently dismantled by wind or once, horribly, of a gray whale being torn apart by sharks. Joseph had been so large; the sheer scope of him had dazzled her from the start. To watch that broad, strong body come to ruin, pare down and weaken, was shockingly cruel, but she swore to give him, no matter what, the gift of herself, her usual self, unbroken, composed and joking and observing the world with sharp-eyed curiosity. He should have his wife, she thought, until the very end, and come hell or high water or sorrow like a screaming bird of prey, she would make certain he did.

John Blanchard had helped lower him into the canoe. It was early morning, just after sunrise, the jeweled hour, the sun a liquid-edged apricot, its light pattering like fingertips over the water, the sky a breath of blue. Joseph's favorite time of day. Edith paddled slowly, then let them just float, suspended between sky and water. She alternated: paddle and float; glide and drift; intention and chance.

Apart from the shearwater, they'd seen few birds, the serenity of the morning punctuated only by two silent flotillas of ducks and one burst of tiny fish skittering like rain across the water. But then, as they rounded a point, they saw them, dozens of them, roosting in the trees, white as laundry: herons, what appeared to be an entire flock.

"I've never seen so many together," whispered Edith. "Never, ever."

"No, never," said Joseph.

Absently, enthralled by the birds, she reached up and slid the kerchief off her head, and in an instant, a light wind kicked off the water and caught in her hair, sliding coolness along the back of her neck. Then, like a massive exhale, the flock of herons lifted itself off the branches and threw itself at the sky, the individual birds, their impossible necks, the white drapery of wings becoming a single event, one noisy, snowy, chaotic glory.

When the birds had blown away like a blizzard, at the moment when the air still held their electric memory, Edith and Joseph turned rapt faces to each other, and Joseph said, reverently, "That was you. You, you. That's what you have been to me. Exactly."

After Joseph died, Edith entered a period of freeze. Numb, wooden, blank-eyed, she moved through first his funeral, then the burial in the bean field cemetery in front of the chapel where they'd been married. His mother, Anne, had been there for his last days, stoic and tender, and after his death she had crumbled and clung—childlike, grief-blind—to Edith until the morning after the burial, when Edith woke to the smell of eggs and bacon. Still frozen, Edith applied fork and knife to the meal, directed the food to her mouth, chewed. Afterward, when she tried to thank Anne, she found she couldn't speak, a condition that lasted for days. So Anne stayed, sat up night after night with her mute, disoriented daughter-in-law, telling her stories about Joseph's childhood. Edith listened without reacting, but some still-working part of her mind gathered the stories up, put them away for safekeeping, all those small pieces of Joseph ready when she needed them, when she thawed.

Which she did, quite suddenly, ten days later, when she was hanging sheets on the line to dry. The bright, salt-tinged early autumn wind tugged at the sheets, surrounding Edith in the scent of lemon detergent and sending her back to her first time in their house, her bridal afternoon, the smell of lemon oil and Joseph waiting for her in the doorway, and she dropped to her knees, felled by loss, clutching the bundle of damp bed linens to her chest like a baby.

So Anne stayed for two weeks more, until Edith could function again, her brain sorting out the world hour to hour: wake, talk, shower, dress, shop for food, prepare food, eat food, sleep. Anne invited her to come live with her in Ohio, saying they could both use the company.

"Also, life isn't easy for women on their own, and I can tell you from experience—long-ago experience but I don't think times have changed much—that small communities like this one can be, well, a little uneasy with beautiful widows."

Edith understood. She'd already felt the wariness and suspicion behind some of her visitors' pointed questions about what her "next step" would be. But even so and as grateful as she was for Anne's offer, she would not leave the house that Joseph had given her, every room of which was a part of him.

"I hate to say this," said Anne, gently, just before she left, "but you will have to make money. I've checked, and you have enough for a few months, but no more. Can you go back to nursing?"

"No," said Edith, pressing her lips together and shaking her head. "Not after my father and Joseph. I can't."

"I understand. So not right away, but soon, sooner than you'll want to, you'll have to find something to do."

Edith put her arms around Anne and pressed her close. "I will," she said. "I promise."

Nearly a month later, at the market, a tourist from Pittsburgh visiting with her family in the off-season, a young mother buying milk for her baby, struck up a conversation with Edith.

"It's only now that we can afford to come, the hotels have gotten so expensive," said the woman, sighing.

"And they aren't homey, either, all those long hallways, and the lobby where I have to keep the kids in check. One day, we'd love to come in summer, for a whole week even, and stay in a real house, but I don't suppose we ever will be able to."

Edith took in the woman's tired eyes, the resigned set of her shoulders inside her sweater, and an idea struck her with all the force of a revelation. She set down the apple she'd been examining and smiled at the woman.

"Why, I have a guesthouse," she said. "Short-term boarders only, vacationers. I'm sure we could work out a rate for the summer. May I give you my address and phone number?"

The woman's wan face lit up. "Well, of all the luck! My goodness. I'll take all your information down right now!" she exclaimed, opening her handbag to rummage for paper, which she found, and something to write with, which she did not. "Does your establishment have a name?"

Edith imagined her precious house overrun by strangers and found it didn't hurt. It seemed somehow right. *Give yourself to something,* Joseph had told her. Maybe this wasn't it, not quite, but it would do for the moment. She reached into her own handbag, pulled out a pen, and handed it to the woman.

"It does," she said. "I call it Blue Sky House."

Chapter Twelve
Clare

"Ave Maria" was pouring out of the open front door of Edith's house, lightening the heavy summer air and tingeing it silver, so I stopped in my tracks on the front walk, shut my eyes, and listened. Near the end of the song, as the voice began to trace an ascending arc so exultant and starlit that it made me want to cry, it cut off and said, "Damn it, Riley, I'm working here! You've called four times in forty minutes. If you miss me so much, why don't you get off your scrawny butt and come see me?"

I laughed. Through the open door, I could see a long, jaunty silhouette, one hand on a cocked hip, the other pressing a cell phone to an ear. As I stood there, the silhouette moved toward me through the house, coming into focus. By the time it got to the door, I saw that it was a girl, probably younger than I was by a few years and worlds sassier, with cherry-red lips, platinum hair twisted into a bun on the very top of her head, and a bright blue bikini top.

"And, hey, if you bring me a pack of Butterscotch Krimpets, I'll be your BFF. And not just for a day but forever and ever." She paused, listening, then rolled her big Betty Boop eyes. "Yes, I *know* BFF forever is redundant? That's why it's *funny*? Just get up and get—"

Spotting me, she broke off.

"Gotta go," she said.

She shoved the cell phone into her pocket and grinned.

"Hi, there. You must be the new owner," she said, walking toward me with her hand out. "My mom said you'd be coming, got word from a lawyer about it, but I thought it was tomorrow. She'll be upset that the house wasn't quite ready for you."

"No, no, I'm early. I guess I got a little impatient," I said. I shook her ring-bedecked hand. "Hi, I'm Clare Hobbes."

"I'm Joliet," she said. "Not like the Shakespeare character, like the town in Illinois where my grandma's from."

"I like it," I said.

"Thanks." She gestured toward the door of the house.

"I just changed the sheets. Wasn't sure what bed you'd be sleeping in, so I took them all home yesterday and washed them. Even though no one ever sleeps here, we do that from time to time, because my mom is super-anal about Edith's house."

"You and your mom own the cleaning service I guess? The one that gets paid out of the trust?"

"Ha! Own! Baby, we *are* the cleaning service. My grandma started it up when she moved here from Joliet. Granny started cleaning this house in the 1960s, before my mom was born. When her arthritis got bad, my mom took over. Her boyfriend, Axel, does all the handyman stuff, repairs, yard work. He even takes care of the canoes; honestly, I think he's obsessed with the canoes. Anyway, I started college last fall. Pre-vet. But I'm helping out this summer."

"Well, thank you for changing the sheets."

Joliet shooed away my thanks with her hand. "I love being here. When I was a baby, Mom would plop me down in whatever room she was cleaning. I guess I kind of grew up in this house."

"That's nice. It's a nice house."

It was. White clapboards, tall windows, a porch that looked like it was once screened in but was now screenless and doorless, a garden lavish with flowers.

Joliet nodded, thoughtfully. "Yeah. I suppose I grew

up in a lot of houses because of the cleaning service and all, but this one's special."

"How so?"

She smiled with her whole face. "Because it's Edith's."

Joliet said this as if no further explanation were necessary, and as a person who had spent all of an hour and a half in Edith's company, I understood completely. "Was she a friend of your grandmother's?"

"No, another company cleaned this house for ten years before my grandmother took over, and of course, by then Edith was long gone. None of us ever met her. In fact, we didn't even know she was alive until we found out that, um, she wasn't anymore, which made us all sad. No, it's just the house itself. You feel Edith all over it. You feel both of them."

"Both?"

Joliet looked surprised at my question. "Well, Edith and Joseph, of course." She said it the way people say Romeo and Juliet or Bogie and Bacall. "How do you not know about Joseph?"

"A few weeks ago," I said, "I had three conversations with Edith, two short, one longer, all during what was supposed to be my wedding weekend."

Joliet narrowed her eyes. "Supposed to be?"

"That's right. I broke it off because marrying the

man I was supposed to have married would've been a colossal mistake. It was Edith who helped me see that."

It was easy enough for me to say this with assurance today, since that morning, I'd woken up to a voice mail from Zach. He was obviously drunk, but even with the slurring, I had no trouble making out his words: "You bitch. You goddamned, heartless bitch. Who the hell do you think you are to play me this way? Someone must've done something seriously shitty to you for you to end up like you are. What do you think of that? Maybe your perfect little childhood wasn't so perfect after all? Hey, you know what? Go to hell." It was the verbal equivalent of being punched in the stomach, and for at least fifteen minutes, I lay balled up on the bed of the hotel room, my eyes squeezed shut, fighting off nausea and fear. It was as if Zach kept taking the five stages of grief and shuffling them, and somehow he kept coming back to anger.

Joliet nodded and scratched her chin, thoughtfully. "That makes sense. You can tell from her house that Edith knew true love, so I guess it would stand to reason that she'd also know untrue love. Or true unlove. Or whatever."

"I loved him. I might still, in a way. But he wasn't the one. He wasn't home to me. Edith could tell."

"So what was she like? Beautiful? Wise? Funny?"

"Yes, yes, and yes," I said. "And calm. I was coming apart at the seams, but she acted like it was all perfectly normal and understandable. 'Understanding' is actually a good adjective for her. And I don't just mean nice. She understood things, saw right to the bottom of them without even seeming to try."

Joliet nodded.

"Strange as it sounds, I think she might have understood everything in the world." I smiled. "Well, that was a weird thing to say."

"Makes sense to me," said Joliet.

"She was frail. She walked with a cane. I didn't know she was sick when we met; I just thought she was old. Only her body was frail, though. Her mind moved fast as anyone's, faster, and her voice sounded like a girl's."

"Go on," said Joliet, then she jumped. Both feet actually came off the ground. "No! Wait! Why don't I show you around the house? You'll see what I mean about Edith; it's like the whole place is a little monument to true love."

"It sounds like a good place," I said.

Joliet smiled. "It is."

It was there, unmistakable. Two chairs in front of the fireplace, tilted toward each other like friends; the matching vintage canoes; the entire third-floor bedroom with its matching bedside flower vases—newly filled, by Joliet, with pink coneflowers—its bed situated so as to offer those sitting up in it curtain-framed views of the back garden and shimmering canal; and oh, that blue sky ceiling, still radiant despite the years. When I told Joliet what Edith had said—*You're his blue sky. When everything else is darkness*—she sat down on the bed and looked up at me as if I'd solved the riddle of the universe.

"I just thought it was to remind them that summer would come. Believe me, it gets pretty gray and drab here in the winter. But this, this is even better. They were each other's blue sky. Oh, be still my heart."

And above all else, there were the photographs, magnificent black-and-whites framed on every wall of the house. All of them were of Edith. Downstairs were seascapes and waterscapes and landscapes, with Edith so organically a part of them you almost didn't register her presence. She might have been a gull, a dune, a pine tree. Upstairs, in the third-floor bedroom, close-ups of her face, high-cheekboned, tan, her dark eyes alive beneath peaked brows, her expression ranging from tender to amused to starkly adoring; in one photo, she had the exact look of someone reading a book she loves. *Joseph,* I thought. *Joseph was the book.*

"You see what I mean?" said Joliet. "Edith and Joseph, Joseph and Edith. Him loving her through the lens, her loving him right back. This house is a frigging love museum."

"It is," I said. "It really, truly is."

"How long are you staying?"

"I don't know. I'm really just here to check the place out. Maybe a few days, maybe a week."

Joliet gave me a skeptical look. "I saw your car. It was packed to the gills, as my mom would say. I bet you'll stay longer than a week."

I felt my phone vibrate and got it out of my pocket. A text from Zach: I'm so sorry about that call last night. Forgive me, Clare. Forgive me forgive me forgive me.

I looked around at the walls of Edith's house and said, "Who knows? You just might be right."

That night, feeling a lot like a girl in a fairy tale, I opened the first locked box I came across—a kind of wooden, oversized jewelry box—trying each key until one fit, and found Joseph Herron's obituary, which I read with sorrow. *War photographer . . . worked with Society of Friends to rebuild Europe . . . photographer for the* Lower Delaware Daily Bee *. . . beloved friend . . . beloved son . . . cared for through his illness and survived by his beloved wife, former nurse Edith Herron.*

Beneath the obituary was a stack of photographs, each a piece of Joseph—a hand, a temple, a hillock of shoulder, the curled corner of his mouth—never a full shot of him, but somehow each photo felt complete and so reverent, as if someone believed that the tiniest part of the man was worthy of the most exquisite attention. Not someone. Edith. On the back of each, just "My J" in small precise lettering and a date.

Beneath the photographs was their marriage certificate, faded and so old the paper was soft as suede. They'd been married here in Antioch Beach. I held the certificate under the lamplight to make out the date, then quickly double-checked Joseph's death certificate, hoping I'd gotten something wrong. I hadn't.

"Oh, no. Let it not be true," I pleaded to the empty room.

Distilled and rare and rampant love everywhere, in every corner of this house and spilling over into the front garden, the backyard, eddying into the canal that led to the bay, all that, and Edith and Joseph had had just two years together.

With tears in my eyes, I picked up a photograph Edith had taken of her husband: his inner wrist, twin tendons running down its center, the narrow valley between them as private, as holy a place as any I'd ever seen.

"*This,*" I said, cradling the photo in my palms. "This is it. The thing you hold out for. You wait a lifetime if you have to."

It felt like a vow, and, for a second, I wished I had a witness, but then I realized that I did. The house was my witness.

Chapter Thirteen
Edith

September 1953

Later, once she had dragged herself far enough out of her swamp of grief to look back, Edith understood that it was the guests who had kept her going. This despite the fact that she resented them, sometimes fiercely, on and off, for at least the first year, resented their presence, outsiders tromping all over her and Joseph's sanctuary, their voices crowding out the memory of Joseph's voice, their carefree, cut-loose vacation happiness reminding her piercingly, hourly of every joy she had lost.

The guests forced her out of bed. They forced her to wash her face, brush her teeth, apply a touch of makeup, and get dressed, not in the blue jeans she'd favored when her house was empty, but in a neat dress or pair of pedal pushers. They forced her to pay attention, to button each button in the right order, to bathe regularly, to not lie facedown on Joseph's side of the bed for hours or days wishing she were dead.

Each morning, she would tiptoe from her attic bedroom and down the stairs, avoiding the creaky spots as she passed the second-floor bedrooms where the guests stayed, and would start the percolator, set the table with her wedding plates and flatware and with little cut-glass bowls of jam and butter, slice peaches or melon or bananas, mix up a batch of drop biscuits, put them in the oven, and then would go out in the backyard with her coffee and sit in a chair, drinking and watching the sun toss coins across the canal and tiny jellyfish beat like gauze hearts just below the surface of the water. For those few stolen minutes, she found she could let go, second by second, of everything that haunted her until her mind was empty as a scoured bowl and all she knew was flavor on her tongue, air against her face, the small, dazzling details of her scrap of world. Then, she would go inside, ready to smile and chat, to fry and pour, to lean over the open oven to check for just the right amount of goldenness.

She was busy, busy, busy, but also—for the first time she could remember—bored. She learned what she would never have imagined: that heartbreak and boredom could be paired. Apart from the guests, most people stayed away. No more cocktail party or dinner invitations, no more of the interminable coffees that she, rocked with loneliness, might even at long last have welcomed.

Out of sheer desperation, despite her terror at how painful it might be, Edith began to venture out alone in her canoe. The first time was a horrible, racked, air-gulping, hair-tearing ordeal, and she swore she'd never go again. But one afternoon, when the guests were at the beach, she found that she missed, down to her bone marrow, the very specific sight of sun glazing the mussel-studded bank of the salt marsh at low tide, that lacquered, rainbow-suffused black. By the third time, she didn't cry. By the fifth, the sensation that Joseph's canoe was gliding along parallel to her own comforted her instead of torturing her. On the sixth trip, she took her camera, and—in narrowing the sprawling, intractable everything into one small, contained rectangle after the next—felt tiny stirrings of hope.

John Blanchard dropped by now and again to check on her with a genial, matter-of-fact concern for a woman living alone that never tipped over into condescension or judgment. In the months following Joseph's death, Edith had a handful of male callers—Donald Smith dropping off a casserole his wife had made; Richie Fulton, barely out of his teens, who cut her grass and trimmed her bushes; old Len Pilgrim, an avid bird-watcher, who came around occasionally to brag about his sightings to the only other person he knew who cared; and a few bachelors and widowers, slick-haired and sheepish, who brought flowers and never got farther than the front lawn—all of whom were subjected to searing, raised-eyebrow scrutiny by Edith's neighbors.

Because of his job, John was mostly, however grudgingly, granted the benefit of the doubt, but Edith knew that even he wasn't gossip proof. Joseph had told her his story: divorced after a brief marriage, his wife a restless type who should never have gotten married to anyone, least of all steady, quiet John, a few years spent living with his widowed sister and her little girl until a couple of years ago when she met a tourist at the boardwalk, married him, and moved away. Single, tall, blond, and blue-eyed, with an unshakable aura of quietude and the ability to deflect flirtation like those new Teflon pans, the women in the town regarded him as either utterly dreamy or the dullest man in the world. How much of this he realized Edith wasn't sure, but she did know that, while he'd sit on the screen porch or at the backyard table and talk for an hour, he steadfastly and politely refused her invitations to come inside the house.

On the first anniversary of Joseph's death, it was John who found her.

Telling herself for weeks beforehand that it would be just another day, that Joseph would be no more lost to her on that day than any other, Edith had planned a short visit to his grave, a bouquet of flowers from the garden he'd planted and a little box of seashells in her hand, and nothing more. This she stuck to, sitting on a folded blanket she'd brought, running her hand over his gravestone, tall and white among the old pocked and tilted ones, and telling him about that morning's canoe trip, how the shy, mica-thin gibbous moon had hung in the sky right along with the freshly risen sun, reminding her of the two of them; about the little girl guest from the week before who could, at three and a half years old, read from the newspaper; about how Edith had matted, framed, and hung his photographs of her so that she could remember being seen through his eyes every day; about the basket of apples someone had left on her doorstep; about how her love for him didn't just abide but grew, fanning like a vine over the walls of the house he'd given her, sending tendrils into every corner of her life.

She stayed dry-eyed and composed, feeling that he was there with her, listening, searching for signs that she was all right. This feeling lasted all day. She came home to her silent house, glad she hadn't scheduled any guests for that day, grateful to be alone. But then, after midnight, the grief rose, many-winged, inside her chest, beating at her ribs, bruising her from the inside out, so she ran out into the rain that had started a few hours before, ran across the highway, and onto the empty beach. Until she felt the wet sand under her soles, she didn't realize she'd forgotten shoes. For a moment, she felt like a crazy person, her last lucid thought before she became one. For hours, she paced the water's edge, sobbing, shouting, and swearing into the noise of the waves.

By the time John found her (she never learned how he knew she was there but assumed someone had called to report a lunatic loose on the beach), she was quiet, dazed, sodden, shivering, raw-throated, her hair like seaweed down her back, her thin shirt transparent.

"Here now, here now," he said.

He draped first his jacket then his arm over her trembling shoulders and gently led her to his still warm, still running car, and drove her home. For the first time since Joseph had died, John came inside.

"Wait here," he said, and she stood in the kitchen, holding on to the counter to steady herself, until he came back with a towel, some wool socks, Joseph's old dark green, cable-knit sweater, and the quilt from the first-floor bedroom. He held the sweater up like a mother dressing a child and dutifully she ducked her head into it; then he walked her to one of the fireplace chairs, wrapped her in the blanket, and asked her to sit, while he built a fire. She put the socks on herself, and once the fire was truly going, he helped her dry her hair.

Then, he sat a few feet away, not in Joseph's chair, but in one he brought in from the kitchen and, in his kind, low, level voice, began to talk. About growing up in Baltimore, about baseball, about his attempts, after his sister moved away, to make bread and piecrust, about the history of Antioch Beach. Gradually, Edith's shivering stopped, the chill and achiness seeping from her body, the firelight dancing over her face, until her bones seemed to grow soft and pliant as candle wax, and she believed she had never been so grateful to be warm. John's voice kept on, long and even as a horizon. In time, it grew fainter. At some point, she interrupted its flow to say thank you. When she woke up, morning lit her windows, and John was gone.

Chapter Fourteen
Clare

The first morning I woke up in Edith's house, a neighbor named Louise Smits showed up at the front door with a pie. Blueberry peach with a lattice-top crust, insanely aromatic, and so fresh out of the oven that she had to use oven mitts to carry it to my house from her own at the other end of the street. Considering it was barely nine o'clock, I figured she must've gotten up at the crack of dawn to start baking, and I was touched and grateful. Even when I began to suspect her visit was less welcome wagon and more reconnaissance mission, which happened within the first two minutes, I remained touched and grateful because I was a pie girl from way back, and Louise Smits's pie was an especially glorious one, purple and gold bubbling up between the latticework like molten heaven. Plus, I had a pretty wide curious streak myself, especially when it came to Edith, and Edith was what Louise had come to discuss.

When we'd dispatched the pie to the kitchen counter, and Louise had refused my offer of coffee (I'd brought two grocery bags of provisions—and, when it came to provisions, coffee topped my list—and had spent no small part of the morning fiddling with the old-fangled electric percolator until it produced a drinkable brew), we sat at Edith's kitchen table to talk. Talking turned out to be Louise's talent. If talking were a sport, Louise would've been a marathoner. I don't think she took more than two breaths during the entire conversation.

"Now, are you a relative of Edith Herron? Ever since we heard that a young woman had inherited this house from her, we've been speculating as to who you might be. A granddaughter was the most common guess among those few folks left around here who even remember Edith existed, although from the looks of you, I'd say more like great-grand. You can't be far out of your teens, now can you? Of course, I never did hear that Edith had a child at all, much less a great-granddaughter. As a matter of fact, I never heard she'd gotten remarried, though of course you don't have to be married to have a baby, not these days, and I guess not even back when Edith would've had hers, although heaven help the girls who went that route. Edith might have, though. She was just that different from the rest of the women in this town, according to my mother. The truth is I never heard much about Edith's fate after she left town. For one thing, my family moved away right after Edith did, December 1956. We were in the process of packing when we heard she'd gone. We went to Arizona for my father's work. From beach to desert, just like that. We rented our house instead of selling, which turned out to be lucky for me. I just moved back to town two years ago, mainly because of my grandchildren. They're up in New York, but they love this place. But even when I lived here, I was just a young girl when Edith took off for God knows where. I don't remember even so much what she looked like because at that age, girls are all caught up in their own worlds, but I heard about her back then, from my mother and her friends, or overheard I guess is the more accurate term. I gathered that everyone expected Edith to leave after her husband died, and no one, not a soul, ever thought she'd open a guesthouse. A woman on her own with all those people, total strangers, male *and* female, coming and going. Made you wonder, I guess. Although according to my mother, Edith was head over heels for her husband, before he died and after, too. My mother said no woman should be that wrapped up in another human being, let alone a man. So *are* you?"

Startled, I said, "Am I wrapped up in a man?"

Louise laughed. "Well, we'll save that question for another time. But I meant are you her great-granddaughter?"

"No. Honestly, I hardly knew her. I was stunned when I heard she'd left me this house. We met briefly just a few weeks before she died."

"Must've been some meeting."

Louise leaned toward me, her eyes alight with questions. But even though I'd told my and Edith's story to Joliet, I found I didn't want to do the same with Louise. She was gregarious and friendly enough but somehow not the kind of person you wanted treading with you on anything like sacred ground. Even having her in Edith's house felt a little uncomfortable. So all I said was, "Yes, it was."

When it became obvious I wasn't going to elaborate, Louise, without taking a deep breath or clearing her throat or any other ordinary preamble to a lengthy monologue, took off full speed ahead.

"But if the folks here thought her opening a guesthouse was scandalous, I can only imagine how they reacted when the real scandal hit. Since the whole affair only came to light after we'd moved, I never got all the details. My mother surely got filled in by some of her friends back home, but she never shared the information with me, probably thought the story wasn't fit for children's ears, and then my mother, poor woman, died when I was only fourteen—car accident—so I never did get grown up enough to hear much. My father remarried after about a year or so. A very nice woman. I called her Marjorie but she became a true mother to me. Not that I didn't miss my mother, of course. Did and do. But anyway, for me, the story of the scandal kind of died with Mom, and by the time I moved back here, this town was so built up and different that most of the old-timers were long gone. I know it involved covering up a murder, though, and the downfall of an officer of the law. I think I do sort of remember the man in question. Tall man. Well respected. At least until the scandal. I'm not sure how Edith was involved, but it had to be something, well, disgraceful, didn't it? For her to just up and leave the way she did. I get the idea that people thought she'd come back when it all blew over, but she never did. I don't know that anyone heard from her ever again. And, now, look at this: here you are, not even a blood relative, living in her house."

"A murder?" I said. "Whose murder?"

"I don't know. After I moved back here and saw this house and got my memory a little jogged, I asked around a bit, but either no one had heard or they weren't telling. As I said, looks like there's no one much left around here who lived through that time period. It was all such a long time ago, and I heard a lot of the families my family knew sold their houses for big money back at the start of Antioch becoming a major resort town instead of just a nice, quiet beach town. You know, *you* could do that."

"Sell, you mean?"

"This place has been kept up beautiful, and it's a desirable location. Not right on the beach, but I'm sure you could get a nice amount for this place."

Until Louise Smits told me this, I hadn't realized just how very much I wanted to keep the house. I shook my head.

"I won't sell it. I don't even know how long I'm staying. I'd been thinking a week, but even if it turns out to be longer, I have to go to school in September. I can't imagine selling this house, though. I think Edith would have wanted me to keep it."

Louise looked skeptical, but she said, "Well, that's good then. There's something sad about an empty house." She smiled at me. "Maybe you're this house's fresh start, Clare. And I don't know if *you're* in need of a fresh start, but maybe this house is it. Isn't that a nice thought?"

"Yes," I told Louise Smits. "It really is."

The Antioch Beach library was like something out of a good dream, if you're the kind of person who dreams about libraries, which I am: pale gray stone with a peaked roofline; a Gothic arch wooden door with spear-shaped, wrought-iron hinges, dull red and very churchy; a cool, high-ceilinged interior full of long windows, the smell of books, row upon row of shelves, and lots of rustling. The rustling—part page turning, part whispering, part shushing, part quietly shuffling feet, part just the books and people breathing—is so much my favorite part of any library that it's possible I imagine more rustling than is actually there. In any case, to my ears, this library was like a dovecote, like a forest in autumn, like a roomful of dancers in tutus.

The woman working in the tiny periodicals room had two sets of glasses, one on her nose, one on top of her head, both on beaded chains around her neck and the no-nonsense expression all librarians worth their salt maintain up until the moment you ask for help finding something, at which point they turn beatific and actually seem to emit light. The name on her desk's nameplate read simply Pat, which struck me as perfect.

"Excuse me," I said. "I was wondering if you might have issues of the *Daily Bee* from December of 1956 through maybe March of 1957?"

Her severe expression softened right on cue, but she raised her eyebrows and said, "The *Daily Bee* is a daily. That's one hundred twenty-one newspapers."

"Really?"

Pat raised her eyebrows again. "You're welcome to do the math yourself."

"No, no, I didn't mean I doubted you. I was just picturing one hundred twenty-one newspapers. Because it's a lot of newspapers."

"It is." She smiled and—*ping*—for a split second, a halo appeared around her head; at least I'm pretty sure it did. "Luckily, two years ago, we received a grant to convert all the papers to digital." She gestured toward a small bank of computers in the back of the room. "Come. I will show you."

Mostly relieved but a tiny bit disappointed—because I'm one of those who likes the feel of paper in my hands—I thanked her and in no time—*click, click, click*—I was immersed in the winter of 1956/1957 and, after hours of reading, backtracking, and note taking, I pieced together the story of the arrest and trial of Antioch Beach Chief of Police John Blanchard.

According to John Blanchard, on the night of Monday, December 10, 1956, even though he was technically off duty, due to a rash of reported car thefts, he was in his car patrolling Birch Grove Street, along which the grandest houses in town—summer homes of wealthy Philadelphians and Delawareans, bankers, politicians, heirs to a chemical company fortune—stood in a row, when he heard a single gunshot. Seconds later, as he attempted to ascertain the source of the sound, before he had time to call in a report of the shot, a woman in a dressing gown staggered out her front door, a baby—a boy, Steven, born exactly one week earlier on December 3—clutched to her chest. The moon was full that night, and when the woman, Sarah Giles, got close to his car, Chief Blanchard could see that she was badly injured, bent almost double, her face battered and bleeding, her neck ringed with red marks, soon to become dark bruises, as if she'd been throttled. When he got out of his car and approached her, she told him that her husband, drunk and enraged, had threatened to kill both her and the baby, had struck her repeatedly with his closed fist before pushing her down a flight of stairs, and that, as he thundered toward the nursery where the baby slept, Sarah had dug out the gun she'd hidden under a chair cushion weeks before and shot him dead.

John Blanchard was familiar with the family. Elliot Giles was the son of wealthy banker turned Pennsylvania state senator Robert E. Giles. While the elder Giles was a pillar of the community, handsome Elliot had the reputation of being charming but reckless and easily angered, a ladies' man who had surprised everyone three years earlier by marrying a young teacher whom he had bumped into, literally, on the steps of the Philadelphia Museum of Art. Since then there had been rumors that all was not well within the marriage, and John Blanchard had himself responded to two calls from the Gileses' neighbors reporting shouting, banging, and other unsettling noises coming from their house. But each time, when he arrived on the scene, all was quiet and Elliot had apologized profusely, saying the first time that a visitor to their home had made unwanted advances toward Sarah and Elliot had had to dispatch him and the second time that he had had one too many Manhattans, had gotten angered by a baseball game he was listening to on the radio—damn Phillies—and had knocked some furniture around. Neither time did John see Sarah Giles, but, both times, he had a "bad feeling" about her well-being, a feeling on which, to his sorrow, he did not follow up.

Because, on that fateful December night, he believed Sarah Giles was telling the truth about killing her husband to save her own life and that of her infant and because he felt concern that a jury might not see the situation in the same light, he made the split-second decision to help her get away and to start a new life free from abuse and fear. He took her inside, and while she dressed, he packed, as best he could, clothes and supplies for her and the baby. Then, he urged her to get into his police cruiser, and because her injuries seemed severe, he took her to the home of Edith Herron, owner of Blue Sky House and the widow of his good friend Joseph Herron. While he was unhappy to involve Edith in his plan to relocate Sarah and her son, his options were limited, and he knew Edith to be not only a former nurse but a thoughtful, trustworthy person. Although he gave Edith no information about the situation and refused to answer her questions, she quietly did what she could for Sarah.

While she was tending to Sarah's wounds, Mrs. Stella O' Shea, who lived at the other end of the street, entered the screened porch at the front of Edith Herron's house. At the trial, Mrs. O'Shea testified that she'd seen John's car parked "near Edith's house" (although he'd been careful to park it down around the corner, not directly in front of her house) and, concerned about Edith, who lived "without a man to protect her and with complete strangers coming and going," had decided to check to make sure all was well. Certainly, the swirling rumors about Edith having more than just a friendship with the police chief played no role in her decision to investigate, since Mrs. O'Shea "never listened to that kind of idle gossip."

Because the front rooms of the house were dark, Mrs. O'Shea decided not to knock, since no one appeared to be home. As she was turning to leave, she heard what sounded exactly like a hungry newborn's cry. Perplexed and concerned and not at all idly curious, she proceeded to look, not only through the front windows, but, leaving the porch and walking around the outside of the house, through all the first-floor windows, and it was as she was standing on an overturned bucket, peering through the back window that she saw, through the open door of a bedroom, what appeared to be a woman lying on the bed. Edith was leaning over the woman applying what appeared to be ointment to the woman's face. This sight so startled Mrs. O'Shea that she lost her balance and fell off the bucket, which clattered against the side of the house. Abashed at the possibility of being discovered peeping—even though of course she'd only had the best of intentions—she ran away, darting just one quick glance over her shoulder to see what she thought was the outline of tall, lanky Chief Blanchard in the window.

Although John did not catch sight of Mrs. O'Shea's exiting the property and found no evidence of anyone outside, he knew that someone might spot his car if he left it on the street for too long, so he wanted to get Sarah and her child out of Edith's house as quickly as possible. He knew that it would be only a matter of time before his fellow police officers found the body of Elliot Giles and began to search for the dead man's wife and child. As soon as Edith finished tending to Sarah's wounds, John Blanchard took Sarah and baby Steven away in his car. The next morning, after dropping them off at what he hoped was a safe location, he came back to Antioch Beach.

The morning after the shooting, Elliot Giles's cousin, Roger, arrived with his wife and three children at the Giles residence for a scheduled visit and found the house locked and apparently empty, despite all three cars being in the garage. Over the next few hours, Roger Giles repeatedly called the residence from a phone at a local restaurant but never got an answer, and, finally, concerned and frustrated, he called the police. When the officers arrived on the scene, they discovered Elliot Giles's body and immediately began searching for Sarah and the baby. Because Mrs. O'Shea had not yet come forward, no one knew of Chief Blanchard's possible connection to the case. Also, at the time, Sarah was not yet officially a suspect but a missing person. One theory, proposed by Chief Blanchard, was that she and Steven had been kidnapped.

The morning of December 12, 1956, Mrs. O'Shea read about the case in the paper, put two and two together, and contacted the police about what she'd seen, giving her statement to one of John's fellow officers. As soon as he learned what she said, John turned himself in, admitting he had helped Sarah and her baby get away, and telling them that Edith had played no role in their disappearance.

When the police went to question Edith, they found a Closed sign on the door of Blue Sky House, and Edith and her car were gone. At the trial John testified that Edith was a deeply private woman who had suffered a terrible personal loss, and he speculated that she'd left town, not to avoid police questioning, since she knew nothing about the death of Elliot or about Sarah's and the baby's whereabouts, but because Sarah and her condition had upset her and she wanted to get away for a few days. When she did not return and the police, despite assiduous searching, could find no trace of her, John surmised that either she had no idea they were looking for her or that, to avoid unwanted attention and because she had no information that would help in the police department's search, she had decided to stay away until everything had blown over.

At the insistence of the powerful Giles family, the trial took place quickly, less than a month after John turned himself in, and everyone expected it to end quickly as well, with the jury finding John guilty and a judge throwing the book at him at sentencing. But somehow—and no one knew how, since, as far as anyone knew, he was neither rich nor well connected—John had snagged himself a top-notch lawyer from a fancy New York City law firm called Wickham-Flaherty, and Randolph Flaherty had left no stone unturned in John's defense. He paraded in witness after witness to attest to Chief Blanchard's courage, work ethic, kindness, and overall nobility of spirit, while another stream of witnesses spoke of Elliot Giles's jealous rages, his violent streak, and what Randolph Flaherty called his "small, twisted, shriveled soul."

Reading through the newspaper reports of the trial, I noticed a shift in perspective, a gradual turning of the tables. Headlines went from "Police Chief Turned Jail Bird" and "Police Chief John Blanchard Refuses to Give Up Murderess" to "John Blanchard Sacrificed Himself to Save Woman and Baby." One editorial admired his implacable demeanor and steady blue eyes and called him saintly; the president of the local PTA wrote an eloquent letter to the editor titled "Sarah Giles Did What Any Mother Would Do!" that ended with the words "God bless Chief Blanchard!" By the end of the trial, John was being regarded as a hero by many local folks and, instead of the fifteen- to twenty-year sentence that the press had seemed sure of at the trial's start, he was given four to six years. I didn't learn how long he'd actually stayed in prison, but none of the legal experts the paper had interviewed seemed to think he would be made to serve the whole term. After the sentencing, an unnamed source at the police department disclosed that, while both Sarah Giles and Edith Herron were considered to be "at large," the department had let its search for them drop.

"We all hope," the anonymous source said, "that wherever those women are, they've found peace and a safe haven."

The library was almost empty. The sky outside the periodical room window had turned to plum and smoke. Twilight. Closing time. I set down my pencil, gathered up my stack of notes—a final rustle—and summoned the memory of Edith in her gardening clogs, clear-voiced and assured, candid and wise and kind, standing firmly on the earth despite her cane, and I felt positive that she had found peace and a safe haven. I hoped that Sarah and her son had, too.

Chapter Fifteen
Edith

Winter 1953

Later, when Edith tried to pinpoint what it was about George Graham that made him stand out from everyone else in the sandwich shop, she realized that, despite his cardigan sweater and lack of tie, the folded newspaper tucked under one arm, it was his utter lack of casualness. Upright posture. Hair immaculately cut, slicked back, impervious to sea breezes. A face like chiseled marble with serious dark eyes. An expensive watch he glanced at more than once, in the manner of one accustomed to being justifiably impatient and to having his daylight hours neatly carved up into important appointments.

Maybe this, the fact of his difference, is why she, who hardly talked—truly talked, not just chatted politely—to anyone apart from John Blanchard, talked to him, a complete stranger in a sandwich shop. The shop itself was the sort of place she rarely went, overpriced, catering to tourists, and just a stone's throw away from the fanciest hotel in town, but that day, a Saturday in late November, she had woken up and felt the urge to be out in the world, to sit in a place with other people. A week later, after she met George Graham for the second time, she would wonder if this unprecedented urge had been the hand of fate pushing her out the door and into that sandwich shop, and even though she would try to laugh off this idea, dismiss it as silly and overly self-involved, she could never fully convince herself that it was wrong.

She asked him what he was reading about. What she actually said was, "Excuse me for interrupting, but you look so engrossed in that paper. If you're reading something interesting, could you please tell me what it is? I've forgotten to bring any reading material of my own, so I'm all at loose ends." It came across as forward, flirtatious even, and unlike anything she would normally say, but she didn't feel mortified. Instead, for the first time in ages and for no reason she could explain, she felt young, a young woman, out and about and lingering over lunch. Young and open and unguarded.

When the man set his paper on the table and met her eyes, she smiled.

"Are you?" he said.

"Well, yes. It's been so long since I've been to a restaurant that I'd forgotten how dull it can be to eat alone in this town."

"You live here, then? Just for the summer or all year round?"

"All year. I run a guesthouse, although I'm a little short of guests at the moment. After October, business slows down."

"You run it by yourself?"

"Yes."

"Interesting."

For a moment, Edith considered telling him why she was going it alone, but somehow, she didn't want to bring up Joseph's death. It had been more than a year since anyone had seen her as anything other than a widow, and even though she would sooner have cut off her arm than forsake Joseph or betray his memory, she felt uncompelled to share her personal history with this stranger whose business it surely was not. For the space of that conversation, she allowed herself to put away her story of loss. She felt bare and stark without it, like a tree without leaves, but also lighter.

"Sometimes, it's interesting," she said. "Often, it's

not particularly. Busy, yes, for which I'm grateful, but not exactly fascinating. My mind gets restless."

That last sentence just slipped out. She had said the same thing to John Blanchard just the other evening during one of their front porch conversations, but, unlike this man, John was a friend, a friend who, for the sake of Edith's reputation, kept mostly to the peripheries of her little world—the porch, the backyard, occasionally but only in broad daylight, the kitchen table—but a friend nonetheless, the only one she had. She waited to see if this man would laugh or be taken aback by her odd statement, but he simply said, "So what do you do with it when it does?"

And, just like that, she was off, telling him about her canoe trips, her hikes through the pinewoods at the water's edge, her new interest in bivalves.

"Did you know that scallops can swim?" she asked.

Now, he did laugh. "I can't say that I did. But then mostly I prefer my bivalves on the half-shell, with a dollop of cocktail sauce. Where did this curiosity of yours about the natural world come from?"

And again—off she went. Her father, her upbringing, her years spent nursing, her love affair with solitude, her abject failure at making cocktail party conversation.

"I never would have guessed that," deadpanned

George (midway into the conversation, they had remembered to introduce themselves, and from that point on, were on a first-name basis).

"Surprisingly, describing the particulars of how a mussel attaches itself to a rock doesn't go well with canapés," Edith said, with a sigh. "Which is probably why I'm not exactly rolling in invitations."

"Nonsense," said George. "All my life, I assumed mussels did it the same way barnacles do. It's even possible I thought mussels *were* barnacles. Now, tell me again about those silky fibers."

And Edith did. On the walk home, she went back over the conversation in her mind. *Look at me,* she thought, *walking around in the afternoon sun smiling to myself like a crazy person.* Her fingers slid inside the neck of her shirt to touch the two wedding rings she wore on a gold chain, remembering the night after Joseph's funeral, how she'd taken off her ring because she couldn't bear to see it on her hand when he no longer wore his. It occurred to her that she hadn't even noticed if George had been wearing one. It hadn't mattered. Edith had not been flirting. She had merely talked to George Graham the way a woman talks when she knows she will never see the other person again. For that hour, she had felt like a normal human being. It had been a reprieve, a tiny space of time in which she'd floated, unencumbered. For that hour, she could have been anyone.

Six days later, he called.

He wanted to reserve a room at Blue Sky House for the following night. Business, he said. She wondered what sort of business a man like that—perfectly cut trousers, watch like something out of a Fifth Avenue window—could possibly have in her little beach town in the off-season. Her first impulse was to say she was booked for that night, but since late October, she'd had so few guests—one traveling salesmen, an elderly couple who liked the beach in cold weather—that she could not afford, despite her frugal ways, to turn anyone down. So she told him yes in as brisk a tone as she could summon, and it wasn't until she went to write his reservation down in her leather-bound ledger that she realized her hands were shaking.

Oh, for heaven's sake, she scolded herself, *he's not coming to see you. You spoke with the man for an hour, mostly about mussels. Don't be ridiculous.*

But the beauty of their conversation in the sandwich shop, the reason it could be light and playful, the reason it had *worked,* was the fact that she had been certain it would never happen again. Immediately afterward,

Edith had slipped back into her accustomed loneliness, skirting around the edges of human interaction. Even John Blanchard had stayed away, as if he'd known she needed time to recall whom she was and how she was meant to live out her days in the wake—and she would be forever in the wake, this she knew—of Joseph's death. Somehow, John was the exception, her only friend; maybe because he'd been Joseph's friend, he'd slipped easily into her days, undemanding, reassuring, always keeping the right amount of space between them. Being with him was as easy as being alone, and sometimes, on piercingly lonely days, easier. With John, her devotion to Joseph was a given. And George Graham, who would be in her house, her and Joseph's house, in a matter of days did not even know Joseph had existed.

Except that George *had* known. She found that out, as she found out so many things, not fifteen minutes after he arrived at Blue Sky House. This time, there wasn't even a pretext of casualness. George stepped purposefully over her threshold in a suit and shirt that had obviously been custom-made for him (even she, with her careless fashion sense, could see that), holding a leather bag so exquisite, it probably cost as much as her car, as if he were attending a business meeting instead of spending a night in a modest little house. As it turned out, this made sense, since a business meeting is what more or less took place at her kitchen table. The second he sat down—his back so straight it didn't rest against the chair, his hands touching at the fingertips, teepee-like—Edith, in her old wool pants and sweater, felt at a distinct disadvantage.

If Edith had worried that George would expect playful banter again, she needn't have. He began, as she later imagined he began all business negotiations, by throwing her off-balance.

"Mrs. Herron, I should tell you right off that our meeting in the coffee shop was no accident. I sought you out deliberately."

His words were strange, but his tone was genial, and Edith was too surprised to feel alarmed or even to notice that he'd called her "Mrs. Herron" when she had never told him she'd been married.

"What do you mean 'sought me out'? You mean you saw me in the coffee shop and decided to approach me? But I'm the one who spoke first."

"No, I mean I came to Antioch expressly to speak with you. I intended to simply knock on your door. My excuse was going to be that I wanted to put relatives up at a local hotel or guesthouse and needed to see if yours would be appropriate. But when you came out of your house and started walking, I got out of my car and followed. I was about to start up a conversation when you saved me the effort."

Edith felt her pulse quicken. She moved her chair a few inches away from the table, and with her eyes, measured the distance from where she sat to the front door. It was only five o'clock, not even verging on dusk, yet. Surely, if she screamed, someone would come.

"You followed me?" she said, keeping her voice steady.

He smiled. "Please. I meant no harm then and don't now. A while back, a young assistant at my workplace mentioned this town and your guesthouse specifically. He and his family stayed here for a week last summer. He told me how pleasant it was, how tight a ship you ran. It surprised him that a woman could run a business so efficiently. He said you were smart, and he described your house to me in some detail. He told me that you were a young widow, a former nurse, who had opened a guesthouse after the death of her husband. By the way, please accept my condolences."

Edith ignored this. "You're saying you knew all of this about me when we spoke in the sandwich shop?"

"I did."

"Why? Why did you seek me out? Why didn't you tell me you'd come to town in order to meet me?"

"First, I needed to see if you would do."

First. What could be second, then? Her imagination raced toward multiple possibilities, each scarier than the last. She pushed her chair back and stood up, her breath stammering inside her chest. "I think you should go."

"Let me explain. Please."

Edith shook her head and started for the door. "You should go now."

She gripped the doorknob, but her hand froze, refused to work. A frightened sob started in her throat.

"Edith, I don't hurt women," George Graham said, speaking quickly. "I save them from men who do. Or I try to, at least. Not by myself, of course. I rely on other people, good people, people who believe women should feel safe in their own homes. People who can keep a secret. I was hoping you could be one of them."

Even though she had no idea what he meant, his voice was so urgent and earnest that it stopped Edith in her tracks. She didn't yank the door open and run out. Instead, keeping her hand on the doorknob, she turned around to face him.

"What does that mean?"

"Come, sit back down at this table with me, and I'll tell you. When I'm finished, if you want me to leave and never come back, I swear to you I will honor that."

"How do I know I can trust you?"

"You just know. The way I knew after we talked in the sandwich shop that I could trust you."

She took him in, his intense eyes, his hands, clasped now, on the tabletop, and she didn't so much decide to trust him as realize that she already did.

"All right, then," she said, nodding and walking back to her chair. "Go ahead. I'm listening."

He called it a relocation system, a neutral and technical term for what sounded to Edith like a manifestly human, risky, and emotion-fraught enterprise.

"Most people think that what happens between a husband and wife in a private home, no matter how unjust or dangerous, is nobody's business but theirs. But I make it my business," he said, his tone turning hard, and for a moment, his affable exterior parted like a curtain so that Edith caught a glimpse of the person underneath, powerful and shrewd and used to getting his way. *You don't afford a suit like that by being nice,* she thought.

George's explanation was full of holes. He said that he identified women whose husbands were hurting them, but he wouldn't say how or where he found them. He told her that he had people in place—scattered in many different places—some of whom drove the women from point to point, some of whom gave them safe places to stay, usually for one night, but he declined to say who the people were.

"Where do they end up, these women?" Edith asked.

"Elsewhere," he said, his face inscrutable. "And safe."

"But don't their families look for them?"

"Of course. Sometimes, the police get involved. The women who have children take them if they possibly can, so by some lights, they're kidnappers. So far, though, and I try to keep track of those we've relocated for at least a year, so far no one's ever been found."

"They leave everything behind?"

"Everything. Their names, their families, their jobs, their homes. Once they get where they're going, we furnish them with new ones."

"New families?"

George smiled a brittle smile. "No. I would imagine that after enough time goes by, they might contact family members whom they trust, their parents or brothers and sisters. They shouldn't. We advise them not to. It's a terrible idea. But I would imagine some do."

"There's something ruthless about this. And about you,"Edith said.

"There's a ruthlessness to any kind of mission," said George, shrugging. "We get them away from their bastard husbands who could end up killing them. Is there a price to pay? I don't doubt that there is. But that's not my concern."

A shiver ran through Edith. To leave everything, everyone behind. She had no one to leave, except John, but she had her house. She looked around at the walls, the photographs, at the house that Joseph had given her, traces of him in every corner, in the very air. She knew she could never leave it.

"I can guess what you're thinking," said George. "But not everyone is happy in their homes. For the women we relocate, their houses have become prisons."

"Am I right in assuming that you want this house, my house, to be a stopping point in your relocation system?"

"It's in a useful location. Your neighbors are used to strangers coming and going. You are a private person with few real ties to your community. You have nursing skills."

Edith startled at this. "Nursing skills?"

"Some of the women have injuries, of course," he explained, coolly. "Occasionally, the children do, too."

Of course that would be true. She nodded.

"I won't lie," he said, briskly. "What I'm asking you to do is risky. But you are just a cog in the wheel. You'll be given as little information as possible. First names only. Everything happens late at night or in the very early morning, before sunrise. You won't know who drives them here or who picks them up. You won't even see the car. I noted a blank spot between houses at the end of your street. No streetlights, no buildings. The car will drop them there, and, if possible, they will walk through the backyards, along the canal, and enter through your back door. No local people will be involved, and the women themselves come from far away. You won't know where, and you will never know where they go once they leave here. There shouldn't be a need to reach me, but, just in case, I will give you a number to call. A woman will answer at any hour of the day or night. You'll leave a message, and I will call you back. But again, this should not be necessary. This is a fine-tuned operation. If you do your part correctly, it will all go like clockwork."

"What makes you think I'll do this?"

"Your mind gets restless, isn't that what you said? I sense that you're a woman who would like to be part of something bigger than running a little place for tourists." He shrugged. "And don't worry, you'll be repaid for any expenses you might accrue. Extra food, medical supplies. If you insist on it, I can even pay you a regular stipend, although most people act purely out of a desire to help."

His imperious attitude and his smug certainty that

she would jump at the chance to be part of his plan annoyed her so much that she was tempted to say no just to prove him wrong. But he wasn't wrong. Edith heard Joseph's voice as distinctly as if he were sitting next to her: *You must promise to give yourself entirely to someone or something because that's who you are. You are a genius at devoting yourself; it's what makes you happiest.*

"Why don't you sleep on it?" said George.

"I don't need to," said Edith. "I'm in."

Two weeks later, on December 19, 1953, a woman's voice—neutral, almost machinelike—on the phone told Edith that the first woman, Margaret, would arrive that night, and, just after midnight, she knocked on Edith's back door. Shockingly young, possibly not yet out of her teens, with a gray wool coat that was much too big for her, clutching a cheap valise that Edith knew was probably full of things she'd only recently been given that did not quite feel like hers (George had said that many of the women left in a hurry, empty-handed), and an old, yellowing bruise on her cheekbone, Margaret stared at Edith with the wide, frightened, bewildered eyes of an injured animal, and on an impulse, even though she was not usually quick to touch people, especially strangers, Edith took the girl's free hand in both of hers, murmured, "Oh, sweet child," and pulled her gently into the house.

Edith would learn that some of the women—and, occasionally, heartbreakingly, some of the children—could not bear to be handled, flinching or pulling away at the slightest touch; some recoiled when she offered words of sympathy; some could not, especially upon first arriving, even meet her eyes. She would learn to move slowly around them, to change their bandages without comment, to offer them food with the efficiency of a waitress in a restaurant, and to wait for a sign—a hand reaching out, a cautious smile, the offering up of a small, personal fact ("My mother has a clock like that one;" "I wish I hadn't left the book I was reading sitting on my nightstand. Can you imagine, fretting about a book at a time like this?")—that they wanted a more human connection. She would learn to take her cues from them. But that night, almost before she had stepped across the threshold, Margaret fell into Edith's arms and clung, her thin shoulders quaking with near-silent weeping.

Because there were no other guests at Blue Sky House, Edith walked Margaret into the living room. When Margaret stopped crying and dropped, exhausted, into the chair Edith offered her, she said, staring into the fire, "He didn't even hit me that often, only when he got really jealous. But it was always in the face. And once you get hit in the face, you're always waiting for it to happen again. Your body gets so tired from bracing itself for the next blow, and it gets so you can't sleep and your mind can't focus on regular things anymore. Even more than the hitting, it was the waiting that got to me."

For a couple of minutes, the crackle and hiss of the fire was the only sound. Then, Margaret turned to Edith with a wry and weary smile. "Well, I always did want to get out of Roanoke," she said, "and here I am."

Over time, Edith would find that, just like Margaret, despite their instructions to hide their history, most of the women would tell her where they'd come from, would let slip a tiny piece of what they'd left behind. She understood this impulse, this laying claim to a past. It was as if they were saying, *Despite my vanishing act, I am not a ghost; I am real, a flesh and blood woman, with a story that belongs to me.*

After Margaret had gone to bed in the little downstairs bedroom, Edith got out a notebook and performed, for the first time, an act that would become a habit: documenting this woman's brief stopover in her own life, setting down, for no one's eyes but her own, a record of this person who would disappear. She knew as she wrote that it wasn't wise, that George would be angry if he found out, but she couldn't shake the conviction that everyone whose life brushed against her own should leave a trace, even if it was just a few, scant, cryptic lines on a page.

In careful, precise printing, she wrote the date, followed by this: *Margaret. Roan. Cont chk. Auburn hair, pale, skinny inside her big wool coat, freckles like sprinkled nutmeg across her nose.*

Chapter Sixteen
Clare

The night I found Edith and Joseph's marriage certificate, his obituary, and her photographs, Zach called me. Even though it was nearly three in the morning, I was still awake, or partly awake, floating, under the blue sky of Edith's ceiling, in a hazy state not only between wakefulness and sleep but between my present and Edith's past. In this dreamy space, it was oddly easy to feel that Edith was close by, not like a ghost or a guardian angel, but physically under the same roof as me, the way, when I was a kid, I would lie in bed and know that my mother was in the house, feel the peace of that knowledge in my bones, even if I couldn't hear or see her.

Even the buzzing of the phone against the bedside table didn't yank me out of this calm, Edith-is-near state, which is maybe why, when I saw who was calling, I didn't ignore it as I usually would have, nor did my heart start galloping like a spooked horse; I just answered.

"Zach, it's really late," I said, quietly, firmly, just as Edith would have.

"I know," he said. His voice was a little high, a little loud and excited, but, happily, he wasn't crying and didn't sound drunk. "I'm sorry. I just—today when I was walking through the park on my way home, I saw this girl, maybe eight years old, walking with her dad, and she was in a costume. This straw hat, maybe a boater it's called? With braids that might have been attached to the hat or maybe she had a wig on or maybe they were real, but anyway, red braids, pretty convincing, and this sort of pinafore dress, and these button boots, and I flashed back to that miniseries you made me watch—I mean, yes, you made me, but then I actually enjoyed it a lot—the one based on those books you loved as a kid, and I walked up to her and said, 'Excuse me but are you . . . '"—he paused, waiting.

"Anne of Green Gables," I said, finishing his thought.

"Yes! And she said she was, and then added, 'Thank you for noticing,' in this very solemn voice, and I said, 'Are you in a play?' and she said, 'No,' politely but also like she was a little miffed at my question, and her dad smiled and said, 'Yesterday was her birthday, and all she wanted was an Anne of Green Gables outfit, a real one, not a ready-made costume with Velcro up the back. So she got this. If she ever takes it off, it'll be a miracle. This kid lives and breathes those books.' And the thing is, the truly amazing thing, Clare, and don't think I'm crazy, but her voice was totally a kid version of yours, and her eyes, they were your eyes, big, brown, same shape, eyelashes, expression, everything. And if you remember, you said the same thing to me about those books, the exact same phrase, that you lived and breathed them. So I took it, I took *her*, this amazing kid who looked like she'd just time traveled from the turn of the century, as a sign."

He paused, audibly winded.

"A sign that you should call me at three in the morning?" I said, not mad, still channeling Edith's firm, kind, implacable calm.

"Yeah, sorry about the timing, but it took me a long time to get my nerve up to talk to you about this, and I wanted to call before my nerve stopped being up, which would probably have happened sooner or later."

"I see," I said. "Well, you're talking to me now. What would you like to say?"

I sat up, leaning against the headboard of the bed, and waited for him to answer, totally and surprisingly unracked by dread or anxiety.

"Let me come see you," he said. "I can get on a plane tomorrow. I just feel strongly that we need to sit in the same room—or maybe take a long walk—and have a conversation. No yelling, no accusations or insults—and I'm obviously referring to me here, not you, since I'm pretty sure you haven't raised your voice even once throughout this whole ordeal—we'll just be two adults talking. How does that sound?"

I waited for the impulse to run for the hills to hit me, but it didn't.

"It sounds—very civilized," I said, truthfully.

"Doesn't it?"

"What were you thinking we should talk about?"

"I don't know, exactly. But I think we should talk, now that we've let go of all the anger. At least, I have. I hope you have, too."

"I'm glad you have. And I don't honestly think I had any to let go of. Lots of other emotions, I guess, but not anger."

"Good! Then it's all settled!"

He sounded happy. More than happy. Jubilant.

"My flight arrives at 10:25 A.M., so I can be at your parents' house by 11:30 tomorrow morning. You want to go to lunch? Or I could bring lunch? You know what? I checked the weather and it's supposed to be nice. So how about a picnic? What do you think?"

His jubilation rose with every word, so that by the end of this he was almost singing.

"Hold on," I said. "Your *flight*? You don't mean you already have a ticket?"

"Yeah, I do. Come on, I knew you'd do this for me; it's how you are."

I wasn't sure what he meant by this, but I didn't demand to know, as I might have done a few months ago. I didn't even feel particularly curious about it. Whatever insights Zach had, or thought he had, about my character, correct or not, they belonged to him. I didn't begrudge him them, but I also didn't need them anymore.

"But still, I might not have actually bought the ticket," he went on, "I just—I don't know, when I saw that little girl, that clinched it. I took a leap of faith."

Buying a nonrefundable airplane ticket because you saw a brown-eyed girl in a boater hat at the park seemed like a dubious decision, even for a hard-core Anne fan like me, and for a moment, I worried about Zach's mental state. But then I reminded myself—and I knew this from my own experience—that if you went out into the world *looking* for a sign that you should do something, a go-ahead from the great beyond or wherever, you were highly likely to find one.

There was a time, even after our breakup, when I would've so dreaded bursting his bubble that I would have told him okay, hung up the phone, and jumped in the car to drive home. But there, in Edith's house, I could instead say, "Zach, I think we should get together and talk sometime. But I can't tomorrow."

"What do you mean you can't?" he said.

"I can't tomorrow."

"You're, what? *Busy?*" An edge entered his tone. Whether it was an edge of hurt or anger, I couldn't tell yet, but I knew I'd find out soon enough.

"I am, actually. I'm sorry, but I really am."

"Clare, this is important. And it's all planned."

"I know, and I wish you'd talked to me about it before you made those plans. Because tomorrow doesn't work. Another day would, I'm sure, but not tomorrow."

In the pause that followed, I could hear Zach taking deep breaths, trying to steady himself, something I knew didn't come easily to him. He tried, he always tried so hard to do the right thing. I wished *he* had the spirit of Edith there to help him; he might have needed her even more than I did.

"Look," he said, finally, "I'm coming anyway. I have the ticket, right? And I don't need to come in the morning. I'll check into my hotel, and you can call me whenever you're finished with whatever you're doing. Or whenever you have a break in your busyness. Tomorrow night, even; it doesn't matter how late. Okay?"

"Zach, coming is just not a good idea."

"Why? You can't squeeze me in? What if it were Hildy? You'd probably drop everything if it were Hildy. Can't you do that for me?"

"I can't. I couldn't if it were Hildy or anyone. Because I'm not home right now."

"You're away? Like for a few days or something?"

"Yes, I'm away."

"On vacation?"

"Sort of," I said.

"Sort of? What is that supposed to mean?" With each word, his voice rose in both volume and pitch. I held the phone a couple of inches away from my ear. "Where the hell are you, Clare?"

No way in the world was I telling him.

"It doesn't matter. I'm just away for a while."

"Wait, wait, wait. You're saying *you won't tell me where you are*?"

"I really just need some time by myself."

"Bullshit," he spat. "If you were alone, you'd say where you are. Who is he?"

So much for letting go of anger.

"I'm not with anyone, Zach."

"God, it's not Dev. Tell me it's not goddamn Dev."

"I think I should go now."

"Seriously, Clare? Your high school boyfriend? That's your rebound guy? You know that's pathetic, right?"

"I'm hanging up now, Zach. Please don't call me again."

"Don't you fucking tell me what to do!"

He was shouting. Zach's shouting had always shaken me; there was a note of something wild in it that reverberated all up and down my internal fault lines. But not this time. This time, without saying good-bye or a single other word to him, I hung up, then went to my phone settings, turned off vibrate, put the phone down on the table, fluffed my pillow into just the right shape, and went to sleep.

After breakfast that morning, in a small locked box under the sink in the kitchen, I found the ledgers. It's how the world works sometimes I guess: you spill your coffee, go searching for a sponge, and find a mystery instead.

There were two of them, one leather bound and official looking, the other just a regular black-and-white marbled-cover composition book, the kind with which, I must admit, I have harbored a lifelong obsession. (Jokingly but also not, Dev used to give me one, along with a box of Ticonderoga pencils, every Christmas, and the sight of the two together—a perfect pairing if ever there was one—never failed to satisfy completely a little part of my soul.) Both ledgers were full of the same almost typewriter-like printing I'd found on the back of Edith's photographs, so clean and precise that, even though the blue ink was faded, I could read every word. Sitting at the kitchen table in a pool of brilliant morning sun, being careful to keep my coffee at a safe distance from the ledgers, I dug in.

I started with the leather one, which turned out to be a list of the people who had stayed at Blue Sky House, their names—including the names and ages of each child, if there were any, and, in the case of a few entries, the name of the family's dog with its breed noted in parentheses, which made me adore Edith even more—the dates they'd stayed, and their home addresses. Most came from Delaware or from neighboring states, but a handful lived in places as far-flung as Ohio, Massachusetts, and North Carolina. At the tail end of most of the entries, she'd written what seemed to be reminders to herself, things like *Youngest child cannot eat eggs,*

Fond of watermelon, Tea instead of coffee, Afraid of the dark; needs a night-light, and *Smokes dreadful cigars but thankfully only outside; put ashtrays on the screen porch,* evidently preparing for the possibility that the lodgers would return. I treasured the bits of Edith's personality that shone through: the plain, clear printing, not a curlicue in sight; the meticulous entries, every one with the same format, no cross-outs or misspellings (the woman even spelled *dachshund* right on the very first try, a feat I never pull off myself), every comma in place; her thoughtful, almost tender documentation of her guests' loves and fears and allergies; and, above all, the hope, on page after page, that they would all come back someday.

The ledger's brown silk ribbon still marked the page with the final entry, the last guest: *November 15–17, 1956; Betty Brownmiller; 715 Chestnut Street, Philadelphia, Pennsylvania; Early bedtime, hot milk.* All the remaining pages were blank, and I wondered, a little sadly, if Edith had known when she wrote those words that Betty would be the last guest ever to stay at Blue Sky House.

Except that what I'd learn from the last page of the next ledger is that she wasn't the last guest.

Even before I got to that page, I'd started calling

it "the shadow ledger." The shadow ledger and the daylight ledger are what the two became inside my head. The shadow ledger's entries were made in Edith's same, now familiar printing and carefully dated, but that's where the similarities between the two ended. Where the daylight ledger was clear and direct and businesslike, the shadow ledger was cryptic and oblique and intimate; where the daylight ledger was complete, the shadow ledger left almost everything—everything practical—out. No last names, no addresses. I even heard the words of them differently as I read: the daylight ledger spoke in Edith's voice, crisp and bell-like; the shadow ledger whispered.

Margaret. Roan. Cont chk. Auburn hair, pale, skinny inside her big wool coat, freckles like sprinkled nutmeg across her nose.

Kitty. Farm. Bns bck, arms. I. Bergman cheekbones, husky laugh, nightmares.

Alice. Port. Br rbs, clav. Cont, abr face. Sang lullabies, voice like an angel, oval nails. Carolyn. Dimples, topknot. Johnny. Drove a toy truck over the floors and up the walls.

Janet. Hamp. Br tooth, cont face. Knitted while she talked, the needles clicking, dove-gray bobbed hair, sweater with acorn-shaped buttons. Peggy. Sixteen, pointed chin, ballerina posture down to her turned-out feet, fierce brown eyes that bode well for her future.

Carol Joan Dotty Ginger Linda Mary Joyce . . .

Rich NNews Char Rich Lou Fred Lynch Norf . . .

Abr chk Cont arms Br rad Cont nck Cont trnk Eardr rup . . .

Swan's neck blue-black hair talks with hands swore a blue streak tall dry humor red lipstick yellow braids Raggedy Ann doll math homework chewed nails green eyes penciled eyebrows loves movies loves baseball spoke in whispers . . .

While much of what I read was code-like, inscrutable, what I could understand was so vivid it seemed to breathe. I found myself turning the pages gently, as if they were precious, as if they might dissolve under my fingertips, causing all the people in them to be lost. The daylight ledger had been interesting, but the shadow ledger made me feel that I was discovering something momentous, like the guy who found King Tut's tomb; one minute you're poking around in some rubble, and the next, you're opening a door to a roomful of gold. A few times, in the middle of reading, I felt so excited that I had to go out and walk around in the backyard. Distracted by wonder and confusion, it's a miracle I didn't step off the edge and fall straight into the canal.

My first theory was that the shadow ledger was a more personal version of the daylight one, Edith's private take on the guests, an aside, like notes jotted down in the margins of a book. So when I'd finished reading the shadow ledger through once, I opened both ledgers and compared the two, entry by entry, date by date. But it didn't take long for that first theory to crash and burn because, for one thing, the daylight ledger began more than a year before Edith made the shadow ledger's first entry, and after that, while sometimes the dates matched up, the names never did.

It was as if Edith ran two guesthouses, one for people with full names and houses on specific streets in specific towns that they'd go home to, and another one for ghosts, mostly female ghosts. Only they weren't ghosts. Ghosts didn't have fierce eyes or freckles; they didn't love baseball or sing lullabies. I thought of Edith's photographs, how one, small, chosen fragment of Joseph could evoke a whole man and a world of love between the photographer and her subject. In Edith's hands, the shadow ledger guests, despite being nameless and rootless, apparently untethered to the ordinary world, became exquisitely human. And what I believed, what seemed clear to me, was that Edith loved *them,* too, although not the way she loved Joseph, of course. What I kept picturing was Miss

Clavel from the children's book *Madeline:* Edith, doing her duty, watching over, keeping track, not turning off the light until everyone was safe.

I called Dev.

I almost didn't because even though I'd maintained my cool through the roller-coaster ride of my dead-of-night conversation with Zach, the next day, I kept coming back to the part where he'd accused me of rebounding with my high school sweetheart. That accusation hit home, just a bit, not because I wanted to rebound with Dev or with anyone—God knows I felt as wrung out and done with romance as I ever had and, anyway, when it came to romance, Dev was definitely and forever off the table—but because what had started the day I'd sat at that enormous, glossy conference table with the equally enormous, glossy (in spirit anyway) Eloisa Dunne and learned that Edith had given me a house, was an adventure. A true blue, strange, astonishing, bona fide adventure. And the person who'd always had adventures with me, my longtime partner in crime (or what passed for crime for two hopelessly goody-two-shoes kids) was Dev Tremain.

I hadn't actually spoken to him since the wedding that wasn't. He'd followed up his wedding-cake-devouring photo with a text that simply read, I'm here if you need, you know, wisdom or whatever. And by whatever, I mean anything. But you knew that already, and then he proceeded, apart from the occasional goofball text, to keep his distance, Dev having always been a person who got, without being told, when a person needed a little space. The night of the day I found out that Edith left me her house, when I was still too stunned to talk about it with anyone apart from my mom, who'd been with me when I got the news, Dev sent a text that said: So get this: this guy I met last week in the sandwich line at Wawa? He just bequeathed me an island. A small one but still: A WHOLE ISLAND. I laughed, out loud no less, and texted back: Always with the one-upsmanship. To which he responded: Wait. Are you saying you inherited something (far less impressive than an island) today, too???

Even though I can see how some people wouldn't like it (he was my ex-boyfriend after all), I'd always found it comforting, Dev's and my being part of the same information pipeline, his knowing things about me without my having to tell him. Even though we hadn't talked about it, I was sure he knew I was staying at Edith's house, just like I knew he was working in a lab at UPenn for the summer, ate lunch at a North Philly falafel place every single weekday, and on Sunday afternoons, played on a men's basketball team that included his former high school biology teacher and his best friend (and my best friend's kind-of-but-not-really-at-least-not-yet boyfriend), Aidan. Neither of us found it weird, and neither of us ever did much with the information we had. We just knew stuff about each other's lives. It was how it was, how it had always been.

But, anyway, I almost didn't call him because I didn't want to give even the tiniest bit of credence to Zach's rebound accusation, until it hit me how stupid and childish this was. *What the hell, Clare? You what? Don't want to give Zach the satisfaction?* I said to myself. *He won't even know.* But then I reminded myself that Zach's knowing or not knowing wasn't the point. The point was that Dev was my friend.

He answered by saying, "You would not even believe what I'm eating right now."

"Falafel."

"Not falafel. The greatest falafel in the world."

"The greatest falafel in the world is in Philadelphia? What about the entire Middle East? What about the falafel in Baghdad?"

"Better."

"What about Dubai? I bet they have really great falafel in Dubai."

"Not this great."

"Is it the tahini?"

"It's the tahini, the falafel itself, the taboon bread. It's everything."

"Can't you just say pita like a normal person?"

"Who would say pita when they can say taboon bread?"

"Everyone."

"Anyway, it's not really a pocket. A pita is all about the pocket."

"Can we stop talking about your lunch now?"

"Yeah, sure, stop when I was winning."

"Winning the conversation about your sandwich?"

"You had no comeback to my pita pocket observation. It was painfully obvious."

"*You're* painfully obvious."

"And we end with another classic Clare Hobbes counterinsult!"

"Turning your own words against you. You'd think you'd know better by now than to argue with the likes of me."

"*You'd* think I'd know better by now."

"I never think you know better."

"True."

"Can you just shut up at this point? Is that possible?"

"Yes."

"Dev, listen."

"Listening."

"This morning, I spilled my coffee and went looking for a sponge because I thought maybe Joliet had left one, Joliet like the city not like the Shakespeare heroine—she's the woman who cleans the house—and so anyway, this morning, coffee, everywhere, so I went looking under the sink for a sponge, and boom."

"Boom?"

"Yes. But it really started before that when the nosy neighbor mentioned the murder and I went to the library, which was the most consummately perfect library ever with this amazing red door and full of rustling like I like, and I sat there and read through nearly a hundred and twenty-one copies of the *Daily Bee,* and I had to do some piecing together and it took me hours, although thank God they had all the newspapers digitized a while back, and, when I was finished working, I looked up and was surprised to see it was dark outside, and my eyesight was doing that underwater thing that comes from staring at a computer screen for too long, but it was all worth it because the story, Dev, it was amazing. Do you have time to hear it? Like is your lunch break almost over? Because I can call back later."

"Did you say murder?"

"Yes."

"I can stay later at the lab if they need me to. Tell me now."

I told him everything. My conversation with Joliet; my conversation with Louise Smits; the two canoes; Joseph's photos of Edith; Edith's photos of Joseph; the marriage certificate; the obituary; the story of Elliot Giles's murder, of John Blanchard's trial, and of the disappearances of Edith Herron and Sarah Giles; the blue ceiling, the percolator, everything. I ended with the ledgers, opening them up and reading Dev a few entries from each.

After I finished, Dev was quiet for a while. I could feel the wheels turning inside his head, and even without seeing him, I knew exactly the expression he had on his face.

Finally, he said, "I guess we're thinking the shadow guests were real people? She couldn't have been, I don't know, taking notes for a book she was writing or something? Or maybe they were just people she met someplace else, like at the beach or in a restaurant or someplace, not people who stayed at her house?"

"I never thought of that. I guess it's possible they weren't guests or even real people at all, but I think they were. There are the dates, for one thing, placed a line up from the guest's name, just the way they are in the daylight ledger, and the two ledgers were together, in the same box, like they were the same sort of thing. A pair."

"A pair," he echoed. "Okay, that's true. Plus, she makes reference to lullabies, right? And nightmares. There are at least two guests with 'nightmares' at the end of their entries. Which seem to indicate that Edith was with them at night. People just don't sing lullabies or have nightmares out in public, and since Edith owned a guesthouse, chances are they were guests."

"Yes, also—" I stopped, my cheeks flushing.

"Also, what?"

"Okay, not to sound crazy, but they just *feel* real to me, real and like they were here, in this house. Maybe it's the details Edith includes that bring them to life for me, but I look around and picture them so clearly, here on the first floor where there's a tiny bedroom, where I bet they slept. I see them knitting and running a toy truck across the floor and singing to a baby. There are these two chairs by the fire, and I can see women sitting there, the firelight on their auburn hair or blue-black hair or—" I sighed. "So, yeah, it does sound crazy."

"Not to me, not really. Brain scientists actually take intuition pretty seriously these days. And even if they didn't—"

"Even if they didn't, what?"

"I take you seriously."

"Well, thanks," I said, sincerely flattered.

Dev cleared his throat. "So let's go ahead with the idea, at least for now, that the people in the shadow ledger were real guests who stayed at Edith's house, but who, for some reason, warranted a different ledger and a different, harder-to-understand kind of entry notation. They were like an undercurrent, this flow of shadow guests, or like Edith's own little parallel universe."

I started smiling at *let's go ahead with the idea,* and as the excitement mounted in his voice, I pumped my fist in the air and shouted a silent, celebratory *Yes!* Because he was back, my adventuring partner, gung ho to grab my hand and jump with me, feetfirst, into mystery.

"Shoot, if only we could find them," I said. "Those shadow guests. Some of them, especially the kids, are sure to be alive someplace. But there's just not enough information to go on."

"No, but listen, listen," said Dev. "Some of them weren't there alone, right? There were other guests, daylight guests, whose stays overlapped with theirs."

"Yes. A lot had overlapping dates," I said. "More in the summer than in the winter, when she probably didn't get that many regular guests. The shadow ledger goes on for about three years, and I haven't counted, but I'd say there were twenty or more times when the daylight guests and shadow guests overlapped."

"And we do have information on those guys, the daylight guests. What if we get in touch with them, and find a way to ask them if they remember other guests being there? Then, we'll know for sure that there were two sets of guests."

"Oh, wow, right," I said, catching on. "And who knows? Maybe they'll remember something about those guests, something that might give us a clue as to *why* they were shadow guests. What made them shadowy instead of daylit."

"It's definitely worth a shot. We shouldn't expect too much, though. Some of them won't live at those addresses anymore. Some of them, honestly, might not live, period. And if they're still around, they'll be pretty old. They may not remember much from way back then. But you know what? Some of them had families, so maybe the kids will remember something, if we can track them down."

"How, though? Should we do one of those reverse-search things online? We can put in names and addresses and try to find phone numbers or e-mail addresses. It's kind of a stalkery thing to do, but we could."

"We could," said Dev, "but we could also just write

letters. Blue Sky House is in Delaware, and I'll bet a lot of the addresses are pretty close by. Delaware, Maryland, Virginia, Philadelphia, or around there. We could say, I don't know, that you inherited a house that used to be an inn and are trying to learn more about its history. Not a lie, just not the whole truth. Most of the letters would either get where they're going overnight or in a couple of days. We could give the people our cellphone numbers. They could call us if they have any information."

"A fair number are Delaware addresses, and most of those are *Wilmington,* actually, where you live. I even recognized one or two of the street names." I had a thought. "Hey, you might even know some of the people, Dev. Or their kids or their kids' kids. For a city, Wilmington's a pretty small town."

"You're right. So why don't I start with them, the Wilmington people, and you can do the others," he said. "We can start tonight even."

Tonight. Suddenly, we were thirteen years old again, gangly and sure of ourselves and full of an almost feverish urgency to begin, begin, begin.

"But how will I get you the addresses?" I asked. "It would also be good if you had the shadow ledger entries that correspond with the dates of the people you're contacting. I could type it all up, I guess."

"You could, I guess," said Dev.

There was a silence during which I was pretty sure the two of us were thinking the same thing. Yes, I could type up everything and send it, which would take a while, especially since there wasn't Internet service at Edith's house, or Dev could come to Blue Sky House. He was spending the summer in Wilmington, splitting his time, the way he usually did, between Cornelia and Teo's and his mother's houses, taking the train into Philadelphia to work every day. Wilmington was a scant two-hour drive from Antioch Beach. He could be here tomorrow morning or even tonight. I knew just how it would be: the two of us sitting at the kitchen table with the ledgers spread open in front of us, Dev's face alternating between pensive and animated in the glow of his laptop, his eyes as full of streaming, darting life as a coral reef. We'd type and leaf through the ledgers and now and then break the quiet to voice ideas that would seem random to anyone else, anyone other than two people who'd been following the stone-skipping trails—bounce, bounce, bounce—of each other's thoughts since they were kids.

It would've been so easy to ask him to come, but, at the very last second, something held me back. I don't know what. I felt not ready, although for what I couldn't exactly say. Not ready to not be alone in Edith's house?

Not ready to not be alone, period? Not ready to be alone with Dev? But that last possibility made no sense, so I discarded it. Still, the fact remained that I didn't feel ready to invite Dev to Edith's house, not yet, not quite.

Just as I was about to say I'd type everything up, go to the library or a coffee shop or something and send it to him, Dev said, "What if you take pictures of the relevant pages with your phone and text them to me? That'll save you some work and save us some time."

I let out my breath, even though I hadn't realized I'd been holding it.

"Good idea," I said.

In the end, over the course of a week, we only got three phone calls between the two of us, but they were enough. We confirmed what I'd known in my bones to be true: the shadow guests were real and had stayed in Edith's house.

One man had been nine, and he remembered getting up early and coming downstairs before his parents woke up. There was a girl sitting in a chair reading a book. She was about his age, maybe a little younger, with dark, curly hair. He remembered that she was embarrassed about her dress because it wasn't pretty and was too big for her. She told him that the dress was "borrowed" and that all her own pretty clothes were back at home. He remembered her mother showing up and telling her to shush, and he wondered why her mother seemed mad when all the girl had done was talk about her dress. According to the shadow ledger, the girl's name was Elaine and her mother's name was Dottie.

Another man, nearly ninety years old but sharp as a tack, had stayed with his family at Blue Sky House three times. He described Edith as quiet and gracious, the kind of person who could produce a bucket and spade out of thin air for the children to take to the beach and who packed a hell of a picnic lunch. On the third visit, he and his wife, Anne, woke up in the middle of the night to the sound of someone "sobbing her heart out," so Anne had gone down to check on Edith. But when she got to the first floor, Edith was standing in the living room, dry-eyed and composed as ever. She told his wife that a guest staying in the downstairs bedroom had had a nightmare but that everything was all right now. By the time his family came down to breakfast the next morning, the guest was gone. According to the shadow ledger, the guest's name was Kitty.

Another woman had been around fifteen when her family spent a weekend at Blue Sky House. A chronic insomniac, she'd been unable to sleep and was lying awake when she heard doors opening and shutting on the floor below. Worried and curious, she'd crept down the stairs to see what was happening and saw a woman with two black eyes—terrible looking, swollen almost shut—standing in the kitchen. She remembered being surprised because she hadn't thought there were any other guests staying there. The next day, she expected to see the woman at breakfast, but even though the girl could hear someone moving around in a back room on the first floor, the woman never appeared. When the girl told her mother about the woman and her black eyes, her mother decided that Blue Sky House must attract a lower class of guest than she'd thought, and they never went back. That shadow guest's name was Mary.

During that week, Dev and I talked every night, about what we'd taken to calling the Blue Sky House mystery ("Pure Nancy Drew," I told Dev, gleefully) and about other things, too. I even told him about my breakup with Zach, although I knew he'd probably heard much of the story already. I hadn't realized how deeply I'd missed this when Zach and I were together: putting my phone on speaker and letting Dev's voice be my company.

The night he told me the story of the woman with two black eyes, I went to bed, tossed and turned, switched the light on and off, tried to read twice with no success, until I was struck so hard by an idea that, even though it was well after midnight, I called Dev.

Before he could even eke out a sleepy hello, I said, "What if Sarah weren't the first? All this coming and going in the middle of the night or early morning. That girl wearing borrowed clothes as if she'd left in a rush and hadn't had time to pack. The two black eyes. The shadow ledger is obviously keeping a secret. It's kept it all these years. What if the secret is that John Blanchard and Edith were running some kind of escape route, an underground railroad for battered women?"

Out of breath, I waited.

"You might be right," said Dev. "Clare, I bet you're right."

My eyes burned, my mouth trembled. When I touched my cheek, I discovered I was crying.

"I think I am," I said.

"Are you crying?" asked Dev.

"It's just that—well, I'm lying here in her house, you know? And I'm thinking who does something like that? Because it would have to have been risky, right? Back then, in the fifties, especially. And I met her, this brave person who did this thing, and I talked to her and now I'm in her house, this house that she gave me that all those women and children passed through, and I miss her so much. I wish she were here, so I could talk to her and—and do something nice for her, give her something, and I will never be able to."

"Maybe you are," said Dev, slowly. "It could be that this is what Edith wanted, for you to find out her story. Maybe this is the thing you're giving her."

Startled, I wiped my eyes and considered what he'd said.

"Do you think it matters, though? Edith is dead. Can it possibly matter when she's not here to know about it?"

And Dev said, "Yes."

Chapter Seventeen
Edith

June 1954

Six months in, John found her out.

When she thought about it afterward, after Alice and her children were gone, after John came back and stood on her porch for the second time in two days, as close to truly angry as she'd ever seen him, and said, "I hope to God you know what you're doing, Edith," she realized he had been bound to find out sooner or later. Because if John Blanchard were good at anything, and he was good at many things, it was paying attention. Also, and perhaps more significantly, he loved her. How far that love went, whether it crossed over from simple friendship into the territory of being in love, she wasn't sure, and he never let on, but she knew this: John Blanchard was her best friend and he loved her. He loved her and looked out for her and, moreover, seemed instinctively to understand when she was sad or worried or hungry for conversation or for the matchless, soul-nourishing camaraderie of laughing with another person. So when she began keeping a secret from him, it made sense that he would know this, too.

The June night that Alice and her two children, a one-year-old girl and a five-year-old boy, were to arrive at Blue Sky House, Edith was more nervous than usual. She'd gotten word the night before that because of some kind of safety concern that forced them to leave the place they were coming from, wherever that was, they would be arriving earlier than was usual for downstairs guests, as Edith had come to think of them, at around ten o'clock, instead of after midnight or just before dawn. Fortunately, there were no upstairs guests booked for that night, but ten seemed so early. Some houses along her street, as sedate as the street was, would no doubt still have lights on; people might even be out, walking dogs or coming home after a late dinner in a restaurant. To distract herself from worrying, Edith kept busy, tidying up the already pin-neat downstairs bedroom, getting the chicken out of the oven and carving it. By now she knew that the women who came either had no appetite or were ravenous, and, if they didn't fall asleep immediately, the children would almost always eat. By 9:45, though, Edith was so jittery that all she could do was sit in a kitchen chair and watch the clock.

At 9:55, a knock at her door—the front door, not the back—scared her so much that she jumped out of her chair. Alice must have gotten her instructions wrong. Heart drumming, hands shaking, Edith opened the door, ready to hustle the three of them in as quickly as she could. But it was John. He wore street clothes rather than his uniform, and in his hand was a book about birds he'd borrowed the week before. His smile vanished as soon as he saw her, and she knew he'd noticed, as of course he would, her flustered state.

"Hey," he said, taking a step toward her, concern in his eyes. "Are you all right?"

Edith brushed her hand over her hair and forced out a laugh. "Oh, my! I guess I was lost in thought when you knocked, and it startled me nearly out of my skin. How ridiculous I am!"

She stepped out onto the porch, trying to keep outwardly calm, while inwardly, she sifted frantically through her options, the best of which seemed to be getting rid of John as quickly as possible.

"Are you sure that's all?" he asked.

"Well, the truth is I feel a bit feverish. I think I'm getting a cold, and I would hate to give it to you. There's nothing so crummy as a summer cold, is there?"

"I'm sorry you're not well. Want me to run out for anything? Orange juice? Tea? Cold medicine?"

"You're so kind, but no. I'm all stocked up on, well, just about everything! Now, you should go before I infect you."

But John stood his ground, and just then, Edith heard a faint knocking on the back door. John heard it, too. He craned his neck, trying to look past her, through the house.

"Was that knocking?" he said.

"Oh, I don't think so," she said, glancing over her shoulder.

The knocking came again, this time louder.

John's eyes met hers. "There's someone at your door, Edith. Are you expecting someone?"

"Well, I—" She paused, her mind racing. "You know, some guests were supposed to arrive this evening, but they never did. I bet that's them."

"At your back door? I didn't see a car drive up."

"Oh, it happens that way sometimes. You know how people can be," she said, airily. "I should really go and let them in. I'll see you soon, John."

She turned to go, but John's hand stopped the door from shutting behind her.

"I don't feel good about this," he said. "I think you should let me go see who it is."

He stepped into the house, just as the back door opened and a tentative voice called, "Hello? Is anyone here?" and then, sharply, "Johnny! Come back here!" Footsteps, and then a small boy with dark hair and a toy truck in his hand appeared, running toward them through the house. When he saw them, he skidded to a stop at the edge of the kitchen and stared, open-mouthed.

"Hello," said John. He smiled and crouched so that he was eye level with the boy. "I see you've got a truck there."

Mutely, the boy nodded uncertainly, but then a second later, he held the truck out for John's inspection. "It's a dump truck," he said. "You can put stones in it. Or dirt."

"Johnny, darling." A woman with a baby cradled in one arm stepped out of the shadowed living room and into the light. John stood up when he saw her, and at the sight of him, she froze, her eyes darkening and darting from John's face to Edith's. She touched a hand, a long, beautiful hand, to her lip, which was swollen and crusted over with blood, and then moved it to her bruised cheek. When Johnny ran to her and threw his arms around her legs, she winced with pain.

"It's all right," said Edith, softly. "This is my friend John. I told him that sometimes guests make a mistake and come to the back door."

The woman drew herself upright and gave John and Edith a smile with her swollen lips that would break anyone's heart. "Please forgive my mistake. Johnny ran around back before I could stop him, and I saw the door and just knocked. So thoughtless of me."

"Don't give it a second thought," Edith said. "It's fine, just fine."

"I just stopped in to drop off this book I borrowed," said John, giving the woman his kindest smile and handing the book to Edith. "I'll make myself scarce, now."

"I think I'll walk him out," said Edith to Alice. "Please make yourself at home."

Out on the porch, as soon as the front door was shut behind them, John turned and said, "Edith."

"I told you it was just my guests," she said, meeting his serious blue gaze. "And it is. There's nothing to worry about."

John lifted his hand toward her, as if to touch her arm, then shook his head and let the hand drop to his side. "I'll be back tomorrow night," he said. "We need to talk."

The following night, he stood on her porch again, and said this: "Three days ago, at the station, we got a wire, one that went out to all the police stations in this area, to be on the lookout for the wife of a high-ranking military man in Portsmouth, Virginia, who had left in the middle of the night with her two children."

Despite the June mugginess, a chill went through Edith. "Oh?" she said, as casually as she could. "Why this area in particular?"

"Apparently, she has family in Kent County. It seemed possible that she would take the children there, but she didn't and is therefore still at large."

Edith swallowed her sigh of relief. Blue Sky House was safe, at least for the moment, but there was still John to contend with. "'At large'? Sounds more like a missing persons case to me."

John shook his head and said, grimly, "She's considered a kidnapper. That woman is a fugitive, Edith."

Keeping a cool head was obviously her best hope of deflecting John's attention from the goings-on in Blue Sky House. Edith knew this; she really did, but still her temper flared. "A kidnapper? They're her own children, aren't they? And tell me this, John, has it occurred to anyone that if a woman takes a risk like that, she must have her reasons?"

John sighed. "Edith, the woman and her children who came to your back door two nights ago match the description of Alice Finlay and her two children exactly, down to the curls on that little boy's head."

Edith averted her eyes, staring off through the porch screen to the yard beyond. Her azaleas were having an especially good year. It was dark outside now, but in the daytime, you could barely see the leaves for the pink riot of flowers. "Did this description of yours mention her fat lip, the bruises covering the entire left side of her face?" she asked, quietly, her eyes on the azaleas. "Did it include her broken ribs and collarbone?"

"No," said John.

"Of course not," said Edith, bitterly. "So I don't see how it could possibly have been the same woman."

"Are they still here?"

"You came to arrest them, is that it?" she said, clenching her hands into fists. "That broken woman and her baby and her little boy."

John took her arm, gently, a kind, light touch, but she twitched it away.

"I don't think anyone really wants to arrest Alice Finlay," said John.

"There are all kinds of prisons," she snapped. "So answer me: Is that why you came, to take that woman and her children back to theirs?"

"I came to see if they were still here," said John, wearily.

She turned blazing eyes on him. "Well, they aren't. They aren't the people you're—hunting down. And they aren't here. They decided they weren't quite up for a vacation right now, so they left just before dawn."

John looked spent, faded, his face drawn into tight lines. He took off his glasses and rubbed his eyes, and Edith recalled another time she'd seen him do this: the morning they'd found the bodies of the poor, drowned Driver twins. Without wanting to, she remembered how tenderly John had lifted Robbie Driver and placed him in the bottom of the boat, but, impatiently, she shook off the memory. That time, John had been on the side of right. He had always, since she'd met him, been on that side, but not tonight, not now that he had become one of the people who wanted to send Alice and her children back to what was surely the opposite of home.

"They weren't the people you were looking for," she said.

"Listen to me." John leaned toward her, gestured with his hands. "These people coming and going in the dark. Strange cars on your street at all hours. If I've noticed, other people will. Just the other day, Walter down at the drugstore remarked to me that your guests must be especially accident-prone with all the gauze and bandages and Bacitracin you've been buying. And my God, what about the other guests, the ones who come in the front door in the daylight? It might take time, but they will notice. And then you'll be a target, and I—" John's voice faltered. "And I can't have that," he said.

Edith found herself breathing hard, on the edge of tears, but she wouldn't break down. She gathered herself. "I understand that you worry about me," she said, softly. "I do so appreciate that. But I'm fine. Nothing is going on here that shouldn't be; I promise you that."

For a moment, they stood staring at each other, Edith balanced on the fine line between evasion and confession, John between personal loyalty and the law. If they slipped, it was anyone's guess onto which side each would land, but for that hour of that night, anyway, they held steady.

"I hope to God you know what you're doing, Edith," John said, fiercely, and then he spun around and left, allowing, for the first time, the screen porch door to bang shut behind him.

For the next week, Edith neither saw nor heard from him. She had put him in a terrible position; she knew that. John took his job seriously, and his reputation as a police chief was golden, unassailable, a fact he cherished. Beyond that, deeper even than that, he was honest to the core, hopelessly honest, he'd once told her, laughing; even as a kid, even to get himself out of sticky situations, he was fundamentally unable to lie. *But you aren't asking him to lie,* she told herself, *you're only asking him to look the other way.* In her heart, though, she understood that for a man like John Blanchard, the two amounted to the same thing. For that whole week, Edith fluctuated wildly between serenity born of the rock-solid faith that he would choose friendship over duty and desperate panic that he would not. In the dark moments, raw-nerved and fearful, she waited, her entire body tensed, for disaster, disgrace, ruin to knock at her door.

What happened instead was this. One morning, a week after John had left and slammed the door behind him, a package appeared on her porch. No stamps, no note, just a neat bundle wrapped in brown paper and tied with twine. Edith brought it into the house and opened it at the kitchen table. Inside were two boxes of gauze pads, three rolls of bandages, three rolls of bandage tape, and a large tube of antibiotic ointment. Edith dropped into a kitchen chair, put her face in her hands, and wept, not only out of relief but also shame at how she had underestimated John. He hadn't chosen to simply look the other way; he hadn't even chosen friendship, not really, because a stranger's damaged face had surely weighed in the balance as much as his affection for Edith, probably more. John had considered all his options, and despite the risks, despite all it would cost his conscience, and she knew it was a great deal, John had chosen to help.

Chapter Eighteen
Clare

"You want to hear something amazing and also amazingly annoying?" demanded Hildy.

"Who would say no to that?" I said.

"Oh, you'd be surprised," said Hildy. "The barista at the Sweet Bean, for instance, the one with the Andrew-Jackson-twenty-dollar-bill hair? He had no interest whatsoever. Actually, if it is a possible thing to have negative interest, and I mean *aggressively* negative interest, this guy did. I asked him the same question I just asked you, and before the words were fully out of my mouth, you could just feel the apathy coming off him like—" She groped around for the proper simile.

"Fumes?" I suggested.

"Radioactivity. When it came to apathy, he was a—whatdayacallit—isotope."

"I don't think all isotopes are radioactive."

"Ah, but you don't know, do you? You know who would know?"

I groaned. "Yes."

"Dev, that's who. Where *is* that Dev when you need him?"

"I know where you're going with this," I told her.

"Where?"

"Where you always go with it."

"Face it, Clairol. He's the lox to your bagel. The gin to your tonic. The Fig Newtons to your cheddar cheese."

"Nobody, not a single human in the history of the world except for you has ever thought for even one second that those last two things go together."

I could hear the shrug in her voice when she said, "It's essentially the same as apple pie and cheddar cheese."

"No. No, it is not."

When I go too long without actually talking to Hildy—or more important, having her talk to me, hearing her actual words in her actual semiblaring, semimusical in-the-manner-of-bagpipes voice—my soul starts to wilt.

"You're talking to him, again," she said, smugly. "Practically every night."

"How would you know that?"

"Aidan was just here visiting me, and he happened to call Dev, and I happened to grab the phone out of his hand."

"And Dev happened to mention that we'd been talking?"

Another audible shrug: "There may have been interrogation involved. Just a tad."

I considered explaining to Hildy that Dev and I were just friends, until I remembered that I'd explained this to her at least three hundred million times before to absolutely no avail.

"So are you going to tell me or not?" I said.

"Tell you what?"

"The amazing and amazingly annoying thing," I said.

"You're changing the subject."

"I'm changing the subject *back*, which isn't the same thing."

"Fine," Hildy said. "So Aidan starts his new job in Washington, D.C., next month, and he asked me to move there."

"Oh! My! God!" I screeched. "Move *with* him? Like live with him? Like you'd live *together*?"

"You're literally hurting my ear."

"Screw your ear. *Are you?*"

"He's renting this apartment, and he said he'd like it if I'd live there with him, but he also said if that idea falls under the heading of moving too fast, there's another apartment for rent in the same building, and if it makes me more comfortable, I could live there."

"So does it?" I said.

"Does it what?"

"Make you more comfortable."

"Hell, no," said Hildy.

I tossed my head back and laughed with pure, giddy, reckless joy. "This is my lifelong dream!"

"You haven't known me your whole life."

"Of course I have, and probably before that, too," I scoffed.

Universal truth: some people you've known since birth and you've just barely met them; others you've known for four years and they've been your friend since before you were born.

"True," said Hildy.

"But how is this amazingly annoying? It's not. It can't be."

"Because: *Washington.*" She slapped the word down like a piece of raw liver onto a butcher block.

"You don't like Washington? It's nice. Where in Washington?"

"Some square or circle or something. But nice or not nice, George Washington was a man. I live in Ann Arbor, the only damn city in the country that's named after a woman instead of a damn man, and Aidan wants me to move. From Ann to a man. Ms. Arbor is turning over in her grave, damn it," she said. I heard a pounding sound; Hildy's fist hitting the table. I'd recognize her pound anywhere.

"You're maintaining that there was actually at some point a woman named Ann Arbor?" I asked.

"Yes. She founded the city. Or something."

"I think Ann was the name of the wives of the two men who founded the city, neither of whom had the last name Arbor. Although even that might just be speculation."

"Regardless."

"And anyway: Charlottesville," I said.

"What?"

"The town where my parents live, where I moved when I was eleven. It's named after a woman. Princess Charlotte who became Queen Charlotte when she married George the Third."

"Hmm."

"And there's a nearby town named Louisa, named after I have no idea, but it must've been a woman, right?"

"Possibly."

"And actually, the whole state of Virginia is named after Elizabeth the First," I said. "Elizabeth the Virgin Queen."

"Now, that's getting kind of personal, isn't it?" said Hildy.

A light clicked on inside my head, the kind with a dimmer switch, dialed down to dim.

Char, Lou, Rich.

"Char, Lou, Rich," I murmured.

The light got brighter.

"Char, Lou, Rich!" I cried.

"What the hell?" said Hildy.

"Hildy, hold on, just hold on, okay? I'll be right back."

I leapt out of the living room chair I'd been sitting in and ran to where the shadow ledger lay open on the kitchen table. I grabbed the notebook I'd been using and a Ticonderoga pencil and started writing: *Roan, Char, Fred, Port, NNews, Lou, Hamp, Lynch, Rich, Rich, Rich . . .*

The light flared bright as a full moon. I grabbed my phone.

"Hildy, listen! Roanoke, Charlottesville, Fredericksburg, Portsmouth, Newport News—God, if Newport News had been a snake, it would have bitten me—

Louisa, Hampton, Lynchburg. Richmond! Richmond! Richmond!"

"Good Lord, you've lost your mind," said Hildy.

"It's Virginia," I sang. "They all came from Virginia! Hildy, I love you, and I'm so glad you're moving to Washington to live with Aidan, Aidan whom I could not love more, and I will call you back and explain everything, but I have to go call Dev."

"Of course, you have to call Dev!" said Hildy, pounding the table again. "You'd be crazy not to always, always call Dev. But call me back so I know you haven't been dragged off to the loony bin, the special one for people who can't stop shouting Richmond, okay?"

"I promise."

"I love you, too," she said.

"Richmond!" I yelped and hung up.

We decided I would pick up Dev in Wilmington on my way home.

When I'd called him to tell him about my Virginia brainstorm, once my words stopped tripping over themselves and he could understand what I was saying, and after the rousing round of verbal high-fiving that followed, he said, "So what's next?" And as soon as he said this, I realized "So what's next?" was my indisputable, hands-down, all-time favorite question. I had not prior to that moment even considered having a favorite question, but at that second, I knew that I did have one, and this was it. It was so game, so chummy, and it just smacked of hope. If "So what's next?" had a face, I would've kissed it on both cheeks.

"Well, I can try to find out if either John Blanchard or Edith had a Virginia connection," I said. "One of the newspaper articles I read said that John was born in Baltimore, Maryland, and moved to Antioch Beach as a young man. I could look up Blanchards in Baltimore and ask whomever I find if there's a Virginia branch of the family he might have visited, I guess, although it's a fairly common name. It could take a while to track someone down. And I haven't stumbled upon anything about Edith's life before she came to Antioch Beach. I might still. There are some of her locked boxes that I've opened but not gone through yet. Some of them were like specimen boxes or something. They had butterflies and other bugs inside, pinned and labeled in Edith's handwriting. One had leaves, pretty crumbled by now. One had shells. The rest of them seemed to just have photographs in them, some hers, some Joseph's. Should I start with the boxes?"

"Clare," said Dev. "What if we just go?"

"To Virginia?"

"Sure. We could stop and see your parents and my grandparents, have dinner or whatever, maybe do a little poking around Charlottesville, and then—boom—go."

I laughed, not because Dev had said something funny, but just because I was happy. I couldn't remember the last time I'd laughed aloud out of sheer happiness, but however long it had been, it had been too long.

"Okay, but go where? We should narrow it down," I said, "because there are a lot of towns on that list. I mean, I have time, but I'm guessing you don't. You have to work at the lab, right?"

"Yeah. I can probably take one day off, not more than that, though. But listen, Richmond is mentioned more than once, and it's the biggest city in the shadow ledger. What if we just go there? Today's Wednesday. I can tell them tomorrow that I need Friday off; you'll swing by and pick me up tomorrow night, and we'll head down. Do you want to do that?"

When Dev gets excited about something, his enthusiasm doesn't just flow, it billows, burgeoning in every direction like the ocean, and I have never been able to resist letting it carry me along. I had no idea what we would do once we got to Richmond. I would have said that the whole enterprise would be like looking for a needle in a haystack, except that I wasn't sure what the needle would even be, but, right then, in the middle of all the billowing, Dev could have suggested that we head to Madagascar (where I've actually always wanted to go) or to the bottom of the Mariana Trench or to a random Walmart (where I never, ever want to go), and I would, without hesitation, have said yes.

"Yes!" I said.

This time, Dev was the one who laughed.

"Good," he said. "Perfect. I'll see you tomorrow night."

The next morning, so early that it was still dark, not nighttime dark, but that grayish, cat-soft dark that happens long after the frogs and bugs stop singing but before the birds start, when the sunrise is still hovering a few notches below the horizon, I got up, threw on some clothes, and went for a walk on the beach. As I set off across the deserted highway, a silver hook of moon still hung in the sky, but by the time I set foot on the sand, it was gone.

Tonight, I would see Dev for the first time since the Saturday afternoon when I had walked into Zach's hotel room and spectacularly blew to bits our wedding and Zach's heart and at least a little of mine, too. And *that* weekend had been the first time Dev and I had seen each other since another Saturday afternoon a few months earlier, one that had been far quieter, far less well attended—just the two of us, no family or friends to bear witness—but equally emotion-fraught, so confusing and painful that almost as soon as it was over, I had gathered up our entire conversation, crumpled it up, and shoved it to the very back of my mind, where it had stayed ever since.

But that morning, with our trip to Virginia just a few hours away, I decided it was time to pull it into the light, spread it out before me, and face it once and for all because my and Dev's friendship had never been the same after that Saturday afternoon. We had hardly talked in the months between the two Saturdays, and the few times we had, the thing I'd shoved into that dark corner of my mind, as much as I'd tried to pretend it wasn't there, had come between us. In recent days, as we'd talked about the Blue Sky House mystery, we'd inched closer to each other and to the friendship we used to have, but that balled-up, shoved-away Saturday was still there, and I wanted it gone.

Here's the thing: I lied when I said I could never resist being carried away by Dev's enthusiasm. There was one time, just one, on a freezing Saturday in January, a week and a half into the new year, when I resisted.

Zach had found out just two days before that his father was dying, and, despite their rocky relationship, he had taken the news hard. Vulnerable, shaky, as twitchy as a squirrel, more fragile than I'd ever imagined him being, he had begged me to come with him to the lake house in Michigan for the bedside vigil, and I had agreed, a decision I didn't even quite regret later, after the trip—and Zach—had turned into a nightmare, because it was just a fact that no one with a shred of compassion could have possibly refused him.

The day before we were scheduled to leave, for the first time since Zach had gotten the news about his dad, I was alone in my apartment, drinking coffee loaded with milk, eating toast buttered all the way to the edges the way I liked it, and trying to store up the solitude and the sweet, sweet quiet, knowing I was sure to need both in the days to come, when I got a text from Dev. It said: Hey, Clare, I'm standing outside your apartment building, of all places. And, because, for my entire life since I'd met him, seeing Dev was always a million times better than not seeing him, I texted back: Why are you standing outside texting instead of walking through my front door?

About five seconds later, he knocked, and I opened the door, and, for the next minute and a half or so was so busy being happy to see him—pulling him inside, hugging him, and saying things like *wow* and *yay*—that I didn't notice immediately how drawn and serious he looked. And pale. Dev's coloring generally tended toward a sort of fawn and russet combination; I could only remember seeing him truly pale on a few occasions, and one of those was when his maternal grandmother died. Dev pale scared me.

"Hey, why do you look like that?" I demanded, holding him at arm's length.

"Genes," he said. And then his accuracy-loving self couldn't resist adding, "Not exclusively, obviously."

The fact that he didn't throw in a few details about epigenetics or the effect of environment on phenotype or whatever worried me almost as much as his wan cheeks.

"Seriously," I said.

"How do I look?"

"Hunched. Mushroom-colored. With blue circles under your eyes."

He smiled a tired smile.

"Extremely handsome, in other words." He rolled his shoulders a few times, wincingly. "I had this brainstorm at 4:00 A.M. and just sort of jumped in the car. I guess I'm a little tired."

"Hold on," I said. "You *drove* here? From Charlottesville? Today? Isn't that like a nine-, ten-hour trip? And what are you doing having brainstorms at four in the morning anyway?"

"It was a *brainstorm,* Clare. You don't plan brainstorms. They just hit and you just get caught in them. Hence the word *storm.*" He gave a wry shrug. "Although this front had been moving in for a while; I just tried to ignore it."

"Could you stop being metaphorical already and tell me what's going on?"

"Okay, but can I maybe sit down first?"

"Oh, Dev, I'm sorry. You must be about to fall over. Come in and sit." I pushed him in the direction of a chair and tugged his jacket off from behind as he walked away. "Do you want anything? Water? Coffee? Toast?"

"No thanks. I should probably just start talking."

Then, Dev sat down in my dark blue velvet armchair, aimed his gray-blue eyes at me like two pretty headlights, and started to talk.

"So I had this brainstorm, and I figured I'd better just get in the car and start driving before I lost my nerve, but I only had to drive about ten miles before I realized that I'd never lose my nerve because if I've ever been sure of anything in my life, I'm sure of what I'm about to say to you."

"And you've been sure of a lot things," I said. "You're an un-wishy-washy person by nature."

"So you understand how sure I am about this."

He did sound sure, but for a second, he looked

downward, his lashes casting tiny twin shadows on his cheeks, and I recognized that this was the moment: the pivot point between the way things had been and the way things would be. And in that still, time-stopped moment, I knew what he was going to say to me.

When he looked up again, he was the usual Dev, flushed and vivid, and he smiled his sudden, direct, radiant, untired smile at me and said, "I love you and you love me, and out of all the things I know, what I know the most is that we should be together."

For a full three seconds after he said it, I knew it, too, with all my heart.

"Oh, Dev," I said.

"And trust me, I get exactly how big a jerk this makes me, since you're with Zach now, but not saying it would be worse. I swear I'd be doing all this even if he were here."

"I believe you."

"Not to downplay my jerk status, but you don't belong to Zach. You belong to yourself. I definitely didn't come here thinking, 'I'll steal her away.'" He spoke those last four words as if they were something bitter he needed to spit out.

"Then what were you thinking?"

"I was thinking, 'I'll ask her to do this with me.'"

"Do what?"

Dev got up out of the chair and sat down next to me, not touching me, but so close that I could see the scar in his eyebrow and the thin tributary of vein running down the right side of his forehead, close enough that I could take in, all at once, the entire familiar terrain of his face.

"All of it," he said. "Everything. Or separate things sometimes but together, next to each other, in the same place."

"You want to live with me? Is that what you're saying?"

"Well, yeah, for starters. Live and everything else. Live, et cetera."

Dev made *et cetera* sound like the best adventure ever. How easy it would have been to reach out and grab his hand and set off on it with him. But I hesitated. I hesitated and he saw me do it and at least half the glow went right out of his face.

"Before you answer," he said, quickly, "please understand that you're not trapped. I would never corner you. If you say no, you won't lose me. That's not a thing that could happen. If you say no, I promise I'll never bring it up again. I'll stay your friend."

He slid his hand under my hair and rested it against the side of my neck.

"I'd miss touching you, though," he said. "I've pretty

much lived in a constant state of missing touching you for the past four years. Please don't say no. Let's be together for the rest of our lives. Don't you want to? It would be so fun. Let's just do it, Clare."

That was my Dev, eyes all lit up, talking about a lifetime commitment like a ten-year-old talks about climbing a tree or starting a secret club. Of course, I loved him. I had loved him since I was thirteen. But oh God, Zach. Zach with his head down, talking about his father in that broken voice, asking me to help him. The men in his family never asked for help, but Zach had asked me. "I can't do this without you," he'd said.

Dev's hand was still on my neck, and I reached up and pressed my own hand against it.

"His father is dying," I said.

In one swift motion, Dev drew in his breath hard, slid his hand away, and stood up, shock all over his face.

"You're saying no," he said, incredulously. "I never thought you would say no."

I jumped up.

"No!" I said. "I mean, I don't know. His father is dying at their lake house up north, and Zach needs me to go there with him. I promised I would. Dev, don't look like that."

I reached for him, but he leaned away.

"Maybe it's good," I said.

"It's not good," he said, drily. "For me, I mean. For Zach, it sounds pretty good. Definitely bodes well for Zach."

"It will give me some time," I said. "To think. To decide."

"To decide between me and Zach?" said Dev, in the same repulsed tone of voice he'd used when he'd said he wasn't trying to steal me away. "To *choose*? What, do a cost/benefit analysis? Is that what you're saying?"

"To decide the best thing to do, for everyone."

Dev shook his head like he was shaking off a sucker punch. "Forget about everyone, Clare. What do you want? Zach? Me? Neither of us? Forget about what we want. Throw that right out the window. Whatever happens, Zach and I will be okay. Just be honest. Say what would make you, Clare Hobbes, happy."

"It's not that simple."

"Yes. It. Is."

I sat back down, cradled my face in my hands, shut my eyes, tried to strip everything else away except what I wanted. Being with Dev was easy. Not because he never challenged me or disagreed with me, because he did. Maybe *easeful* is more what I meant. We fit. I never laughed more with anyone than I did with him. I never felt more myself. We could say anything to each other.

But what about Zach? How many times had he told me I was his entire family, his one and only shot at joy, redemption, being good, his one and only shot at everything? Dev was wrong about him. If I left, Zach would not be okay.

"Could you really do that?" I asked Dev. "Just go back to the way we've been for the past four years? Be friends with me?"

Dev stared down at me, and, just like that, I could tell he was angry. The shift was almost imperceptible, but I saw it and I knew how it would go: no wildfire flaring, no raised voice, no bruising silences, no meanness for the sake of meanness. Just a deliberate, resolute, ruthless pulling away.

"So that's the trouble with me," said Dev. "That's my mistake."

"I didn't say that. "

"I should lie and tell you no, right? That would help my case. But I don't lie to you ever, so yes, sure, I'd stay your friend. What else would I do? Not talk to you? Not see you anymore?"

"Please don't be mad."

"I won't die. I won't live the rest of my life in dire misery, either. But that doesn't mean we don't belong together."

"I can't leave him right now," I said. "He's lost his mother and his sister. His father is dying. I couldn't live with myself if I left him now."

"When, then?"

I threw up my hands. "I don't know! How could I know?"

"So this is how it goes. We miss out on being together because I'm not broken enough."

"That's not fair."

"No," he said. "Not fair at all."

Dev turned and walked away from me, lifted his coat from the back of the kitchen chair where I'd left it, and put it on. I knew the way his hair grew; I knew how he shrugged on a coat, with that quick flip right at the end; I knew exactly how wide his shoulders were. All the tiny, precious details, the variations that separated Dev from every other person on the planet, the universe had entrusted these to me, and here I was, letting them all go.

Just before he walked out my door, he said, "I meant what I said. I'll go on being your friend, and I'll never bring up any of this again. Neither will you. It's gone. Erased. It never happened."

By the time I was ready to start back to Edith's house, the sunrise had unleashed its colors on the world, sent them shooting across the sky and sliding across the water, and the low sun was turning the grass-spiked dunes gold. The gulls were wheeling in from wherever they'd been to perch on the empty lifeguard stand, gray-winged and noble as eagles, while under my feet, the sand was already relinquishing its coolness. Now was the moment for regret, for cursing myself for being a fool, the moment for guilt and self-disgust and shame. That's what I'd expected when I set out this morning to take the past head-on. But now, to my surprise, mostly what I felt for the girl I'd been then was tenderness. She'd been confused, but she hadn't been careless. She had done her best. And on her wedding day, when she had finally seen the light, she had walked straight into it, which was surely worth something. Even if no one else in the world ever forgave her, not Zach or his family or even Dev, I could.

I did.

Then I asked the girl I was right at that second, "So what's next?" and the words were as sweet as spun sugar on my tongue.

Gold-leaf sand stretched out before me; the green waves unfurled themselves over and over under the lucent sky. For the second time in twenty-four hours I laughed simply because being this particular person in this particular world at this particular moment was cause for joy, and then I put on my shoes and went home.'

Chapter Nineteen
Edith

Winter 1955–Spring 1956

The first time coincided with the first snowstorm of the season, a few days before Christmas, flakes pouring dense as flour, and, when Edith stood alone afterward at the back window and watched her yard become mute and smothered and finally lose itself under the anonymous weight, she found there was no piecing the events together, no first this, then this, then this. She had neither decided nor been persuaded. George had merely shown up at her door, breathless, red-cheeked, snow on his shoulders and inside the brim of his hat, and said, uncertainly, "I walked from the hotel," and her desire had bolted out of hiding, huge and fleet and hurtling forward, forward, carrying Edith in its slipstream.

During future encounters, she would be deliberate. She would relish undressing him, this man whose clothes seemed so intrinsically part of who he was, her fingers easing buttons from their holes, unknotting his tie, negotiating his belt buckle and slithering his belt free a loop at a time, sliding off his layers of wool and silk and fine cotton, feeling her way like a blind woman, her eyes locked on his, refusing to rest so much as a fingertip against his skin even as he strained his body toward her hands. When she got to the last layer, she would close her eyes and rest her cheek on his chest, feeling his heat through the thin, ribbed cotton of his undershirt. Only when he was naked would she touch his bare skin or allow him to touch her. Naked, George was transfigured, was someone else, was anyone, no one.

Edith, who had not so much as held hands with a man before Joseph, learned the acute, concentrated pleasure of sex with a man she did not love. George's body was a means to an end and an instrument to play. They met several times a month, always in the downstairs bedroom, George knowing better than anyone when that room would be empty. She didn't ask about his wife, although she knew he had one. She didn't ask how he managed to get away so often. She didn't ask him anything or ask anything of him, except to instruct him, occasionally, as to what part of her to handle or enter or take into his mouth, exactly how, and for how long, words he liked to hear and, after listening, to obey.

The second time he came, he brought a bag with him and spent the night; propped up on an elbow, watching him sleep, she marveled at her own abstraction. For a day or two, after he left her house, he came back to her in flashes, pure sense memory; her nerve endings resurrecting him in precise and aching detail. But that was all. When he arrived, always without warning, she burned her desire out against him over and over; when he left, she never asked when he'd be back.

Sometimes, after they were finished and he'd gotten dressed again, she would photograph him, the real George, a distant, elegant, dark-haired man.

After the first few times, he began to talk to her, the two of them lying together in bed, his voice threading faintly through the dark as if from far away. He told her about the places he'd traveled, about the restaurants and the hotels, the museums and boats and women. Once, he told her, with no emotion at all, that he and his wife were unable to have children. Another time, he described his first love; he was sixteen, she was twenty-one, his cousin's friend from college visiting for the summer. "She went back to school and never even wrote. Dashed my heart to pieces," he said, laughing.

And then, one night, four months in, he told her the story of his parents.

His father beat his mother, regularly, brutally. George's first memory was of hearing his father shouting during the night and then, afterward, his mother crying in the bathroom, something she would do again and again, her throat-wrenching sobs nearly masked by the thunder of water into the tub. For years, with almost clinical accuracy, his father was careful to leave bruises only in places her clothing would cover, but when George was eight, for reasons unknown to him, his father's rages became less frequent, but wilder. He would hit his wife in front of the maid, in front of George, with his fists, yes, but also, sometimes, with whatever was closest: a frying pan, a shoe, a candlestick, his briefcase. On one occasion, he threw a five-pound bag of flour at her head. On another, he beat her with the heavy, black telephone until the phone cord snapped from the wall. Whenever George witnessed this, he would be sick afterward, his stomach yanked into knots, but he never tried to stop it from happening.

"Maybe I wasn't brave enough," said George to Edith. "But what I remember is feeling that it was just the way things were in my house, and nothing in the world could ever make it stop."

A handful of times, a neighbor or a passerby called the police. The uniformed men would come to the family's grand house purchased with his mother's money, tuck their hats under their arms, and stand in the marble foyer, speaking to George's father, who could turn on charm like throwing a switch, his laugh big and rollicking. If George's mother were presentable enough, she would appear, would stretch her mouth into a smile, offer the officers tea, say she was fine, fine, fine, even if her hands were shaking, her eyes red from weeping. And the police officers would nod and tell them all to please be quieter and to have a good night. On occasion, the officers would apologize to his parents for disturbing them.

When George was ten, a night came that was worse than the others. George's father arrived home crazy with rage over something that had happened at work. He slammed George's mother against the wall, her head jerking backward hard. George remembered the sound of it, bone on plaster. He remembered the streak of red on the wall as she slid to the ground, unconscious, looking dead, her head lolled to one side. He remembered blood on her mouth; she must have bitten her tongue. George's father nudged her with his foot, shouted at her to wake the hell up, and finally, she opened her eyes, blinked, and looked straight at George who was across the room, watching from his hiding place between the closed velvet drapes; she smiled at him to reassure him, her little boy, that despite the blood and her oatmeal-colored face and the way her head wobbled on her neck, she was fine.

The next morning, his father left for a business trip, and once he was gone, George's mother washed her hair, pinning it so the lump on the back of her head didn't show, and packed two suitcases, one for her and one for George. They rode a bus—his first time ever on a bus; he could still remember the smell of the seats—to a church on the other side of town. Although she and George's father had been married at a different church, one up north where they had met, she had grown up going to this one, had always taken George on Christmas Eve and Easter Sunday. It was a place his father never went.

There was an elderly rector and another, younger priest. Neither had been there when George's mother was growing up, but the rector remembered meeting her father. "A humane man," he said. "A philanthropist. A rich man who felt a true responsibility to the poor."

Dry-eyed, George's mother told them about her marriage; she included terrible details without flinching; she called her life "hell," a bad word, one George had never heard her say. She told the priests that she couldn't bear for her son to spend another minute in that house for fear it would scar him or, worse, turn him into the kind of man his father was. The old rector held her hands between his large, wrinkled ones, prayed with her, said that she and George could stay two nights, or maybe three, however long it took to catch their breaths, regain their balance.

"But after that respite, I must ask you to go back," he said. "Marriage is a sacred bond and a deeply private one. Use the time here to think of ways to talk with your husband and also to avoid angering him. He's gone astray, lost his moral compass, but the fact that he never hits your boy is a sign that he has a good heart. A man like that can be reasoned with."

George remembered that the old rector's voice and eyes were sorrowful and kind. But the young priest got angry with him.

"We cannot, in good conscience, send them back!" he said, through gritted teeth.

"But they can't stay here forever," said the old man, sadly. "She will have to go home eventually, and the longer she stays away, the worse it will be, the wider the rift. He is her husband."

In a flat voice, George's mother thanked them. She

said they would just go home that day. "Three nights will make no difference," she said.

"Try to persuade your husband to come to church with you next Sunday," said the old man, as George and his mother were leaving. "Help him to heal. Help him find his way back to God."

The young priest walked them to the door of the church. He was red-faced and his mouth was trembling; George thought he might burst into tears. He braced himself for seeing a man cry, but it never happened.

"I'm so horribly sorry," said the priest. "I wish there were more we could do. If you think it would help, I could offer counsel to you and your husband. To preserve your privacy, I could even come to your house."

George saw his mother's lips twist, as if she were laughing at the young man, but she didn't laugh. She just said, in the same flat, dead, empty voice she'd used before, "Thank you for your kindness."

They went home. That very evening, his mother made telephone calls to people up north, and when George's father returned a few days later, she told him she had arranged for George to go to boarding school. To George's amazement, his father agreed to the plan, and even though it was the middle of the school year, fifth grade, George went. His mother rode the train with him. They ate from china plates—china on a train!—as, out the window, state after state blurred by, smears of green and brown punctuated by steeples and roofs and occasional roaring tunnels. Before his mother left to go back home, she hugged him hard, whispered, "I love you more than life itself," in one ear and "Be brave," in the other.

George came home for three weeks out of every year, one at Christmas, one in the spring, and one in the summer. He never saw his father hit his mother again, but he never stopped hating him, hate upon hate upon hate. For eight years, George stockpiled rage. On his eighteenth birthday, two things happened: he found out he had been accepted into Yale and he came into his inheritance, money left to him in a trust by his mother's parents. His mother called him at school to wish him a happy birthday. A week later, she overdosed on sleeping pills. No one called it suicide, but George knew.

"She waited until I had the means to take care of myself," he told Edith. "When I went back for her funeral, I told my father that I was finished with him, to never contact me again, a request he honored. Six months later, he remarried and moved out west. A year later, he was dead. A stroke. Apparently, he had been an alcoholic for decades. I never knew. I can't remember even seeing him take a drink. Isn't that strange?"

In the dark, Edith nodded.

"He cried at her funeral. Can you believe that? Somehow, I couldn't shed a single tear, but that bastard cried like a baby."

There was a catch in George's throat, his first display of emotion. Edith tensed, waiting for more, but the moment passed so quickly and completely that she wondered if she'd imagined it. His dispassion should have put her off; no one should have been able to tell a story like that without sorrow or anger, but she wasn't put off. She was relieved. She didn't want to see this man as fragile. His breaking down, her comforting him, the intimacy of it would have been a sham, would have looked too much like love. She wished he hadn't told her the story of his parents; if she could have given it back to him, every word, she would have.

He left a few hours later. That night, Edith removed her clothes and surveyed her body in the mirror and felt, for all the world, as if she were staring at a stranger. For more than four months, she had made love to a man she did not love, and not loving him had been good. But it wasn't good anymore. She wasn't ashamed; she was just finished. The next time he came, without malice, she asked him to leave and to never come again, and without malice, he had gone.

Chapter Twenty
Clare

As soon as Dev got into my car, he said, "Breaks, contusions, abrasions, lacerations, ruptures!" not in the lions-and-tigers-and-bears manner you might expect with such a grim list but gleefully and accentuating each word with a karate chop to the dashboard.

Unaccountably, it was exactly the right thing to say.

I'd been nervous on the drive from Edith's house to Dev's mom's house. Not sweaty-palms, heart-clanging nervous; no high school orchestra warmed up inside my brain as sometimes happened. But my thumbs fluttered; my legs vibrated; three separate times, I caught myself humming a song that had nothing to do with the one coming through my car's speakers. After ten miles of this, I was faintly exasperated with myself. By thirty, I had become the most irritating person I had ever met.

And by the time I hit fifty, I was threatening to pull over and dump myself out on the side of the highway.

"You're just lucky you're driving," I said aloud, "or you'd be gone, baby, gone."

While it was true that I had spent a little face-to-face time with Dev at my nonwedding, it had been very little time, and for most of it, we'd been with at least one other person, so our attention had been divided, although looking back, I understood that the other people had been a minor distraction compared to the elephant in the room, the elephant being, of course, the fact that I could not possibly, in this lifetime or in any other, marry Zach. So when you factor in the other people *and* the elephant, Dev and I had almost not been together in real life that weekend at all.

Since then we'd been together on the phone, yes. In texts, yes. We'd been comfortable and jokey and chatty and even, once in a while, serious, more and more so with each conversation or exchange, until, by the time I pulled up in his mom's driveway, we were very nearly back to the business of being the Dev and Clare of old, minus being in love, of course. Which is exactly why I was nervous because, as everyone knows, nothing makes you feel stupider than being familiar and totally at ease with a person over the phone, only to be stilted and shy and awkward when the two of you are finally physically in the same room. Or car. Cars are so much worse.

But Dev's litany of bodily injuries turned out to be—if you'll excuse the lame joke—just what the doctor ordered. "Breaks, contusions, abrasions, lacerations, ruptures!" and—poof—the awkwardness vanished.

"Nice to see you, too," I said, starting the car.

"Br rbs, clav. Cont, abr face," said Dev, more or less, and then again, "br rbs, clav. Cont, abr face!"

"Wow. This is going to be a long drive," I said.

He said it again, loudly.

"Increasing the volume never helps in these situations," I pointed out.

He said it again.

"You know what would help? Vowels."

He rapped on the side of my head with his knuckles, lightly but not that lightly. "Clare. Pay attention."

As I rubbed my head, he began to say it again, very, very slowly, but before he finished, it hit me. "Oh!" I said. "Oh, oh, oh!"

"Finally. Geez."

"The shadow ledger! The stuff after the town abbreviations! She's listing their injuries!"

"Yup," said Dev.

"That's wonderful! I mean, it's awful. But how did it take you so long to figure it out?"

"And by that you mean, *Way to go, Dev!*"

"You start medical school in two months, at a fancy-pants school, no less. Correct?"

"What's your point? And I would not call it 'fancy-pants.'"

"Why not?"

"Because it's not 1910 and I'm not ninety-seven years old. For starters."

We went on like this for very close to all of the four-hour trip. Somewhere in there, I noticed that Dev's hair had grown out since the nonwedding and that he was back to doing the thing where he'd rake it impatiently off his forehead with his fingers as if it had fallen there just to annoy him; and, after we'd stopped to switch places, that he still drove with just one hand on the wheel despite all those years of my admonishing him about safety, safety, safety; and, when dusk fell outside the car where we sat talking, that his eyes, when he glanced over at me, matched the sky exactly.

Even though it was just after ten o'clock at night when we got to my parents' house, everyone was there. Besides my mom and Gordon, there were Dev's paternal grandparents, Ingrid and Rudy Sandoval, and Dev's maternal step-grandparents, Ellie and Dr. B. Brown. They all lived in the same neighborhood, the one I'd moved to with my mother when I was eleven, the one in which Teo and Cornelia and their brothers and sisters had grown up, and the one Dev had visited so often that it was his neighborhood as much as anyone's.

The first time I talked to Hildy about these people, and their children and their children's children, and their various relationships to one another, she had pretended—very convincingly—to tear her hair out by the roots and had then thundered, "Enough! From now on they are 'Leftover Night.'"

"What? No. Why?" I'd said.

"On the seventh day, God created Leftover Night! Except it wasn't God. I think it was my dad or possibly my mom or maybe my older brother, Stephen. Anyway, in our house someone would cook dinner six nights out of seven, and on the seventh night, whoever's turn it was would have to make a dish that used up all the leftovers from the other nights. So what we'd get was this mishmash of stuff that should absolutely not have worked, but somehow almost always did. That's your family." As usual, it was hard to argue with Hildy. From that moment on, we called them Leftover Night.

How bone-deep sweet it was to be with them, to sit at the big dining room table together eating the dishes they'd all brought to share, everyone running roughshod over one another in conversation, ending one another's stories and sentences, mercilessly interrogating and forcing food on me and Dev. I met Dev's eyes a couple of times across the table and could tell he was thinking what I was thinking: that it was good—as it had forever been and forever would be good—to sit at that table and be Clare and Dev, the doted-upon children, beloved by all these loud, teasing, bossy, outstandingly kind people.

After dinner, Dev and I took a walk around the neighborhood. It was well after midnight. The streetlamps burned, their blue-white glow pooling, at regular intervals, on the white sidewalks, but most of the windows of the solid, broad-shouldered, brick and stone houses were dark, their lawns spreading solemnly around them. A mailbox stood sentry at the end of every driveway. The big trees sang with cicadas. Dev and I knew every house. We knew every tree and all the places where their roots buckled the sidewalk. We'd known for so long we didn't even realize we knew; it almost didn't count as knowing. Every block of this place was jam-packed with the kind of memories you don't have to conjure up because you *are* them. Here, nostalgia was rendered moot. Walking here, Dev and I could be fully in the here and now.

"It's crazy what we're doing, isn't it?" I said, with a laugh. "Just heading off to Richmond, like we know where to look and what we're looking for."

"We'll trust our instincts. Hey, I told you that scientists are taking intuition seriously, didn't I? Have faith, Hobbes." Then he shrugged and smiled down at the sidewalk. "But, yeah, it is a little crazy."

"Fun, though," I said, after a pause. "Even if we don't find anything, it's fun to be doing this."

Dev walked along, looking straight ahead with his hands in his pockets, not saying anything for so long that I began to get nervous again.

"I mean, *I* think it's fun to be doing this," I said.

"Together," said Dev, giving me a gentle—fairly gentle—elbow to the ribs. "Get it right. It's fun to be doing this together."

"Clare and Dev are on the case!" I said, shooting my fist in the air.

"Dev and Clare," corrected Dev.

We kept walking.

"We're lucky," I said. "To have all of them. Our family. Even when we're not with them, we have them."

It was the understatement of the century, but I counted on Dev to know what I meant.

"They're a constant," he said. "Like pi. Wherever you are, pi is pi."

"A constant. Like a turtle's shell, a home you carry around with you everywhere."

"That, too," said Dev.

I was the one who thought of churches. Later, Dev would always say he was, but I was the one who *brought up* churches in the first place, and since we were all about intuition, even though I hadn't specifically mentioned churches as a place to look for clues, the fact that I'd mentioned them at all was clearly my intuition subtly pointing us in the right direction. Or more or less the right direction.

We were driving through Richmond, following our intuition because that's what we'd agreed to do and also because we didn't exactly have anything else to follow, when I said, "There are a lot of churches in Richmond. It seems like on every corner, there's a church."

It was just a tossed-off comment, the kind of thing you say when you're driving through an unfamiliar city searching for you-have-no-idea-what located you-have-no-idea-where. But about thirty seconds after I said it, Dev snapped into full-on ponder mode, brows knit, face still, lashes batting, eyes focused. I could almost see his brain working: holding an idea like a Rubik's cube, turning and twisting it, *click, click, click,* until all its parts were in the proper place.

When I saw the last click happen and the tension leave his expression, I said, "Okay, give it to me. Not just the end result, but the whole train of thought."

It was something we had always done, a way, maybe, to stand inside each other's heads for just a moment. I remembered my own voice saying to Cornelia and my mom about Zach, "Sometimes, I think he won't be satisfied until he climbs inside my head and lives there." But this was different. Zach wanted to take possession, at least that's how it felt; Dev and I just wanted to watch the machinery turn. "It's like being inside a clock tower," I'd told him once, and he'd replied, "Or like watching the doughnut machine at Krispy Kreme."

"Okay. Sanctuary," said Dev. "What's the first thing that comes into your head?"

"A safe place," I said. "A haven."

"Same with my head. But I'm pretty sure—and I'm not great at Latin—but I think it comes from the word *sanctuarium,* and I think—*arium* means a container, like a terrarium is a container for a little piece of the earth, and *sanctu* means sacred. So a container for something holy."

"Like the sanctuary of a church," I said. "The part where the altar is."

"Hey, whose train of thought is this anyway?"

"Sorry."

"So where did I go next? Oh, right. Like the sanctuary of a church, the part where the altar is."

I punched him in the arm.

"Ow. Okay, so maybe that's the original meaning of the word, but now it also means—"

"A safe place. A haven. Like I said."

"I thought it before you said it, but fine."

"I said 'churches' before you thought any of this, but fine."

Dev rolled his eyes. "Moving on. I'm just guessing but the word probably came to mean that because churches became safe havens for people."

"Oh, oh, like Mother Bethel African Methodist Episcopal Church! In Philadelphia! I went there!"

"If that was a stop on the underground railroad, you just completely hijacked my train of thought," said Dev, shooting me a baleful glance.

"Oh. No. Nope." I shook my head decisively. "That's not what it was. It was something—else."

Dev heaved a very large sigh. "*Anyway.* Back in the fifties, before they had women's shelters—at least, I don't think they had them then or definitely not many—where would a battered woman go for sanctuary?"

"Yes! We should go look at churches," I said, whacking the dashboard.

"It's still a shot in the dark, just to walk in and ask if there's anyone who remembers anything that might help us. But it's less a shot in the dark than driving aimlessly around the city."

"And what do we have to lose?"

"Nothing. Let's do it. We'll look up churches on our phones and just start."

For the next three hours, that's what we did, went to church after church, skipping the ones built after 1953, and asking the people we met there whether they knew anything that might suggest that the church was part of an organization, possibly secret, that helped abused women escape to safety. I suppose we could have called instead of going, which might have saved time but wouldn't have felt nearly as much like an adventure.

By the fourth church, I'd mostly given up on finding out anything about Edith's shadow ledger guests, but I liked the churches anyway. There were grand ones with domed ceilings and gold fixtures and dazzling stained glass; there were simple white clapboard ones with tidy box pews and no-nonsense wood floors; there were historic ones with brass plaques dropping names like Robert E. Lee and Jefferson Davis. We went to the church where Patrick Henry gave his "give me liberty or give me death" speech at the Second Virginia Convention, and both of us got the shivers imagining him there, burning with audacity and eloquence, as Thomas Jefferson and George Washington listened.

I loved the symmetry of the pews, with the aisle straight down the middle. I loved the vocabulary: apse, chancel, nave, pulpit. I loved the small, tucked-away chapels. I loved how stepping into each cool, hushed interior was immediately peaceful, like morning coffee at your kitchen table or sitting in your backyard watching the fireflies begin their light show in the lilac bushes along the fence. I loved how I could say these things to Dev and he smiled and only made fun of me a little but not like he really meant it.

Everyone was nice, and no one knew a thing about John Blanchard or Edith Herron or an underground railroad for abused women.

And then a secretary at an Episcopal church said, "We need more places like the one down the road. Everyone in danger should have a safe harbor, a sanctuary."

Sanctuary.

Her use of the word set my intuition pinging, only faintly pinging because it was a completely reasonable, even obvious word choice, but a faint ping is better than no ping at all. I looked over at Dev, and after a second, he shrugged and nodded.

"Why not?" he said.

The Andrew Pfeiffer Women's Center and Shelter had just celebrated its thirtieth anniversary, which made it pretty old but not old enough for our purposes, and all the people who worked there had clearly been born decades after the 1950s, so, right away, it seemed like a dead end. A very, very good and worthwhile dead end, though, because the Andrew Pfeiffer Women's Center and Shelter turned out to be a kind of clearinghouse for hope. In addition to sanctuary, the center offered mental health services, legal advocacy, a twenty-four-hour hotline, homework tutoring for children, and financial counseling. The staff there helped women get jobs and mortgages and go back to school. They even allowed dogs.

The director was a woman named Selby Abbott; she was tiny, blond, wore dark jeans and a simple white shirt, had an aristocratic Tidewater accent, ramrod-straight posture, and the frankest, most unwavering gaze I'd seen in a long time. She could not have been nicer to us, but, even so, I got the feeling that Selby Abbott was someone with whom you would not want to mess.

After we'd introduced ourselves, and Selby had led us back to her immaculate office, she said, "Welcome to Andrew Pfeiffer, Clare and Dev. What's your story?"

and even though we hadn't told our full story at any of the churches, I found, suddenly, that I wanted to tell it to Selby.

"Our story," I said and paused.

"Go ahead," said Dev.

So I told as efficient a version of it as I could—glossing quickly over the part about leaving Zach practically at the altar—and I was on fairly firm ground until I got to the part about the city abbreviations and our trip to Richmond because, as I described it all, out loud and to a complete stranger, I realized how flaky and impulsive it sounded, how much like a fool's errand. But the crazy thing is that, while Selby had appeared fully engaged from the very start, when I got to the Richmond part, she leaned toward me, locked her attention in even harder, and when I'd finished, she said, "Oh. My. God," not as in *Oh my God, you two are idiots,* thank goodness, but more like *Oh my God, this is amazing.*

"What?" I asked.

She opened a desk drawer, rummaged around for a few seconds, pulled out a brochure, and handed it to me.

"It's Andrew," she said, excitedly. "It has to be. Okay, maybe it doesn't *have* to be, but I really think it is."

The brochure was for the center's thirtieth-anniversary gala and fund-raiser.

"Go to page four," she said, "and read."

Dev scooted his chair closer to mine, took one side of the brochure in his hand while I held the other, and, with our heads almost touching, we read.

The center had been started by an elderly woman and her friends. The woman was Lillian Pfeiffer, the widow of the Reverend Andrew Pfeiffer who had died just the year before. Reverend Pfeiffer had been a remarkable man, although almost no one realized exactly how remarkable until after his death, when Lillian finally told his story.

One day in the early 1930s, when Andrew was a young assistant rector, a woman and her son had come to his church. The woman told Andrew and his superior, the rector, that, beginning about a year after they'd been married, her husband, a wealthy man prone to wild rages, began to beat her. She told Andrew and the rector that the beatings were getting worse and that she feared for her life and for her son, who looked to be about nine or ten. She asked them to help her. Despite the terribleness of her story, the rector sent her back home to work on her marriage. Although Andrew never found out what became of the woman—and indeed did not even know her name—her story, her palpable fear and sadness, and, as she left, her air of utter hopelessness haunted him for decades.

Almost twenty years later, around 1950, when his and

Lillian's children were teenagers and he had a church of his own, Andrew became part of a secret relocation effort for victims of domestic violence. He organized a wide network of carefully chosen ministers and rabbis and other like-minded people who identified abused women and their children in their communities and sent them to Andrew Pfeiffer's church. They would arrive in the dead of night and stay a day or two in a back room until a car came, picked them up, and took them far away, to safety. While Lillian knew the basics of what was happening, for her own safety Andrew never gave her details. She didn't know the names of any of the other people involved; she didn't know who the women were or where they came from or where they went when they left Andrew's church. While she cooked food for Andrew to take to the women and children, she never set eyes on a single one of them.

Not until I came to the end of the story and heard Dev say, "Ow," did I realize I'd been holding on to his free hand, squeezing it tighter and tighter as I read.

"Sorry!" I said.

I dropped his hand and, as he shook it out and flexed his fingers, with what I regarded as more drama than necessary, he said to Selby, "I'll bet you're right. It all fits. The time line is right. But did Lillian ever mention the names John Blanchard or Edith Herron? Like maybe it was John who picked the women up and drove them away?"

Selby shook her head. "She never mentioned names, at least not to the reporters who wrote the articles about Andrew, and if she mentioned them to my predecessor, I never heard about it."

"Wait," I said. "You never met her?"

"No. I didn't start working here until 2000. I believe Lillian passed away in the midnineties."

I sighed. "Oh, I was hoping we could talk to her."

"Yeah," said Dev. "She might have been able to tell us something, some little detail, that she didn't tell the reporters."

Selby's face brightened. "Well, hey, her daughter Abby Stewart is on the board of the center. Why don't you give me a cell number and I'll see if she wouldn't mind calling you? Would that help?"

I smiled. "Yes! That would be great, actually. Thank you so much."

"Yes, thank you for everything," said Dev. "No one would've blamed you if you thought we were crazy, and here you are going above and beyond."

Selby clasped her hands under her chin. "Andrew Pfeiffer is kind of a household god around here." She grinned and instantly looked about eleven years old. "Plus, I spent a good chunk of my childhood being obsessed with Nancy Drew. I just love a good mystery."

"Ditto," I said, laughing. "On both counts."

Dev and I ate dinner at a Thai restaurant because it was the first place we came to that we could agree on, the only drawback to Thai being that we couldn't share, since my philosophy about Thai food is that if your tongue doesn't practically burst into flames while you eat it, it isn't worth eating, a philosophy with which Dev adamantly—and wimpily—disagrees. When we'd eaten ourselves right to the edge of oblivion and were toddling out to my car, my phone rang—or vibrated actually—and I looked down at it expecting to see Zach's name on the screen. During dinner, he'd texted four times, and each time, he'd written exactly the same words, ones that sent a chill up my spine and caused me to glance over my shoulder and at the restaurant's big plateglass window, even though I knew what he wrote couldn't possibly be literally true: I know you're with him right now.

But this was a number neither my phone nor I recognized, area code 804. Abby Stewart.

Dev and I got inside the car and Abby Stewart let me put her on speaker, so that when she broke the news that she'd never heard anything about a John Blanchard or an Edith Herron from her mother, had never heard any names at all, Dev and I were able to be disappointed together.

"Even though this was all going on while I was in high school, I never knew a thing about it until after my dad died and my mom told me. I do know that my father was just a cog in the wheel, a big cog for sure—he took a lot of risks—but he wasn't the one running the machine. He wasn't the mastermind; another man had the idea and sought my father out, recruited him I guess you could say. When the women and children left my father's church, not even my father knew where they were going. A car picked them up and took them away. My mother didn't share that information with the reporters because she didn't want them digging around, trying to find the guy. She only told me that he existed shortly before her death."

"Who was it?" asked Dev.

We held our breaths.

"Someone with deep pockets," said Abby Stewart. "My mother told me that my father never used his name in front of her, just referred to him as Mr. Big City. He was from someplace up north, she said. My father said he was a man with power and money and a load of rage. He'd channeled it toward doing good, obviously, but it was rage nonetheless. My dad said a man with that much anger must have had firsthand knowledge of domestic violence."

"Do you know how long your father was part of this operation, this underground railroad?" I asked.

"Until the midfifties, I think. Fifty-six, fifty-seven. It ended abruptly. For reasons unknown to my dad or my mom, Mr. Big City just called the whole thing off. My dad felt guilty about stopping, but the tide was already turning. In the early sixties, my dad and other like-minded people began to establish shelters, small ones, and my dad spent the rest of his life working to educate his congregation and the public about domestic violence. He was a good man."

"He was," I said.

"And your mother was obviously a good person, too," said Dev. "She helped establish the women's center and everything."

"She was tireless." Abby Stewart chuckled. "And relentless about raising money to keep the place up. People used to say that Lillian Pfeiffer could squeeze money out of a stone."

"Thank you for talking to us," I said.

"It's my pleasure," she said. "I mean that. I haven't talked about my parents much recently, although I think about them and miss them every day. I'm truly grateful for the chance to tell someone about them. Now, you have to promise to let me know if you find out anything else. And, oh Lord, let Selby know, too. You've got her interest piqued. That woman loves a good mystery."

We promised. After we hung up, we sat for a minute, not talking.

"Rich, powerful. It doesn't sound like John," said Dev.

"I know." I could hear how crestfallen that *I know* came out, but even so, my tone didn't come close to conveying how let down I felt.

"Hey," said Dev, tugging a lock of my hair. "We found out a lot on this trip, didn't we? A lot more than I thought we would."

I looked at Dev. Of all the people whose bubbles I hated bursting, Dev topped the list, but it seemed wrong not to tell him what I was thinking. I groaned.

"Okay, I hate saying this, but if I don't say it, I might fret about it for weeks, and I might do that anyway, but since we're in this thing together, I just think I should say it. What do you think?"

"Go for it," said Dev. "We can at least fret together."

"Well, isn't it possible that Mr. Big City's machine and Edith's shadow ledger aren't related at all? That it's just a coincidence? There's nothing here really to absolutely connect Edith or John to any of what we've dug up."

"I agree that some kind of irrefutable proof would have been nice, and, sure, it's possible that what you're worrying about is true, but I don't think so. Mr. Big City called it quits at right around the same time as Edith left and John got arrested. Everything fits too well. They were all in it together."

Even though I knew Dev couldn't be 100 percent sure of that, not as sure as he sounded, I felt relieved anyway.

"So Edith and John were other cogs in the machine. The shadow guests stayed at Blue Sky House for a night or two and then someone, maybe John, took them to wherever they went next," I said.

"Probably not John, though," said Dev. "It could have been, but it might have aroused suspicion, the police chief leaving town mysteriously on a regular basis. Mr. Big City probably sent a car to Edith's house, too."

"And Sarah and her baby? How do they fit? I mean, they kind of don't. Sarah wasn't from Virginia; she was a local woman; she had killed her husband; and she wasn't written down in the shadow ledger. All of that makes her different from the others."

"Okay, so Sarah and the baby weren't part of Mr. Big City's escape machine, not at first. Relocating her and her baby was a spur-of-the-moment decision, and I think it probably all unfolded a lot like John said it did in court."

I nodded. "What he left out was that he and Edith had done it before; there was a system in place. They just slid Sarah and her baby into it."

"You'd make Nancy Drew proud," said Dev. He raised his palm, and I slapped it.

"You, too."

But neither of us sounded especially happy. We should've been triumphant because Dev was right when he said we'd found out a lot. But mostly what I felt was deflated, even sorrowful.

"I think . . ." I began.

"What?" said Dev.

"Well, maybe this is it. We've figured out all we can figure out."

He smiled and leaned over to bump my shoulder with his. "Unless you want to go scour every major northern city, looking for Mr. Big City."

"Sounds fun, actually," I said, then I sighed. "I just wish we'd learned more of Edith's story."

"We don't know the middle part, all those years. I guess we'll never know it." Dev brightened. "But we know how it ended."

My eyes filled with tears. "We know that whatever

happened during those years, she survived it all. She lived on, even after leaving everything she knew behind. She became an amazing person."

"And she left you her house," said Dev.

"She was taking care of me, a woman she didn't even know." I wiped my eyes and smiled. "Like she took care of all those other women. She was worried about me, so she gave me a safe place."

"A sanctuary."

Outside the car, dusk had ended, and the summer night surrounded us. Pinprick stars floated above the trees edging the restaurant parking lot. I couldn't find the moon.

"So this is where Edith's story ends, I guess," I said.

"With you," said Dev. "You're Edith's happy ending."

"Honestly, right now, I feel sad."

"Hey, happy endings aren't allowed to be sad."

I suddenly understood that, yes, I was sad that we hadn't found out all of Edith's story, but that wasn't the entire reason.

I wanted to ask Dev my favorite question. It was there, hovering above us, singing itself over and over, like a mockingbird, waiting for one of us to ask it, but what I realized right then was that if you didn't have an answer to it, the question lost its magic. And if the answer were "Nothing," "So what's next?" became, in an instant, the saddest question in the world.

"I wish this weren't over. I'll miss—" I found I couldn't look directly at Dev, so I stared out the windshield. "The search," I finished.

After a few seconds, Dev said, "I'll miss that, too."

Chapter Twenty-One
Edith

December 1956

Before she noticed the smear of blood on his tan windbreaker, before he had spoken a single word, Edith knew, not exactly what he was going to say to her, but that whatever it was would change everything. Tranquil John, John of the steady voice and unflappable nerves, cerulean-eyed, eye-of-the-storm John stood on her porch, lips pale, weight shifting from foot to foot, hands rubbing together as if he were trying to warm them. Indeed, he was shivering, head to toe, shivering in bursts, as if electric shocks were running through him. And because it troubled her, the sight of him cold, and maybe also because she wanted to buy a moment, to postpone knowing whatever frightening thing he had come to tell her, she opened her front door wider and said, scolding him, "That flimsy jacket's not enough for this weather. For heaven's sake, come in."

He came in and she shut the door behind him, but the shivering persisted. She saw the blood, then, a handprint like children make in school on his jacket, dashes of it on his white shirt, still a wild red, fresh blood, and panic shot through her.

"Oh, God, you're hurt." She reached toward him, but he stepped back, dodging her touch.

"I'm fine." He stared down at the blood as if he were seeing it for the first time. "I shouldn't have come. I don't want to visit this trouble on you, but I didn't know, I couldn't think what else to do," he said.

"Of course, you should've come," she said.

He shook his head. "However this thing plays out, if you're involved in it, you'll be at risk. More than you've been so far."

John pressed his hands to the top of his head, trying to calm himself. When he dropped them to his side, the shaking had abated, but he looked at her with stricken eyes. "You can say no, and, God help me, Edith, you should say no. Just say that one word, and I'll go away and never mention this again."

Edith remembered John on the beach in the pouring

rain, how he'd found her wandering in the storm and brought her home, how he'd warmed her and talked to her and stayed all night.

"You're my true friend and I'm yours," she said. "Whatever you're asking, I'm saying yes."

"You can still say no after I tell you."

"I won't."

Suddenly cold, she pulled her hands inside the cuffs of the sweater she wore, one of Joseph's. Now that it was winter, she'd taken to dressing this way when she was home alone, her body cocooned, lost inside Joseph's oversized clothing, safe and warm.

"I parked my car in the dark place down the street," said John. "There's a woman in it with a newborn baby. She shot her husband, not half an hour ago. The man's dead, Edith."

The rest of the miserable story tumbled out. By the time John was saying, "Anyway, I was hoping maybe you could do for her what you've done for the others," Edith was already putting on her coat.

Her name was Sarah. For a woman who had recently given birth, for any woman, Sarah was thin—stark jawline, broomstick arms, her back a frightening relief map of bones—and more horribly hurt than any woman who had ever passed through Blue Sky House. John carried her from the car to Edith's back door; Edith carried the baby, Steven, who did not cry but merely regarded her with his almond-shaped eyes.

Edith centered the baby on the cot in the corner of the room, as John placed Sarah gently on the bed, leaving the room immediately afterward so that Edith could examine her. Sarah's face was ashen where it wasn't bruised or bleeding, one eye purple, swollen shut, her throat, back, breasts, rib cage, arms, legs covered with bruises like ink stains, some of them new. Edith gently dabbed some ointment on her split lip. Edith heard a clattering sound outside and froze, but when John didn't reappear, she assumed it was just the wind and went back to her examination. When Edith pressed carefully on Sarah's abdomen, Sarah moaned.

As soon as John came back into the room, Edith pulled him aside and said, "I'll do what I can, but her distended abdomen, the pain, those dark purple splotches on her stomach could mean she's bleeding internally. She should be in the hospital," said Edith.

"If we take her to one, she's sure to be arrested," said John. "Her husband was rich, well connected. Word of this will spread like wildfire."

Sarah's eyes were shut, her dark hair shining against the pillow. *She must have been beautiful,* thought Edith. And then, bitterly, *Sometimes, beauty is a curse.*

"She has no fever, not yet," she said. "We may have some time to work with, but I just don't know. I can't know the extent of the damage."

"Wherever the car takes the other women," said John, "there must be hospitals."

"There must be," said Edith, "but I don't know where they go or how long it takes to get there. I don't know anything; that's how this works."

"We should ask her what she wants to do," said John.

Edith walked to the bed, and said, "Sarah." The woman opened her good eye. It was a remarkable color, ice blue, almost silvery, and, despite everything, alert, to Edith's relief. Sarah listened to Edith and then said, "I won't go to a hospital. If I'm in prison, what will become of Steven?"

She could barely get the words out. *A bruised larynx,* thought Edith.

"Do you have family who could take him?" Edith asked.

Sarah laughed, a terrible, broken-down wheeze of a laugh. "My husband's people would never let that happen."

She reached out and clutched Edith's hand and said fiercely, "They are fiends, all of them, cruel and heartless. Would you want your child raised by people like that? If I die or get caught before we get to the safe place, promise me you'll never let Steven go back to them. Promise me you'll find good people to raise him."

Edith couldn't bring herself to tell Sarah that she wouldn't know where she was going or whether she and her baby ever arrived. Instead, she said, "I'll find a way. I promise."

She turned to John. "We shouldn't wait until morning. If she's leaving, it will have to be tonight, the sooner the better."

John nodded.

"I need to make a phone call," said Edith.

For the first time, Edith called the number George Graham had given her. A woman answered, took Edith's information, and hung up. When ten minutes passed without George calling her, she began to pace, her hands clasped hard against her sternum, and, for the first time in years, to pray. Ten minutes later, the phone rang.

She spilled Sarah's story out in one long stream. It was the first time she'd spoken to George since she had ended their relationship, but she didn't have time to feel awkward. When she was finished, she waited for George to give her instructions, tell her when the car would arrive. Instead, his voice came at her like a knife.

"Don't be foolish, Edith. Do you think the driver of

that car waits down the road for me to call him? He's hours away; even tomorrow morning would be too soon, and that woman and her baby need to get out of your house tonight."

"Get out? And go where?" asked Edith, confused.

"I don't know. Figure something out. Jesus God, Edith, a murderess? A man from a prominent family? A woman people might recognize and with an infant? People will be looking for her. They're probably already on the hunt. I need your house, Edith. Don't you understand that?"

"I understand that her husband would have murdered her if she hadn't killed him first. You haven't seen the horrible damage he did to her."

"Then she should be in a hospital. Have that police chief take her there. Immediately."

"No. I promised her I wouldn't. If I do that, she'll be arrested."

"*You* promised?" he said, acidly. "It was not your place to promise."

Edith said nothing, and when George spoke again, his voice was calmer.

"I'm sorry, Edith. Listen. Have the police chief take her to the hospital. Have him do it right away, and if she is arrested, I'll help her. I will get her the best lawyer money can buy. I know lawyers who could get the devil himself off. But she has to swear not to mention you or your house to anyone. That's my one condition. Be sure she understands: if she does mention your house, if she says anything about it at any point, I will withdraw my assistance, and God help her then."

For the first time, Edith felt shame at having ever put her hands on this man. She sat down heavily in the chair near the telephone, trying to gather her scattered thoughts. After a moment, she took a breath and said, "No."

"Damn it, Edith."

"She could lose her baby. Her husband's family could find a way to take him from her."

"And what about all the other women and babies? The ones still out there who I haven't saved yet? I've spent years putting this system in place, fine-tuning it; if the police start looking too closely, it could all collapse and take you and me with it."

"I'm sorry, but no."

"Do what I say!" he said, loudly.

"If you can't send a car tonight, tell me where to take her. I'll drive her and the baby myself."

"You must be insane. I'm not telling you anything."

Edith sat for a moment, thinking, then said, "If you don't, I'll spill the beans, every last one. I know the first names of all the women who have come through here. I know where they're from because they always tell me. It won't take the authorities long to find you and to blast everything you've built to hell."

"How dare you?" he hissed. "You think you can blackmail me?"

"I don't think I can. I'm doing it. Right now."

After she hung up the phone, Edith leaned over with effort and let the blood flow to her head. When the stars shooting across her vision had disappeared, she stood up and walked into the bedroom.

"There's been a change of plans," she said. "The car can't get here in time. I'm driving Sarah and Steven."

"What?" said John, sharply. "Where?"

She held up her notebook. "I have directions to a safe house in Canada. It will be a long drive, so we should leave right away."

"Oh, no," John said. "Not you. I'm taking her."

"It could take days to get there and back, John," she said. "You have a job. People will wonder where you are; they might even get suspicious. I don't have any guests scheduled for the rest of the winter."

John's eyes glinted. "I don't care, Edith," he said. "I won't let you do this."

"Be reasonable. A woman no one cares about going on a trip won't raise any eyebrows. The chief of police disappearing will. And what will you do? Take your police cruiser? Take my car and leave yours here for everyone to see? It won't work. If you're not concerned about yourself, think of Sarah and the baby. They'll have a better chance of getting where they're going if I take them."

"Edith," said John, his voice ragged with emotion, "what if you're caught?"

"We won't be. Even if someone stumbles onto our trail, which is very unlikely, the directions I've been given are designed to throw people off. Back roads, small towns, swinging wide, looping back. It's not the fastest route, but it's safe. And at the border, there will be an officer in place who is part of the system."

"I'm the one who brought her here," said John. "I should go."

"Thank you for wanting to. But you must see that it doesn't make sense. You'll take care of things here, think of a story to explain my absence if the need arises. I'll be back before you know it, and this will all be over."

"No," said John, quickly. "Give me the address of the house in Canada, and I'll send a wire, letting you know when it's safe to come back."

Startled, she said, "Why? Why wouldn't it be safe right away?"

"It will be," he said. "But just in case."

As Edith wrote the address down on a piece of notebook paper, she found her hand was shaking, which surprised her. All through her conversation with George, she had stayed collected, but now, here with John, she felt close to breaking down. She took a few long, steadying breaths before she tore the page from her notebook, folded it, and handed it to John, her eyes meeting his.

"I'll wait to hear from you," she said.

"I should never have brought you into this," said John. "I'm so sorry."

"Nonsense," she said, smiling at him. "You gave me a choice, remember? I chose this."

John nodded, wearily. "All right. All right."

"You should go now," said Edith. "I can get Sarah and Steven to my car by myself, and the longer you stay, the longer your car sits empty on the street, the greater the risk."

At the door, John turned to her, his expression unguarded, stripped bare and so full of love that she had to hold back a gasp. A thought flew into her head: *Oh God, what if I don't see this man again?*

But she would. She would.

John moved toward her, as if to kiss her or take her in his arms, but she put out her hand.

"Good-bye," she said. "I'll see you soon."

He took her hand and pressed it to his mouth, and then John Blanchard was gone.

Chapter Twenty-Two
Clare

I couldn't let it go.

I didn't even know what I hoped to find. Mr. Big City's identity? Proof that Sarah and her baby had found sanctuary in the end? John Blanchard's story after he was released from prison? The missing fifty-plus years of Edith's life?

Yes. No. I didn't know. And, more important, I didn't know why it mattered so much, so *extraordinarily* much to me. Apart from understanding that what urged me on was more than simple curiosity, I understood nothing else about my own motivation. I tried asking myself, *What if you answer all your questions, fill in all the blanks, what will it give you, what will it change?* But all I came up with as an answer was: something.

Maybe it was the house that spurred me on.

Maybe it was Edith, the Edith of Blue Sky House who had loved Joseph, who had slept with him under the blue sky ceiling, who had paddled a canoe, who had collected leaves and bones, who had suffered Joseph's death, who had run a business, who had given refuge again and again, who had written down the names of the shadow women and their children in order to make them real, to bear witness, to say that nothing is ever truly erased.

Or maybe it was the Edith of my wedding weekend, sharp-eyed, clear-voiced, human and also spun together out of earth and sky, giving me courage, persuading me to find a way to lift my home onto my shoulders and carry it with me.

I searched for their names, collected Herrons and Blanchards, but never the ones I wanted.

I researched Wickham-Flaherty, the New York law firm that had represented John during his trial, but it had closed in the 1960s, after the tragic deaths of John's lawyer Randolph Flaherty and his son, Randolph Flaherty Jr., in a sailing accident. I wondered how a small-town police chief would even know about the existence of Randolph Flaherty, Esquire, and I wondered how he could possibly have paid him. I wondered if Mr. Big City had signed those checks, if New York were the big city of Mr. Big City.

I kept thinking that as soon as I found something, I would call Dev. But I didn't find anything, so I didn't call. He didn't call me, either. We hadn't spoken in the four days since I'd dropped him off at his house on my way back from Richmond. I wasn't angry at him. I didn't not miss him. My nights were emptier without his voice in them. But I just kept hearing that question: *So what's next? So what's next? So what's next?* And I imagined that Dev felt like I did: suspended in the empty space where the answer should have been.

Then, one evening, he called.

Before he even said hello, he said, "Are you okay?"

"I'm okay. Are you okay? Because you don't sound especially okay."

"How do I sound?"

"Worried. Or no—mad. Actually, both. Morried? Wad?"

"You do sound weirdly okay," said Dev.

"Gee, thanks."

"So what's up with your Facebook page?" he demanded.

"Now you sound mostly just mad. Also, what are you talking about? I almost never go on Facebook," I said. "I jumped on briefly right after—"

In the car making my getaway from my nonwedding, I'd taken down the "Engaged" status I'd only ever put up at Zach's (very persistent) prompting, but I didn't feel like sharing that bit of information with Dev.

Dev didn't say, "Right after what?" for which I was grateful. He said, "How long ago was that?"

"Back in June and everything was normal," I said. "Everything on Facebook, I mean."

"Get on your computer and go to your page. Right now."

"No Wi-Fi, bossy person. And, hey, you're on Facebook even less than I am. How did you happen to be looking at my Facebook page, anyway?"

There was a pause. "Irrelevant. You're missing the point here."

"Well, maybe if you made a point, I would stop missing it."

"Just get on your phone and look at your Facebook page, Clare."

"Are you speaking through gritted teeth? You know, that might work for Clint Eastwood, but, honestly, it makes you a little hard to understand."

"Clare."

"Fine."

"After you look, call me back." He hung up.

"Dev was looking at my Facebook page." Even though there was no one in Edith's house with me to hear it, it was still satisfying to say out loud.

But as soon as I took a look at the page, this satisfaction, along with every other remotely positive feeling, evaporated.

I hate myself for what I've done to Zach. And to me. My life is so empty.

I guess you never realize what you have until you've thrown it away like it was garbage.

First his mother left him, then his sister Ro left him, then his father, now me? I feel like a sadistic monster.

I can't get Zach out of my head. His face. His voice. His body against mine.

I would do anything to get him back. Anything anything anything anything.

The thought of never being with Zach again makes me wish I were dead.

I just need this pain to end.

Post after post after heartbroken, regretful, semisuicidal post, all put up an hour ago. The proximity in time creeped me out, made him feel somehow near me, lurking, which I know didn't make sense, but I was rattled, and by rattled I mean I felt like either taking a shower or throwing up or both, if not simultaneously, but instead, I deleted my account. Then I shot off a text to Zach:

What the hell is wrong with you? Was that supposed to be a joke? Because it wasn't funny. As I'm sure you know.

I called Dev back. "It had to be Zach. He's the only person who knew my password. I guess I should have changed it back in June, but I'd forgotten he had it."

"Well, he didn't forget," said Dev. "Obviously."

"I'm sorry you were worried."

"Morried," said Dev, correcting me. "Wad. And *I'm* sorry I was both of those completely nonexistent adjectives."

"That's okay. For the record, I don't feel any of the things he posted. Not a whit."

"No one says 'whit,'" said Dev. "But, hey, that's good news."

"Mentally and emotionally, I'm tip-top."

"Which is more than we can say for Zach."

"Thanks to me," I said.

"Nope, you can't take credit for this. Creepiness of this magnitude had to be in there, waiting to happen. Sooner or later, it would have."

"I hope so. No. I mean I hope not. I don't know what I hope, but while we were eating dinner in that Thai place?"

"Yes?"

"He texted me the same text four times: I know you're with him right now, I know you're with him right now, I know you're with him right now, I know you're with him right now."

"You didn't tell me that," said Dev.

"I didn't want you to get morried the way you do."

"Seriously. Do you think he did know?"

"Of course not. How could he?"

"He could have had you followed, hired a private detective or something."

I laughed. "Zach might be crazy, but he's not *that* crazy."

"It would be good to know," said Dev, "just exactly how crazy he is."

My phone vibrated in my hand, and I took it from my ear and looked at the screen. Zach.

"He's calling me. I should get it," I said.

"Okay. But Clare? Don't tell him where you are."

"I won't. Don't morry. He doesn't even know this place exists."

He claimed to be drunk, a claim I had no trouble believing, since I could practically smell the alcohol through the phone. He said he'd been drinking more lately, which his brother, Ian, said was understandable, even normal, even wise, at which point I wanted to remark that his brother, Ian, might not be the ideal go-to person when it came to identifying wisdom, but I refrained. He talked about numbing the pain and blunting the anger, but then he mentioned that he was angrier than ever, not every second, but in spurts. He talked about his sister, Ro, about how, for some reason, he couldn't stop thinking about her, about how all his conversations with Ian seemed to lead back to Ro. He said he'd only written on my Facebook page what he *wished* I were feeling—presumably including the "wish I were dead" sentiment—but knew I didn't feel, unless deep down I actually did, which he suspected was true, since he knew the two of us would end up together in the end, and if he knew this, he bet I knew it, too, deep down. I told him, again, that I would always care about him, but that I could never be with him. He ignored this. I told him that maybe he should consider going to a doctor, talking to someone, getting some help. He ignored this, too. I apologized, again, for hurting him. He didn't ignore this. He said that I should be sorry, that he hoped I'd be fucking sorry for the rest of my goddamned life, and then he hung up.

"How about I make a quick visit? Just to be sure you're safe," my mother said when she called later that night. "I heard about the Facebook thing."

I sighed. "From Dev?"

"From Cornelia who heard it from Hildy who heard it from Aidan who heard it from Dev."

"*I* only heard it from Dev an hour ago," I grumbled, sounding exactly like my fourteen-year-old, privacy-deprived, indignant self.

The next day, when my mother arrived, in a whirlwind of sunglasses and linen and knife's-edge pleats and blondness, I ran out so fast to throw myself into her arms that I nearly mowed down a squirrel. When she'd managed to untangle her elegant limbs from my hug, she took off her sunglasses and smiled, and I was struck for the hundred-millionth time by how my mother would have looked exactly like Grace Kelly if only Grace had bothered to be just a teensy bit more polished.

After we carried in her sleek overnight bag and the four tons of groceries she'd brought, I gave her a tour of the house, which I'd begun to think of as *my* house, although somehow this didn't seem to make it any less Edith's. My mother oohed and ahhed and ran her hand along some things and gazed at other things and got solemn and expressed reverence in all the right places. We made sandwiches and picnicked at the beach and then went for a long walk on the sand, during which my mother in her black one-piece swimsuit, raffia sunhat, and a silk sarong knotted around her hips with the same nonchalant, maddening perfection with which she knotted scarves around her neck, turned the heads of men—and plenty of women—a third her age, a phenomenon she noticed not one whit.

That evening, she treated me to the best table at the best restaurant in town. We sat on the bayside deck, feasted, and watched the sunset outdo itself, no doubt turning on the magnificence for my mom, who clapped and called out "Bravo!" just as it hit its rose-gold, magenta, and blue-opal peak.

We talked and talked. She already knew about the Mystery of Blue Sky House, of course, but I told her again anyway, filling in all the details and updating her on the recent Richmond developments.

When I was finished, and we were forking up strawberry pie, my mother smiled and said, "You and Dev always did love to puzzle things out together."

"He'll tell you that he solved all the hardest parts, but really it was me," I said.

"I suspect you solved them together. Two heads are better than one, especially when they're your and Dev's heads." She paused then said, gravely, "I'm glad you two are back on track. We're all glad."

I narrowed my eyes at her. "Just as long as you—all of you—are clear as to exactly which track we're talking about."

"You're friends, I know." My mother blinked, innocent as a baby. "But why do we need to rubber-stamp your and Dev's relationship—or any—as one definite, limited thing?"

"I don't know about *any*," I said. "But this one is rubber stampable. Trust me."

"I trust you. Now, if only you could learn to trust yourself."

"Meaning?"

"You're such a good girl, and I love that about you. But what if you put aside what's appropriate or expected or even noble—and you know how I like nobility—forget rules and rubber stamps and boundaries and just follow your instincts?"

"Are you going to start in about how brain scientists are taking intuition seriously these days? Because I've heard that one."

"From someone very smart, I expect," she said. "Who has lovely gray eyes and your best interests at heart."

"They're blue-gray, actually," I said.

"Ah," said my mother, infusing that single syllable with so much complicated meaning that the only thing to do was ignore it. "Anyway, rubber stamp notwithstanding, I'm glad you two are having fun."

"*Had* fun," I said, wistfully. "I guess I'm suffering

a little postadventure depression right now. I wish it weren't over. It somehow doesn't *feel* over. But it is."

"Maybe it's not. The world is big and life is long. You never know," said my mother, giving a shrug that managed to be chic and wise and jaded and careless all at once. It was the kind of shrug for which words like *insouciant* and *urbane* were created.

And even though I *did* know, my mother's shrug was so persuasive that I allowed myself to have a tiny bit of hope.

Later, back at Blue Sky House, we sat on the living room rug with glasses of wine, and I opened the boxes of Edith's and Joseph's photographs, including a few I'd never actually gone through.

"These are marvelous. I love the exuberance of his, the way she seems like a wild bird or a goddess. Clearly, he worshipped her. But I think I like hers of him even more; they're so personal and intimate that I almost feel guilty looking at them. Who knew a photo of the back of someone's head or the inside of his wrist could be so passionate?" said my mother.

"I know," I said, reaching for a stack of photos from one of the previously unexamined boxes. I shuffled through them and then laid them out, one by one, in front of me on the rug.

"Hey!" I said. "These aren't Joseph."

"Are you sure?" said my mother.

"This man is dark haired, too, but much slimmer, narrower in the shoulders. Joseph was a big, muscular guy. And the—I don't know—*tenor* of them is different from the Joseph pictures."

My mother slid over to look, but after a glance, she scooted back to her own patch of rug and the Joseph photos she had arrayed before her. "I see what you mean. Those are clever, arch. I prefer these."

This new batch contained fragments of a man, as did the photos of Joseph, but even though they were just as close-in, they were somehow much more distant. Cooler in mood, more full of angles and straight lines, more full of *things* rather than focusing on the curved, pliant, warm-blooded terrain of skin and sinew. A man's hand holding a glass, his nails smooth, his shirt cuff almost blindingly white, an odd signet ring—flat, dark, square stone, heavily carved sides—glinting on his left pinkie. Fingers holding a wool fedora by the brim. A polished wingtip with a slice of sock-covered ankle. Tip of chin, glimpse of neck, knot of tie. Knuckles of a hand that gripped the oval handle of a leather bag, a hint of a name—unreadable—stamped in what looked like gold beneath the handle. Blurred man in a suit standing at the back window, elegant shoulders, dark hair. Dark, I noted, so not John. I remembered reading in the newspaper articles about the trial that John Blanchard was blond.

When I turned the photos over, I saw that each had a faint G.G. penciled in the right-hand corner with a date underneath. I was right about the photos not being of Joseph; all of them were taken during the winter and spring of 1956 when Joseph had been dead for over three years. I took out the daylight ledger and examined the entries spanning that time period but found no one with the initials G.G. Then, I went further back and there it was, many months earlier: *George Graham.* Nothing more. It was the only entry in the entire ledger with no address. If George Graham had come back during the winter and spring of 1956, he hadn't come as a paying guest.

I went back to the photos. Could this man have been Edith's lover? It was true that the photos had an air of detachment, but the person in them would have had to have known she was taking them. He and Edith had to have been familiar with each other for her to get so close to him.

"These clothes and shoes and things," I said. "They look expensive. And formal, not the kind of thing people typically wear for a beach trip, even in winter."

"Let me see," said her mother, holding out her hand.

"Yes, tell me what you think. You're the style star."

It was true; even with her reading glasses resting on the tip of her nose, she looked ridiculously glamorous.

I restacked the photos and handed them to her.

She stopped on the one with the oval-handled leather bag, set the photo on the floor, and tapped it with her long forefinger.

"Mark Cross," she said.

"You mean the name stamped on it?" I said. "You can read that? But I thought the man's initials were G.G."

"Mark Cross is a leather goods designer, very expensive. It shut down in the 1990s but was resurrected a couple of years ago. In its new incarnation, the company reissued a lot of its older, classic designs. That's why I recognize this duffel; it was one of the reissues."

"Is the company based in a particular city?" I asked. "Maybe a northern city?"

"There was a store on Fifth Avenue. No longer there, but back in the 1950s I'm pretty sure it would have been."

My mother continued to look through the other photos, but I held on to the Mark Cross one, my heart starting to beat hard.

"Okay, Mom, what if G.G. was Mr. Big City? I mean, maybe it's a long shot, but he was here; Edith knew him well enough to take all these photos; assuming he's

George Graham, he came the first time not long before the first shadow ledger guest arrived; and Edith either didn't know his address or was keeping it a secret. Also, the lawyer who represented John Blanchard came from an upper-crust New York firm, and doesn't it seem likely that if John, one of the cogs in Mr. Big City's machine, got in trouble while being a cog, Mr. Big City would do whatever he could to get him out of it?"

"Oh, my God," gasped my mother.

"I know! It really could be him."

But when I turned to look at her, her gaze was riveted on a photo in her hand.

"Mom? Did you hear what I said?"

She looked up at me, staring absently through her glasses, and shook her head.

"No, no, I didn't. Sorry. But, oh, Clare."

She turned the photo she held around so that I could see it. It was the one of the man's hand holding the glass.

Wide-eyed, her voice so breathless I could barely hear it, my mother said, "The ring. Clare, I know that ring."

Chapter Twenty-Three
Edith

December 1956

For the first eight hours of the journey, Edith made things happen. She pressed the gas pedal, and the car accelerated. She pressed the brake, and the car rolled to a stop. She drove through towns, noting their names, the dark gas stations, the church steeples piercing the sky. She drove along deserted roads and watched her headlights carve a tunnel of light for the car to travel through. She passed stands of trees, roadside motor inns with partially burned-out signs. She spoke words of reassurance to Sarah, who lay propped up with a pillow and wrapped in blankets in the backseat, her baby in her arms. She ate a sandwich. She stopped twice, briefly, to stretch her legs, change Steven's diaper, consult her road atlas, and check on Sarah, who both times eked out a smile and a hoarse, heart-cracking "I'm fine." Edith grew impatient, wanting to go faster, stick to bigger roads, take a straighter shot, but the only priority greater than getting to where they were going as quickly as possible was not getting caught along the way, so she reasoned with herself, stuck assiduously to the speed limit and to her winding, circuitous route.

But just as the sun came up, things began to happen *to* Edith. The world outside the car windows changed, wavering like a heat shimmer, leaning in to press against the sides of the car or circling around it like a carousel. And the car began to drive itself, hurtling along at fifteen miles an hour, crawling at forty, or sitting motionless as the buildings and road signs and trees rushed by it in a blur. To keep herself awake, Edith began to sing, and the songs chose her instead of the reverse. Sometimes, she sang without knowing she sang, talked without topic or direction. When she stopped at a gas station, she told the attendant that Sarah was her sister who had recently been in a car accident, that they were going to visit relatives in Maine; she babbled brightly on about blueberries, lobster, bears, and moose, until the attendant said, "You seem a little fatigued, ma'am. Might want to check into a motel and get some sleep," and she said, "As soon as we get to the next town, I promise we'll do just that." She didn't keep the promise, but she came close, pulling the car into a motel parking lot and lying down across the front seat.

Four hours later, a sound woke her. She thought at first it was the baby crying, but it was Sarah, groaning in pain. When Edith turned around, the sight of the woman knocked the wind out of her like a punch. Sarah's eyes were unfocused, her face glazed with sweat, and she trembled as if an invisible person had her by the shoulders and were shaking her until her teeth rattled. Edith got into the backseat, coaxed water and aspirin down Sarah's throat. With great effort, she kept her voice low and soothing, but fear was charging through her, beating out a loud prayer inside her head: *Just let her live, just let her live, just let her live, I'll do anything if you just let her live.*

In the end, that fear is what saved Edith: jolting her out of her fog into an acute, raw wakefulness, sharpening her senses, jerking her attention back on track whenever it began to stray. And Edith believed forever after that it was the baby who saved Sarah. Quiet for the first two-thirds of the trip, as his mother grew sicker, he transformed into a bundle of steely will, of raucous demand, his throaty, mechanical cries making the air inside the car pulse like a migraine as he insisted on his own survival over and over and over. Even when his mother muttered, delirious with fever, wild-eyed as an animal, or when she seemed to slide into and out of unconsciousness, some tiny, clear piece of her remained to hear him, to hear him and to answer. When Sarah was too weak to hold her head upright, she pressed her son into the curve of her body with an unflagging grip. When she no longer seemed to know where she was, she lifted her shirt and nursed him.

By the time they got to the border checkpoint, Edith was so tired that, for a panicked moment, she forgot the words George had told her to say to the guard, but just as she was rolling down the window, she remembered.

"We've come all the way from Latrobe to visit our northern cousins," she said, smiling.

After a quick glance at Sarah and Steven in the backseat, the guard delivered his line: "Latrobe? Isn't that where the banana split was invented?"

"It is," said Edith, with a sigh of relief. "It is, indeed."

Because of the indirect route, the trip took over twenty-four hours, so that it was dark when they arrived at the safe house. Edith didn't know what she'd been expecting—a mansion? A fortress?—but the sight of the farmhouse set back from the road in a copse of maples took her by surprise. It was so ordinary, so peaceful with its mailbox, its brick walkway, its gabled roofs, its amber porch light, its shaded windows like closed eyes.

The young doctor who lived there came out to meet them. He'd been expecting them. "Oh, Lord," he said at the sight of Sarah. "I'll need to get her to the hospital tonight."

At Edith's alarmed expression, he said, "Don't worry. There are people there who know, who help. Friends. My mother is a friend, too. She's waiting inside."

The next half hour moved around Edith like a dream. She handed over the baby. She heard bathwater running, saw clean pajamas draped over the back of a chair, smelled bread baking. But, reeling with exhaustion, without bathing or eating or changing her clothes, still wearing her winter coat, she tumbled onto the bed and slept.

When she woke up, it was the afternoon of the following day.

The doctor's name was Thomas Farley. His mother introduced herself as May.

Edith took a bath in a claw-foot tub as big as a rowboat, sinking into the steaming water up to her chin. The air smelled of talcum powder and rosewater, and Edith wished she could stay right there all day, cradled and weightless, the hot water coaxing the ache and stiffness from her muscles. She washed her hair and dressed in the clothes she'd hastily packed, another of Joseph's sweaters and a pair of blue jeans. Examining her reflection in the bathroom mirror, she shook her head and said, "Aren't you a sight," and then, following the fragrance of bacon, she went down to find May.

When she walked into the kitchen, May turned, spatula in hand. She was diminutive, pink-cheeked from the hot stove, her gray hair cropped. She should have been a cute old lady but somehow she wasn't. May gave Edith a fleeting once-over, and then, without remarking on her appearance, turned back to the stove, where an egg danced in a skillet. She flipped it in a glory of sputtering and said, grinning, "I know it's almost four o'clock, but I figured it was breakfast time for you."

"Thank you," said Edith. "I'm ravenous and that smells like heaven. But how is Sarah?"

"*After* you eat," said May, sternly. "And no rushing. I can only imagine what you've been through, driving all that way through the cold and dark with a sick woman and an infant. First and foremost, your body needs nourishment."

She placed a plate of eggs and bacon and fresh buttered bread before Edith, and then stood watching while she ate it. For all her kindness, there was something commanding about May, rooted there in her kitchen, keen-eyed and upright and stalwart, like a soldier or a lighthouse. Not until Edith had eaten every bite—and it didn't take long—and May had taken her plate away and brought her a mug of tea thick with cream did she sit down next to Edith at the table, fold her hands before her, and say, "About Sarah."

"Is she all right?"

"Not yet," said May, shaking her head. "She's got a rough road ahead of her. They had to take out her spleen, and that's a long recovery all by itself, but she's got an infection as well, which has sent her into shock. An infection without a spleen to help fight it off . . . well, I won't sugarcoat it; Thomas is worried sick."

Edith's chest tightened and she grabbed onto the arms of her wooden chair.

"Don't do it," said May. "Whatever you're second-guessing yourself about, just don't."

"I had to try to bring her here," Edith said, gasping. "She insisted. But there was a time when we stopped and I slept because I was just so tired that nothing felt real or made sense, and when I woke up, I knew, I *knew* she had taken a turn for the worse, the much, much worse, and I shouldn't have slept or I should've taken her to a hospital right then and—"

May held up her hand. "Stop. You should have done just what you did."

"But—"

"She deserved her chance at freedom and a good life. And she may get it, yet. She's young and has got good doctors and has her baby to live for. Sarah shot her husband to save her baby's life and her own. Any woman who can do that has a fighting chance at the very least."

"She can't die. She just can't."

May reached out and moved a lock of Edith's damp hair off her cheek, a brusque, tender act that made Edith, for the first time since she was a little child, miss her mother, of whom she had not a single clear memory.

"Don't let yourself get worked up," said May. "It isn't good for you."

Impulsively, Edith took May's hand. "May, I promised Sarah that if anything happened to her, I would make sure Steven ended up with good people. I swore he would never live with her husband's family. She said they were fiends."

"Then Steven will be raised by her husband's family over my dead body," said May. She stated it like a simple fact, and Edith thought that it was the very absence of malice in her voice that made her fearsome.

"Over mine, too," said Edith. "But I might have to leave before—before we know if Sarah will get well. As soon as I get word from back home that it's safe, I'll need to go back. If I stay away too long, people will begin to wonder about me."

"Wherever you are, Thomas and I will make sure you keep your promise to Sarah. You have my word on that."

Edith smiled. "You remind me of my friend John, who brought Sarah and Steven to me. The way you keep so calm and certain, as if there's a peaceful river running through you."

May smiled back. "Oh, but really it's fierce and wild. It's all I can do to keep it in check. I'll bet John's river is that way, too."

The next morning, when Edith came downstairs, May told her that Thomas was bringing Sarah and Steven home.

"Oh, but that's wonderful," said Edith, confused by May's grave expression.

"No," said May. "She's still very, very sick. Thomas said she had no business being anywhere but a hospital."

"Why then?"

"One of the student nurses who doesn't know about what we do accidentally entered Sarah's room with a tray of food, despite the quarantine sign. Thomas and another nurse, one of ours, were in there with Sarah. They had forgotten to lock the door, you see. It's hard to do everything right when you're exhausted, and that quarantine sign should've been enough, but it wasn't."

"Oh, no," said Edith.

"It may well be nothing. Thomas said the student nurse just blushed and stammered an apology and left, but even so, he thought it best to bring Sarah home."

Later that morning, Thomas carried her into the house in his arms, stepping gingerly, jarring her as little as possible, but Sarah's face was gray with pain, and she winced with every step. Still, Edith believed she looked a little bit better than she'd looked during the drive to Canada, more lucid. When her eyes met Edith's, she moved her mouth, and although no sound came out, Edith knew Sarah was saying thank you.

Thomas took Sarah into the downstairs bedroom just off the living room, a room more like a closet, windowless, and too small to contain more than a bed and a leather armchair. May had made up the bed and set a crib for Steven in her own bedroom. Thomas would spend nights in the armchair, keeping watch.

After Sarah fell asleep, Thomas came into the kitchen, sat down at the table, and his mother brought him a plate of food. In the daylight, his face was drawn, exhausted, but still remarkably boyish; Edith thought that if he was out of his twenties, it wasn't by much.

But when he spoke, he sounded like an old man: "I wish to God I hadn't had to bring her here. I wish to God."

Two days passed without any word from John.

"I'm sure a letter is on the way," said May. "Don't worry."

"I won't," said Edith.

Even so, that night, Edith did worry, and the worry sent her mind darting like a dragonfly, unable to settle. Because sleep was impossible, she drew on the robe May had lent her and went down the back stairs in the dark, her feet feeling their way on the worn, silken wood, her hand holding firmly to the banister. When she got to the kitchen, she gasped at the transformation night had wrought on the cozy room. Moonlight spilled like mercury through the black branches of the maple tree outside the window, figuring crazy shadows on the walls and on the strawberry-print tablecloth, shadows that writhed and rippled as the wind blew. The linoleum gleamed like steel and burned the soles of her bare feet with cold. Edith felt heavy and dark in the middle of the mutable, quicksilvered room, like a rock on the bed of a flowing stream, and, as she stood there, she was filled with the presentiment that something was about to happen, something frightening, that she was about to be tumbled loose by a current and carried away.

You're ridiculous, she scolded herself, *you're safe here in this house,* and, as noiselessly as she could so as not to wake Thomas or Sarah or the baby, she began to open cupboards, searching for a water glass, but before she found one, she heard, from outside the kitchen windows, what she instinctively recognized as the crunch of footsteps on frozen grass, and panic gripped her.

They've found us, she thought bleakly. *We're caught; all that driving was for nothing; oh, poor Sarah, poor Steven, poor little baby.*

The silhouette of a man in a hat materialized at the kitchen door, and then he was turning a key in the lock, and then he was pushing the door open, and then he was standing in the kitchen staring at her and saying, "Jesus Christ, you nearly scared me to death."

George.

"Oh, George," she whispered, pressing her hand to her heart. "Thank God it's only you."

"Don't thank God, yet," he said, grimly, and switched on the kitchen light.

Her vision swam in the flood of brightness, and she lifted a hand to her eyes to shade them. When she took her hand away, George was looking at her with a strange mixture of surprise and confusion, as if he'd expected someone else entirely. Under his gaze, she felt naked and intensely conscious of the fact that she hadn't set eyes on him since the morning after the night they'd made love for the final time. Reflexively, she pulled the robe more tightly around her.

"Edith," he said, softly.

She lifted her hand to ward him off, but he didn't move in her direction. He just stood.

"Turn off the light," she said. "And please keep your voice low. Thomas sleeps in a chair in the downstairs bedroom where Sarah stays. We don't want to wake him, poor man. Or Sarah."

George turned off the light, and the two of them stood in the moon-drenched kitchen, waiting for their eyes to adjust, for the other to come into focus.

"What did you mean by that?" Edith asked.

"By what?"

"'Don't thank God, yet.'"

In the moonlight, Edith watched his face go from soft to hard.

"John Blanchard is in police custody," he said.

"John?" said Edith. Light-headed, she pulled out a kitchen chair, almost toppling it over, and fell into it like a sack. "For what?"

"What else? Helping a murderess and kidnapper to escape."

"How?"

"You were seen, the two of you. In your house. With Sarah."

Edith raked her fingers into her hair and shut her eyes. "Oh, no."

"You should have sent him away as soon as he showed up with her and the baby," George said, coldly.

Edith opened her eyes and stared at George Graham, trying to balance all the contradictory parts of this man who had spent money and years making women and children safe and yet who could dismiss Sarah and Steven as if they were nothing.

Finally, she said, "You never see their faces, do you?"

"What are you talking about?"

"Or hear their voices. You don't know the color of their hair or how they jump at noises or flinch when they're touched. They aren't real to you. They aren't even stories, are they? They're what? Names on your list? Tally marks?"

"You're talking nonsense."

"But your own story, you keep that one close, don't you? And all the characters in it are flesh and blood."

George turned his face away.

"I'll bet you remember the color of that minister's hair, the one who sent your mother away when she came to him for help."

"Enough," he said, through tight lips.

"You didn't see Sarah, the shape she was in, and with a newborn baby. No one could have sent them away."

"I take your point, Edith," said George. "And still here we are. John caught like a rat in a trap. Your house compromised forever, useless to all those women who need help. And you and Sarah—" He broke off.

Edith reached up and rubbed her temples, tried to clear her head. She said, "They'll come after us, won't they? Sarah and Steven and me."

"They're already looking," said George, and then asked, sharply, "did you tell Blanchard where you were going?"

She nodded.

"Good," he said.

She lifted her head. "Good?"

"Yes. I don't know the man, but he seems to be the noble type. I'm sure he'll do what he can to steer the authorities in all the wrong directions."

"You're right," said Edith. "John's not a liar by nature, but he will lie to help us."

She imagined John, her friend, the most decent, innately kind person she knew, locked in a cage like an animal.

"Good."

"But I'll have to go home eventually," said Edith.

George sat down at the table with her and she watched him look at her, taking her in, his eyes growing distant and thoughtful, and then, after a few moments, something shifted, snapped into place, and Edith understood that she had just seen him make a decision.

"If you go home," he said, "you will be arrested and will almost certainly go to prison. At some point, you will be given a choice: tell them Sarah's whereabouts and be granted some sort of leniency or refuse to tell them, in which case . . ." He shrugged.

That shrug made her want to slap him. How easy it would be to allow herself to hate him, to turn him, in her mind, from a man into a monster. But what good would that do? And anyway, it would be a lie. Edith thought of Sarah's husband. It was possible that there were monsters afoot in this world, but she knew that George Graham was not one of them.

"Ordinarily, if you left now, you wouldn't know where Sarah and Steven were because, before you'd even arrived at home, they would have been transported from here to their next place," said George. "But moving Sarah in her condition is obviously impossible. She and Steven will be here for weeks, maybe longer."

"I would never tell them where she was," Edith said.

"You'd be surprised at what you might do if you

were facing a long prison sentence," he said. "So going back wouldn't just be disastrous for you; it could put Sarah and Steven in danger, as well."

"I wouldn't betray them."

He seemed not to have heard her. "I'm sure John Blanchard will buy you some time. There's no need to leave right away, but you can't stay here forever. Neither can Sarah and Steven. When the police realize they've been misled, they'll eventually start looking in the proper direction. You had to have stopped places on the way; people saw your car."

She remembered the gas station attendant, politely listening to her exhausted ramblings. She nodded.

"Who knows? It's possible that they'll never trace you or Sarah to this house. It helps that you're in another country now. But they might find you," said George.

"So what am I supposed to do?"

"Stay until you—until you're ready and all the plans are in place. And then let me relocate you."

Edith fell back in her chair, stunned.

"You mean never go back?"

"I've done it for many women, as you know. And I'll be honest, fugitive life is hard. You will spend years looking over your shoulder. Some of the women, especially the ones with children, even regret their decision to leave; although so far, none have been desperate enough to go back."

She shook her head.

"But my life. My entire life is back in Antioch. I have nothing else anywhere else. No family. No real friends. No work. My clothes, my cameras, my boxes of important things, I've brought none of that with me here."

Confused and frightened, she thought that if only she explained her situation as clearly as possible, he would see that she had to go back.

"Edith, don't you understand that life as you've known it ended the moment you took Sarah and her baby into your house?" said George, quietly.

"John's life, too. How can I let him take responsibility for everything?"

"It can't be helped." Edith heard a note of regret in his voice.

"*You* help him," she said. "Whatever I do, wherever I end up, you help John however you can. Will you do that?"

"Yes," said George.

She nodded. "Thank you."

"You're welcome."

"And what about my house? It's more than a house to me." *It's Joseph. All that I have of Joseph.*

George sighed. "I can do whatever you want me to do about your house. Sell it or—"

"No!" said Edith, forgetting to whisper. She lowered her voice. "Never."

"As you wish. I'll do whatever you want."

"Please don't speak as if I've decided."

Edith's hands lay palms down on the table. George reached out as if to hold one of them, but then just set his own hand on the table between the two of hers.

"Edith, you were wrong about me. Those women *are* real to me, all of them, even though most of them I never see."

Edith scanned his face, and noticed, for the first time, how tired he looked.

"I shouldn't have said that," she said. "It was unfair."

"You're real to me," said George, quietly. "I know the color of *your* hair, and I want you to have a life. Let me help you."

Edith sat still, struggling to absorb what was happening, but then she heard May moving around on the floor over their heads. At any moment, she might come down the stairs.

"Think it over. Take your time," said George. "I'll be back in a couple of weeks. And when you've decided, I will put it all in motion."

The full meaning of what they had been saying to each other hit her all at once, and the world seemed to spin.

Edith had written down the names of the bruised and hollow-eyed and homeless, but who would make a record of her name and where she'd been? Who would catalog her injuries, document the tilt of her black brows, her laugh, her two hands cradling a coffee cup or knotting back her wayward, wind-tangled hair?

Nothing is decided, she reminded herself, *nothing.* But when she closed her eyes and tried to hold on, to her house, her canoes, her kitchen table, her boxes, her blue ceiling, Joseph's photographs; when she tried to reach her hands around all of it, it was as if every solid, holy thing she'd ever loved had turned to water and was already pouring through her fingers and rushing away, away, away.

Chapter Twenty-Four
Clare

Compared to Edith's boxes, the box my mother held out to me was pretty drab, no golden, swirl-grained oak or fragrant cedar or mahogany shiny as a mirror, no black lacquer tops or velvet linings: just rubber-band-colored, fireproof metal with a round lock on top, the key stuck inside it. But this had been my summer of finding truth in locked boxes, and this one just might be the last, so I took it from my mother's hands with the care and respect you'd offer any holy grail, any *sanctuarium*. I set it on the coffee table in my parents' living room, and all of us gathered around: my mother, Gordon, Cornelia—who was in town dropping off her children at her parents' house for a week of, as she put it, "unfettered joy, limitless pie, and irreversible spoiling"—Dev, whom I had picked up on the way down, and I.

And slipping in at the last minute to look over my shoulder, tall, slim, dark-eyed, handsome, dead for more than ten years, and invisible to everyone but me, was my father, Martin Grace.

My parents had divorced when I was a toddler, and while my father was alive, until the day he left for London, where he died in a car accident, whenever I was with him, I was the one who felt invisible. He wasn't mean. On my rare visits with him, he joked and teased and bought me things. He called me "Clare-o the Sparrow." He just didn't love me, and I knew it, and once he had died, I knew he never would. That could have been the end of our story, but then, one day, when I was twelve and won a writing award in school, I realized that even if he'd never loved me, I could love him. And that's when I began to edit him in. That night, when I stood on the stage in the school auditorium, receiving my award, I found an empty seat in the audience, near the back but close enough for him to see my face, and I put him into it. *Hello,* I told him in my head, *I'm glad you're here.* Dances, Christmas dinners, my high school graduation, even at my rehearsal dinner, he was there, a slender presence, half in shadow, stopping by just long enough to absorb the small allotment of love

I beamed in his direction and then disappearing like a trick of light.

Now I told him, silently, *This is your box, and I am glad you're here,* and then I reached out and turned the key and lifted the lid.

Photographs. Of course, photographs. Photographs always. I almost laughed at how appropriate it was. One of Martin at three or four years old, sitting on his mother's lap. She is tiny and fair haired and smiling directly into the camera lens, while my father's dark-haired father stands behind the two of them, his hand on his wife's shoulder, his face angled downward because he's looking at his son. Another photo of my father in a high school track uniform, kissing a trophy, his parents standing behind him, caught in midclap. Another of my parents on their wedding day, my mother swanlike and radiant in a narrow cream-colored suit with a portrait neckline, her hair in a French twist, my father cutting a Cary-Grant-like figure, chin dimple and all, in his coat and tie.

I handed the photos to my mother, who glanced through and handed them to Cornelia, who held up the wedding photo and said, "How did you two look like this? Wasn't it the late eighties? Where is the cotton candy hair? Where are the gargantuan square shoulders?" and my mother laughed.

"Keep going," said Dev to me.

"I just really want it to be the same ring," I said. "And as long as that ring box I see in the bottom of this box stays closed, it might be the same ring. But if I get it out and open it and it's not the same ring, then it definitely won't be."

"Remember when we were fifteen and spent an entire day at the pool talking about Schrödinger's cat?"

"We were such nerds. How did we turn out to be so cool?"

Dev laughed. "Good question." Then, he nodded toward the box.

I took out the black suede ring box, stared at it for a few seconds, then handed it to Dev.

"You open it," I said. "I'm way too nervous."

He grinned and handed it back. "Not on your life. There might be a dead cat in there."

"This is no time to talk quantum physics," said Cornelia, shaking a finger at Dev.

"*I* was going to make a Pandora's box joke," said my mother. "But in the interest of time, I decided not to."

"Clare," said Gordon, gently. "Could you please open the damned box?"

I opened it.

It was the ring from the photograph. Same flat, square stone; in the photo it had looked brown or black, but in real life, it was a shade or two darker than apricot jam ("Carnelian," whispered Cornelia). Same deeply carved gold sides: a shield on one side, a rampant lion on the other. Inside, still just barely legible, were the initials GLG.

I slid the ring onto my forefinger, then reached into my shoulder bag and pulled Edith's photo from between the pages of the hardback book I'd brought to carry it in and keep it flat. I handed the photo to Dev, who held it up by its edge with his right thumb and forefinger. With his left hand, he reached out, scooped up my hand, and lifted it, balanced on his palm, to his face. For a moment, I thought he was going to kiss it, but he just narrowed his eyes, looking. The tiny twinge of disappointment I felt at his not kissing it took me by surprise, but I forgot all about it—or mostly—a second later when Dev said, "It's the same ring. Definitely. And with those initials inside, it couldn't be any other ring, could it?"

"No," said Gordon, taking off his glasses and bending over to look. "It's without a doubt the same ring."

"I can't believe it," I said. "Dev, it's the same ring!"

Dev smiled, an event as sudden and breathtaking as a white heron breaking from the marsh grass to wing over water, brighter than snow. His fingers closed over mine and squeezed, and for a split second, all I knew was his face and his hand holding mine, and there was no ring and no photograph and we were the only two people in the room.

"How cool is that?" he said, and he let my hand go.

I saw my mother and Cornelia exchange one of their two-second, thousand-word glances, and then Cornelia clasped her hands under her chin, eyes shining, and said, "Very."

There was one more item in the box. Neither hope nor a dead cat. It was a manila folder held shut with a paper clip. Inside the folder was one slip of paper: an adoption certificate.

I didn't read further than the header before I stopped, reached over, took Dev by his T-shirt sleeve, and pulled. "Get over here," I said, and he walked around the corner of the table, and together, we read.

"Oh, my God," I breathed.

"Holy shit," breathed Dev.

"Gareth Grace," I murmured.

"G.G.," murmured Dev.

"Tell us!" barked my mother.

We told them.

On December 29, 1956, in a Canadian town called Canterbury Mills, Gareth Lambert Grace and Louisa Cole Grace of Rye, New York, adopted a healthy baby boy, Caucasian, eyes brown, hair brown. In the spaces for the boy's place of birth, for his mother's name, and for his birth date, the same two words were typed: *UNKNOWN, FOUNDLING.*

As I read and for at least twenty seconds after I finished, no one moved or said a word. We all just stood around the table, swaddled in an awestruck hush. But after that one rapt moment, I got busy putting all the puzzle pieces together inside my head, and I could tell from the expression on Dev's face that he was doing the same thing. After about ten seconds of this, our eyes met.

"We should fill in the blanks," I said.

"Birthplace," said Dev.

"Antioch Beach, Delaware," I said.

"Birth date."

"December third, 1956."

"Birth mother."

My eyes filled with tears. "Sarah Giles."

Dev smiled and bumped me with his shoulder. "Go on. Sarah Giles, who?"

I lifted my head and told my family, "Sarah Giles, my grandmother."

We all moved into the family room, Cornelia having suggested that comfy chairs and sofas lent themselves to the task of processing revelation far more readily than did standing around a dining room table. As usual, she was right.

"Food would help, too," said Gordon, and a few minutes later, he was carrying in wooden carving boards covered with cheeses, smelly and not-smelly, soft and hard, and prosciutto sliced so thinly you could see through it; baskets of cut-up baguettes; bowls of blueberries and strawberries and olives; and a big plate of molasses cookies he'd baked the day before.

"I love you, Gordon," I said, popping a blueberry into my mouth. "With all my heart."

"I love you, too," he answered, dropping a kiss on the top of my head. "Now, partake, people."

We didn't just partake. We gorged. We relished. We destroyed.

Finally, my mother said, "Clare, I don't know why I never gave you that box of your father's things before. I've been trying to decide whether or not I kept it from you on semipurpose because of some kind of deeply buried resentment I harbored toward your father, and the answer I've come up with is that I honestly don't think so."

"No," I said, "that doesn't seem like something you'd do. Your resentment is never deeply buried. If it isn't buried in a *very* shallow grave, it's alive and well and walking among us."

"My thought exactly," said my mother. "We just moved so soon after your father died, and there were so few personal items. Most everything was sold, the furniture, the apartment, the artwork. All the proceeds went into a trust with the rest of what he left you, the money you'll get when you're twenty-five. Anyway, I forgot all about that box and that ring until I saw Edith's photo. I even forgot that Martin was adopted. His parents were dead when I met him, and he wasn't big on discussing personal information. He told most people that he was born and raised in Rye, New York, but, now that I think back, he did mention the adoption to me once or twice, right after we got married. Anyway, I'm sorry about the box."

"That's okay," I said.

"It's lucky that I left the key sitting in the lock. Not particularly security-minded, but lucky. I'm sure I would never have been able to track it down."

"I'm pretty sure that if you couldn't find the key, Clare would've yanked that box to pieces with her bare hands," said Dev.

"And teeth," I said.

"So Gareth Grace, who you think called himself

George Graham, was Mr. Big City?" said Cornelia. "Is that what we're thinking?"

"It all fits," I said. "He and Louisa are from New York, too, not far from the city."

"And Gareth worked in Manhattan," said my mother. "Finance, banking, some money thing. I remember that now. Not sure about a Richmond connection, but we have a name, so it should be easy enough to track down."

"Oof. Trying to put everything together in the right order is making my brain hurt," said Cornelia. "Can someone tell me, in a slow, step-by-step manner, how Sarah and her baby ended up in Canada?"

"Dev, you start," I said. "My brain's a little sore itself."

"Okay," said Dev. "So the night Sarah killed her husband, we'll assume things unfolded the way John described them at the trial. Sarah and Steven weren't meant to be part of Gareth's escape system, but when John found Sarah distraught after shooting her husband, he took her to Edith's for medical treatment and so that she and the baby could be relocated. Then, he drove her to the next safe house on the route, which must have been in this Canadian town Canterbury Mills. Gareth probably didn't drive with him, but he must have met them there, either because that's how it always worked or because he already had the idea of adopting Steven. We don't know what happened between him and Sarah, but I'm guessing that either she died of her injuries or she decided that her kid would be better off with Gareth and Louisa."

"I can see how that could've happened," I said. "Sarah was a fugitive. If she'd gotten caught eventually, who knows what would have happened to Steven?"

"But how hard," said my mother. "What a devastating choice that would have been for Sarah."

"All right, but I'm confused about something," said Gordon, scratching his head. It was a thing I loved about Gordon: he actually scratched his head when he got confused. "John Blanchard says he took Sarah away and was back at work the next morning. But there's no way he could've driven to Canada and back that fast."

"Maybe he put the two of them on a train or something," said Dev. "Although Sarah was apparently really injured, probably in ways that would have attracted attention. And he knew the police would be looking for her, so public transportation wouldn't have been a great idea."

"Or maybe," said Cornelia, slowly, "he didn't take her at all. He just told the police he did. Wouldn't Gareth have sent a car with an anonymous driver the way he usually did? And if that were the case, John wouldn't have mentioned it at the trial because he wasn't about to give away Gareth's relocation system."

"Yeah, I didn't even think of that," said Dev. "Bet you're right."

"Good," said Gordon. "My second point of confusion is fuzzier."

"Go for it," said Clare. "We're on a roll."

"Well, none of this is a coincidence, right? Edith was at the wedding—"

"Nonwedding," I said, automatically and then grimaced. "That's, uh, what I call it, although usually just inside my own head."

Gordon smiled. "Edith was at Clare's nonwedding on purpose. She probably read about it somewhere."

"Oh, God," I said, covering my eyes. "The stupid newspaper announcements. In more than one paper, too, with a photo and everything. I was mortified. Who announces an engagement? But Zach said it was a tradition in his family. Like the Barfields are the Kennedys. Like anyone would care."

"Well, *someone* did," observed Dev.

"Oh. Right," I said. "Well, if those ridiculous announcements brought Edith into my life, I guess they were a good idea after all."

"So here's my confusion. While I personally would give Clare a house or anything else under the sun that she wanted," said Gordon, "why would Edith? Sarah was just a woman who seems to have spent a few hours at her house and then disappeared forever. Why would Edith give her granddaughter a house? Why would she even make a point of showing up at her wedding almost sixty years after she'd met Sarah?"

I sliced off a piece of Bucheron, popped it into my mouth, and contemplated Edith. Finally, slowly, I said, "I think they belonged to her, all of the women and children she helped, at least a little. Not in an ownership way, but I think she felt responsible for them. That's why she kept the shadow ledger, to keep track, to help her remember them, even after they disappeared. I think it's how she was."

Dev said, "But she couldn't literally keep track of them because they did disappear. She never knew where they went or who they became."

"All except for Steven. She knew that Gareth adopted him and took him back to New York. She knew that he became Martin Grace. She kept track of him because she could. And then she kept track of me."

After a pause, Dev said, "You know, we promised we'd tell the Richmond people—Abby and Selby—if we ever found out more of the story. We should call them."

I met his eyes. "We will. But why don't we wait?"

"For what?" asked Dev.

"Until we get back from Canada."

Chapter Twenty-Five
Clare

About two hours into our road trip from the airport in Bangor, Maine, to Canterbury Mills, as we were driving our tiny rental car through a tiny town full of tiny lakes, a dozen of them, like twelve dropped silver dollars, I realized that I was completely happy. And if the town seemed like something caught in the past, with its simple black-roofed houses and its single downtown street lined with storefronts (bakery, coin laundry, drugstore, shoe store, movie theater, coffee shop), a white church at one end, I was fully—mind, body, and soul—rooted in the now, as present in the present as I had ever been.

Dev was driving, one tan hand on the wheel. We had the windows open. Dev's hair shifted around in the breeze. We had talked straight through the flight and through the rainy first hour and a half of the car ride but the rain had stopped, and now we were sitting in a loose, amiable silence surrounded by the crayon-bright, washed-clean world. Right then, what lay behind—all those mistakes I'd made—didn't matter, and what lay ahead—all those blanks we hoped to fill in—didn't matter either. The moment was complete—a brimming glass, a terrarium—and every question I'd ever had felt answered.

"I wish I could keep it," I said.

"What?"

"This."

Dev's profile didn't move a muscle, but a pink flush appeared in the center of his right cheek.

"So keep it," he said.

When we got to Canterbury Mills, we parked the car on a side street and walked around, sticking to the neighborhoods and the little offshoot country roads because we figured that those were more likely places for a safe house than the downtown. I think I half expected a brass plaque nailed next to a front door or a historical marker stuck in the middle of a front lawn saying something like: *This house harbored Sarah Giles and her baby, Steven, and a lot of other people. It was a* *good place.* Of course, we came across exactly nothing like that, but somehow just walking down those streets and seeing houses that could have been that house gave me something I hadn't known I was missing.

"Maybe that's what I'm really searching for," I told Dev. "I mean, answers about whether she survived her injuries or where she went when she left here would be wonderful, but now that we're here, I realize that mostly what I want is for Sarah to feel real to me. Like those Civil War battlefield field trips we'd take as kids. Pretty much all you got was grass, rickrack fences, maybe a statue or two, but being there in that field, you could picture the battle: the smoke and shouting, the gunfire and the boys dying on the ground. You could feel history prickling the skin up and down your arms."

Dev stopped in the middle of the sidewalk and turned to face me. It had happened before over the years I'd known him: I'd say something and Dev would regard me with a pure, almost clinical interest, as if I were a math problem or a scientific theory or a microscope slide or a zoo animal. Which sounds off-putting and possibly creepy, I know, but somehow wasn't at all. In fact, I'd always liked it: being from time to time a thing that piqued his intellectual curiosity, sparked his neurons, got his wheels turning.

"Literal prickling?" he asked.

"Yes. Like sleet hitting my skin and bouncing off. Little stings."

"So do you feel Sarah here? Is *she* prickling up and down your arms?" he asked. He looked down at my bare arms, and I lifted them, pale side up, elbow side down, for his inspection.

"Yes. And Steven and Gareth. And Edith, too, even though she was never here," I said.

"That's interesting," he said.

"It's not like ghosts," I said, quickly. "More like an interplay between place and imagination and nerve endings. Or something."

"Which *could* be like ghosts, I guess. What people think of as ghosts. I wish I could see what parts of your brain are lighting up when this happens."

"Whatever is happening, it helps me, the prickling, the unseen things becoming real. It solves something. Fills in a space. I don't mean it fills a hollow place inside me. It's more like those ovals on a standardized test: it shades in an answer to a question I hadn't known I'd needed an answer to," I said, and then laughed. "Yeah, that sounds weird."

Dev shrugged. "Good weird, though."

We kept walking, side by side, the noon sun resting on our shoulders and on the tops of our heads.

"But hey," I said, suddenly. "What if she *was* here?"

"Edith? You're thinking this because of the prickling?"

"More like the prickling got me thinking about how Edith might have been here. Remember how Gordon asked why Edith would leave me her house when she'd only been with Sarah and Steven for a few hours, and I said that I thought she felt responsible for those two the way she did all the other shadow ledger people?"

"Sure, I remember."

"Well, that *could* be all it was because I really do think Edith had this big, capacious Miss Clavel soul."

"Who's Miss Clavel?"

I waved his question off. "But what if it were more than that? What if, for some reason, Edith drove Sarah and the baby to Canada? And on the way or after they got there, Sarah died. I don't want to believe that Sarah died, but it would help to explain why Edith felt so responsible for Steven, why she would keep up with him for so many years: Edith is the one who gave Steven to Gareth."

Dev kept walking, lost in thought, his hands in his pockets, his eyes on the sidewalk in front of him. He nodded. "That would explain why she disappeared from Antioch Beach around the same time Sarah and the baby did. She left with them."

"Right, and, at some point while she was gone, she found out that the neighbor had seen her and John with

Sarah and that John had been arrested," I said. "She knew that if she went back, she would be, too."

"So she stayed gone," said Dev. "Forever."

We walked on, side by side, our strides matching, our two shadows stretching down the sidewalk, preceding us, sometimes getting lost in the clutter of other shadows—trees, lampposts—but always emerging, clear-cut and together. From time to time, our arms brushed each other, our shoulders bumped. Out of the blue, the thought came to me that I had first held Dev's hand when I was thirteen years old, and that, touching or not touching, together or miles and miles apart, I had never really let go.

I said, "Edith and I talked a lot about having a safe place, a home. Carrying your safe place around with you, like a turtle. I hope that, wherever she went, she brought Blue Sky House with her."

Remembering something else Edith had said, I stole a glance at Dev.

"She also talked about people," I said.

"She did?"

"She said the ones who look like home are home. They're where you go."

After a while, Dev said, "Did she say you carry the people around with you, too? Even when you're away from them?"

"I can't remember if she said it or if I just thought it."

"Either way, I agree. That happens. I've done it." He didn't look at me.

"Where did you carry them?" I asked.

"Her," said Dev, correcting me. "And—everywhere."

We checked at two churches and at the hospital at the other end of town to see if anyone knew if there had ever been an orphanage in Canterbury Mills, but no one had ever heard of one. The middle-aged woman working at the hospital front desk said that it was possible abandoned babies had been dropped off at the hospital in the 1950s, but that records from that long ago would be in storage somewhere—she didn't know where—if they still existed at all.

It was when we were coming out of the Canterbury Diner, having sat at the lunch counter and devoured two pizza-slice-sized wedges of sour cherry pie, that Dev said, "Too bad there's not one of those public parks like in the movies where all the old-timers hang out and play checkers and reminisce so that we could go ask them if they'd ever heard of a safe house for battered women or the story of a mystery man who came to town empty-handed and left carrying a baby."

I stopped short on the sidewalk in front of the diner, whacked Dev on the shoulder, and said, "Bingo!"

"Okay! Jeez. Or bingo," said Dev, frowning at me and rubbing his shoulder. "Although people usually play bingo in fire halls or church basements or whatever. Checkers is more of a park thing."

"No, I mean 'bingo' as in 'you're right!'"

"You don't hit people who are right. You high-five them or shake their hand or hug them. You don't hit. But hell, yeah, I'm right. What else would I be?"

"You have no idea what you're right about, do you?"

"Nope."

"*Old people*," I said. "We need them, a bunch of them, preferably. A critical mass."

"A critical mass is the minimum amount of fissile material you need to start a nuclear reaction," said Dev.

"The fact that you just said that out loud tells me, once again, that you did not get beaten up nearly enough in middle school."

I seized him by the elbow and U-turned him back into the diner. Our tiny, adorable server, Audra, who had flirted shamelessly with Dev back when we were customers although she could not have been older than sixteen, and who had the phrase "a murmuration of starlings" tattooed on the inside of her right wrist, stood behind the counter reading a hardback biography of Harry S. Truman so thick that I wondered how her scrawny little, bird-boned, bird-loving wrist could hold it.

"Excuse me," I said.

Without even glancing up, Audra said, "It didn't stand for anything."

"What didn't?" asked Dev.

"The S. That's why there's sometimes no period after it," said Audra.

"His middle name was just the letter S?" said Dev.

She lifted her big, green, kohl-rimmed eyes from the book, aimed them at Dev, raised her eyebrows, and said, "Indeed." Then she smiled and batted—actually batted—her sooty lashes and said, "Are you back for more—pie?"

Dev laughed.

"No," I said, giving him a stern look. "We were actually wondering if there's a retirement community or maybe a nursing home around here."

"Well, she's a fun date," said Audra to Dev.

Dev laughed again, and I elbowed him in the ribs.

Audra sighed and swiveled just her eyes in my direction. "Yes. Greenbriar Community. My grandma lives there."

She gave us the address, and I typed it into my phone.

"Thanks," said Dev, and he shot her a grin that almost sliced his face in half.

"Anytime." Audra leaned a few inches closer to him. "At all."

As we walked out of the shop, I growled, "Stop grinning like that. You look like a shark. And anyway, she can't see you anymore."

"But you can." Dev's grin got wider and sharkier. "Maybe we should stop by on our way out of town. Get a piece of pie for the road."

We found our critical mass of old people sitting out on the sunlit patio in front of the retirement community. Four of them sat in rocking chairs; one woman was on her knees planting pansies in a flower bed; and two of the men were actually playing checkers, which caused Dev to do a (thankfully) abbreviated victory dance, which I ignored. When the rocking-chair people saw us, one of the women—she wore jeans and an Obama HOPE T-shirt—stood up and said, "Come over here where we can see you."

Dev and I obeyed. The woman assessed us, head cocked, hands on hips, then turned to her friends and said, "Do these belong to any of you?"

The flower-bed woman squinted up at us. "Not me. They're cute, though."

"I'm Dev and this is Clare, and we're actually not from around here," said Dev.

"Well, of course, you're not," said one of the checkers players, irritably. "We'd know you if you were."

The Obama woman gestured to a couple of empty chairs. "Pull up a chair and stay awhile."

We did. The gardening woman tugged off her gloves, slapped the soil from her knees, and pulled up a chair, too.

"I'm Tess," said the Obama woman. "These people are Mattie, Cleve, Paul, and Kate. The ones who can't be bothered to get up from their game are Jack and Pete. They're chronically grumpy."

"True fact," said Jack, without turning around.

"So what's your story?" said Kate, the gardener.

Even though I'd given my spiel three times, at the hospital and both churches, here, with all those avid eyes on me, I was suddenly nervous. I cleared my throat.

"Um. So. I recently found out that my father, who died when I was eleven and who I didn't really know that well, was adopted. He grew up in New York, but he was adopted here."

"When was this?" asked Tess.

"December of 1956."

I watched all those sharp eyes grow foggy and inward looking for a moment, as all of them traveled back—or tried to travel back—over fifty years. When they seemed to have all returned, I went on.

"Was it a local girl in trouble?" asked Kate.

For a second, I didn't know what she meant, and then, starting just under her ribs, she drew a downward curve in the air with her hand in a universal symbol for pregnant.

"Not local," I said. "We think she was, um, just passing through. Her name was Sarah Giles."

They all exchanged looks, and then Tess shook her head. "Doesn't ring a bell."

"We think she might have come with a friend, Edith Herron. And my grandfather, who came up from New York, the man who adopted Sarah's baby, his name was Gareth Grace, but people here might have known him as George Graham."

"An alias? What was he?" called out Jack. "A damned spy?"

I opened my mouth to answer, but Kate called back, "None of our business, Jack Powell, so zip it."

No one remembered a man named either of those things, and no one knew anyone named Edith Herron. I looked at Dev, my heart sinking.

Seeing my disappointment, Tess said, "Names are the first thing to go. You'll find that out one day. But I can still place a face. Do you have a picture of any of these people?"

I reached into my bag and took out two photos, one

Joseph had taken of Edith walking on the beach and one of Sarah that I'd printed out from Antioch Library's digitized newspaper articles about the trial.

Everyone passed the photos around. There was a lot of head shaking, and then, just as Tess was handing the photos back to me, Kate said, "Let me see that printed-out one again."

She held it at arm's length and narrowed her eyes.

"This one looks a bit like Dr. Farley's daughter, Gwen. Pretty girl. Similar eyes. But mostly it's that widow's peak. You don't see really defined widow's peaks like that very often."

Tess peered at the picture.

"Now that you mention it, that does look like Gwen," she said. "With that hairline that makes her face look like a valentine."

A small thrill of hope ran through me. "Does Gwen still live around here?"

"No," said Kate. "Moved to Boston years ago. I think it was Boston."

"Oh," I said.

"Comes up to visit every summer with her family, though," said Tess. "Or used to."

Her family. Dev's eyes met mine.

"Who do they visit?" he asked.

"Well, old Dr. Farley, of course, Tom Farley. And his wife."

"They're still alive?" I said.

"Well, who the heck visits dead people?" shouted Jack.

"Alive last I heard, and I would've heard if they weren't, I think. Never knew Tom's wife very well. They live pretty far out in the country, and she always kind of kept to herself, especially when her kids were growing up. Had five or six of them. I guess they kept her busy because people hardly ever saw her for years. Got out and about a little more after they all moved away. Nice enough to talk to, but private, I guess," said Tess.

"Didn't want you poking your big nose in her business, I'll bet," said Jack. "Can't say I blame her!"

"Do you know her name?" said Dev. "Tom Farley's wife?"

"Why, Sarah. Sarah Farley," said Tess. Her eyes widened. "Well, I'll be damned. You don't suppose . . ."

"He was a doctor," I said to Dev. "Like Edith was a nurse. A doctor fits."

"Do you know if Sarah came here from somewhere else?" Dev asked Tess. "Like maybe the United States?"

Tess rubbed her chin, thinking. "I can't recall. Can you, Kate?"

"I don't remember going to school with her or anything, but then she's quite a few years younger than we are."

"Who isn't?" said Jack.

Tess slapped her forehead. "Chicago!"

"Really?" I said. "Are you sure?"

"Not positive. But I think so. Tom grew up here but trained with a doctor in Chicago. I think Sarah was his sweetheart down there, and he brought her up one spring to marry her."

"Oh," I said, a little glumly. "Spring. Spring doesn't fit."

"Might not have been spring," said Tess, soothingly. "Although that's what I remember."

"Your memory's as full of holes as a leaky boat," bellowed Jack.

"Hey," said Dev, touching my wrist with one finger. "It's worth checking, right?"

"Go inside and get me some paper, Jack Powell," demanded Tess, "and I'll write down directions to the Farley house."

Jack got up with a groan and shambled, mumbling all the way, toward the door of the building.

Kate said, "And what about you two? Are *you* getting married?" She swished her forefinger back and forth between us.

Dev smiled and rubbed the back of his neck. "Us? Uh, actually—"

"Hey," I told Kate, cutting Dev off. "You never know."

Out of the corner of my eye, I saw Dev swipe a surprised glance at me.

"Nope," said Kate, smiling. "You never do."

It was a white farmhouse, deeper than it was wide, with black shutters, a front porch, and a single dormer window in the center of the gabled roof. The window reminded me instantly of the eye at the top of the pyramid on a dollar bill, which shows you how whirring and discombobulated my brain was. *Don't be an idiot,* I told myself, *it looks nothing like that.* But even so, as Dev and I sat in the car and looked at the house, I couldn't help feeling that it was looking back.

"You ready?" said Dev.

"I don't think so," I said. In my ears, my voice sounded like it was coming from the bottom of a well.

"Oh. Well, that's okay. We can sit here for a while or leave or whatever you want."

"No, I want to go knock on the door. I really do. I want to meet Sarah. It's just that my lungs seem to have stopped working, and my legs seem to have turned to wood, and I really don't see how, under these circumstances, I'm going to get out of this car," I said, my voice bouncing and echoing off the stone sides of the well.

"Hey," said Dev. "Clare."

I sat rigid, staring at the house.

"Look at me," said Dev.

"Okay," I said but my neck couldn't remember for the life of it how to do that.

Dev reached over, took my chin in his hand, and gently turned my head so that I faced him. "What are you afraid of?"

"Nothing. I'm not afraid."

Dev waited.

I sighed. "I don't know. It just feels weird to have a grandmother. I never expected to have one. And she never expected me. What if she isn't happy to see me? What if I don't see any of myself in her? What if she sees me and remembers giving her baby away and gets upset?"

Dev moved his hand so that it was cupping the side of my face, but, of their own accord, my eyes shifted sideways toward the house. "She'll be happy to see you," said Dev.

"If I don't go in, if I just stay here in this car and then leave, she'll always stay the person who was glad

I came. But if I get out and go up to that house, she might become someone else."

Dev laughed. "Old Schrödinger again. There's a live cat in this box, Clare. I just know it."

The dormer window eye regarded me coolly. It gave nothing away.

"You do?" I asked.

"Yes."

"Well, don't just sit there. Help me do this," I said.

"Look at me."

With effort, I pulled my attention away from the house. There was Dev's face, his smooth brown skin and his hair falling on his forehead and his eyes, dusky Blue Ridge blue. And maybe because we were in a new place or because my brain was swirling around like a murmuration of starlings, even though I had seen his face more times than anyone could count, it was new, too.

"Your eyelashes," I said, marveling. "They go all the way around, like a ruffle."

Dev smiled. "Did you think maybe they'd stopped?"

I breathed in and my lungs filled all the way up with air.

"You'll go with me?" I said.

"Where else would I go?"

"Then I'm ready."

Halfway up the brick walkway, I took Dev's hand or

maybe he took mine, and we walked, our breath making clouds in the cold air.

As I knocked on the door, I realized that I had no idea what I would say.

"Oh no," I said. "What should I tell her? I haven't even—"

But there she was, in a light blue sweater that matched her eyes. Sturdy, very wrinkled, her steel-gray hair coming to a point at the top of her forehead like a valentine. Her eyes were light blue. Mine are dark brown. She was short and solid. I am tall and rangy. I searched for myself in her face but didn't find me.

"Hello," she said, uncertainly. "Can I help you?"

"My grandfather was a man named George Graham," I told her.

For a moment, her expression went blank. Then she smiled, dimples appearing, like magic, in her cheeks. "Oh, you," she said, tears making her eyes shine. "You. After all these years. You beautiful girl. Come in, come in, come in."

She made us tea with honey. Holding the steaming mug in my hands and drinking the tea made me feel like a child with a sore throat who someone good was taking care of. We told her the story, tag-teaming it, beginning with my nonwedding, and Sarah sat with her shining eyes and didn't speak, except to murmur, now and then, "Oh, dear Edith, dear, dear Edith."

I finished up with Tess giving us directions to Sarah and Tom's house, and when I stopped, Sarah said, "What a journey Edith sent you two off on!"

Dev said, sheepishly, "Well, just Clare, really. She didn't know I'd be coming, too."

"Hmm," sniffed Sarah. "I wouldn't be so sure. Edith was a person who knew things. Well, I suppose it's my turn now?"

"Yes, if you don't mind," I said.

"All right then. I got sicker after Edith and George—or Gareth rather—left."

Heartsick, I thought with a pang, *because she had given her baby to Gareth.*

"I had an infection that wouldn't go away, so I stayed here for weeks and weeks, suffered setback after setback, and then, one day in mid-March, I woke up and realized that I would live. I was as weak as a newborn kitten, but I got out of bed and walked out into the living room, just inching along until I got to the nearest window. I stood there, hanging on to the window frame, shaky and fragile but feeling alive from head to toe, and I saw crocuses opening up in the yard, yellow and purple, and, for the first time not just in weeks but in years, it was as if spring were happening inside of me, too. I got better." She smiled. "And Tom and I fell in love. We didn't have far to fall, either; after all those weeks together, we were more than halfway there."

"So you stayed," I said.

"He wanted to marry me right away, but I couldn't let him. By that time, we'd gotten word that John Blanchard's lawyer had turned him into a hero—the hero he truly was—in everyone's eyes, but part of me still waited every day for the knock at the door, for them to catch me and make me go back. And then, one day in May, Tom said, 'Sarah, I think it's time to let go of that worry,' and the strangest thing is that, as soon as he said it, I did let it go. Just like that. And Tom told everyone that his sweetheart from Chicago had come up to marry him, and right out there in the backyard of this house, we were married. When George left here for the last time, on that night just before Christmas, he told Tom he wouldn't be sending people here anymore. I was the last. He said it was too risky. And maybe it was, but also, of course, he had the baby to think of. Babies change you. They change everything."

Here, Sarah stopped and the tears in her eyes spilled down her cheeks, just one brief rush of weeping, before her face cleared and she wiped the tears away.

Carefully, carefully, I said, "I can understand about the baby. A woman who worried that she might always be a fugitive, I can understand why she would've given her child to someone else to raise. Always looking over your shoulder would be hard enough without worrying that your baby boy might be caught, too, and given to strangers or worse. Gareth was rich and trustworthy, and he and his wife didn't have any biological children, so it made sense."

"Yes," said Sarah, softly.

"It was an act of love," I said.

"Yes, that's exactly what George—Gareth—said."

Shyly, I said, "So you. You're my grandmother."

And then Sarah turned wondering eyes on me and said, "Oh, no. He didn't say those things to me. Is that what you thought? Dear girl, he said them to Edith."

Even before my mind understood what her words meant, my body did. It began to tremble. Dev took my mug from my hand and set it on the coffee table, and then he slipped his arm around my shoulders and I reached up and grabbed his hand and held on. I opened my mouth to speak, but nothing came out. Mutely, I turned to Dev.

"The baby Gareth Grace adopted wasn't Steven?" said Dev.

"No, Steven stayed right here with me and Tom. He was at our wedding, in his grandmother May's arms. We told people that right before I moved up here to be with Tom, my sister died shortly after giving birth and gave her baby boy to me. But he was my son. Steven lives in Montreal with his family. He's a doctor like Tom."

"So—*Edith*?" I said, in a voice that was barely more than a whisper. "The baby Gareth adopted was Edith's?"

"Yes, Edith's. She'd risked everything for me and Steven," said Sarah, her eyes teary again. "And that made her a fugitive, too. George—Gareth—helped her disappear and start a new life like he'd done with the others, but he persuaded her to give her son to him."

"I don't—I don't understand," I said, gasping. "No one ever said anything about a baby. The newspapers never mentioned it."

"She was near the end of her pregnancy when she brought me here. Bad off as I was, I knew it that night in her house, as soon as I saw her. She was one of those tall, whippet-thin women, quite like you actually, the kind who can just about cover it up with clothes, even at the end. I expect most people couldn't even tell. But I'd just had a baby myself. I knew. I never said a word to her about it, but I knew."

"She delivered the baby here in this house?" said Dev.

"Yes. I didn't know until afterward because I was having a bad time that night. I wasn't aware of what was going on around me. But I saw the baby later, the next day. The prettiest little boy. Big dark eyes. I can still see his face. And the next night, when Gareth came here and talked to Edith, it was on the sofa you're sitting on right now. I was lucid then, lying in the next room, and I heard Gareth talk her into giving him the baby to raise."

"Poor Edith," said Dev.

"I can't believe it," I said, and then I was seeing her again in her gardening clogs and her blue dress; I was hearing her ringing voice: *Courage, dear heart.*

"No, actually I can believe it," I said. "It was Edith. Edith, all along. That's *why.* The wedding, the house, everything. That's why."

Sweet joy swept through me like a flock of birds, a murmuration of starlings, an exaltation of larks. Dev squeezed my hand.

"Gareth said something else that night," said Sarah.

"What?"

Her eyes gleamed, silver-blue as the silver-blue summer sky outside the kitchen window.

"Edith was crying, so bitterly, poor girl, and Gareth swore to her that he would take the best care in the world of her son. He told her that of course he would, of course, because the baby was his son, too."

Chapter Twenty-Six
Clare

Dev came to Edith's house early on an azure-soaked, gold-dusted, jade-green Friday evening in mid-August, and even though our plan had been to leave for North Carolina right away, as soon as he saw the canoes, he said, "Look at those. How can we not take them out?" with his own special brand of arms-thrown-open, face-to-the-wind, conspiratorial, little kid enthusiasm, and I said what I vowed from that day forward to always say to his proposals, however spontaneous or goofy or madcap or impractical, which was yes.

We glided through water that was sun-spangled steel blue from a distance and tea-colored up close. We wove, parting ways and coming back together, again and again. We talked and didn't talk. We startled birds and were startled by birds. We steered in single file through a narrow channel, the mussels gleaming like spilled oil on either side, our paddles brushing the feathery reeds and marsh grass, and then we slipped out into a wide-open pool edged with woods, where we drifted in a hot, hazy, rustling, bird-call-scattered quiet. I tipped back my head and let myself be entranced by the sky.

When I came back to earth, I saw Dev across the shining water, at least fifty yards away, and I understood that some things you decide and some things you choose and some things just are. Dev and I just were.

And then he was calling out, "Come over here and watch these water bugs with me. You know it's surface tension, but it still looks like a miracle," and I took up my paddle and, as fast as I could, even though the two of us had all the time in the world, I made my way to where he was.

When Edith departed from Canterbury Mills, she left behind her baby and her entire life and her name; by the time she got to the tiny town in western North Carolina, sixty miles outside of Asheville, that Gareth had found for her, Edith Herron had become Edith Waterland. When Thomas Farley got home and found Dev and me, Edith's granddaughter, sitting in his living room, he told us this; it was all he knew. After just a little Internet searching, Dev and I found her, not in the original town she'd been sent to, but in one just an hour's drive away. A town that was hardly a town at all, just a handful of houses near a lake. The fact of the lake made me happy: Edith Waterland near water, where she belonged. On the other side of the lake was a summer camp, and I imagined the campers' shouts and laughter winging like birds over the water to where Edith sat or hung laundry or read in a hammock in her yard. I hoped the sound of children was sweet to her; I hoped it didn't hurt. Apart from an address, we could find out nothing about her, and, after all my digging and sleuthing, my burning need to discover her complete story, I was at peace with the blank pages, all the missing chapters. I knew what I needed to know: Edith had loved my father enough to give him away; she had loved me enough to find me.

Still, I wanted to see her house. Just to see it, to stand and look at the place she had lived, her last safe place, although surely not her only one. Edith carried Blue Sky House with her wherever she went; I felt sure of it.

Dev showered while I packed the car. We would spend the night with our families in Charlottesville and then would drive the seven hours to Edith's house the next day. When our bags were in the trunk of Dev's car, I clipped some hydrangea blooms from the plants in Edith's garden, wrapped the stems in wet paper towels and aluminum foil, and walked out into the newly fallen dark. A few steps from the car, I heard not so much a sound as a shift in the night noises, and I turned to see a figure half stumble from the shadow of the dogwood tree in the front yard. Tall, broad shouldered, lurching toward me. A scream caught in my throat, and I dropped the flowers.

"Clare, goddamnit, it's me."

Zach. Drunk. Angry. His words slurring. Before he reached me, I stuck out my arm. He ran into my open hand and staggered backward.

"What the hell?" he said. "I thought you'd be glad to see me."

"How did you know I was here?" I asked.

He laughed. "I've known about this place for a while now. Your little love nest."

"How?"

"I've been staying at Ian's in Baltimore. Getting myself together, which is working out pretty well, as you can see." He made a bitter sound. "Ian hired someone to track you down."

Cold anger filled me. "*Hired* someone? That's sick, even for Ian."

Zach waved his hand in front of his face, dismissing what I'd said. "He hired a guy to watch your parents' house a few weeks ago, waiting for you to show up." In the dim light, I could see his face break into a grin. "And then, you know what?"

I kept silent.

"You did," said Zach. "Showed up with your pathetic little boyfriend and then went to Richmond with him to do God knows what, and then you came back here."

I thought of a stranger watching me open my front door, peering at me through windows, treading all over my sacred ground. I thought of the trip to Canada, of him trailing us all that way. I shuddered.

"And?" I asked, relieved when my voice came out hard instead of shaky.

Zach shrugged. "Since then I've been waiting for the right time. And this morning, I said to myself today's the day."

I felt relieved that the guy hadn't tracked us to Canada, but then I turned and saw Zach's car parked on the street.

"You drove here? In this state? You know you could've killed someone, right?"

Zach, who never so much as tailgated, who drove sixty miles per hour on the *highway.*

"That would've been on your head, Clare. Like everything else."

"You have to stop this craziness, Zach. Having me followed? Driving drunk? Hacking my Facebook page? This isn't you."

"You left me. Like my mother. Like Ro. *Women aren't supposed to leave!*" he shouted.

I had never had anyone look at me with such pure, black meanness in his eyes. I backed toward the car and groped for the door handle, but my fingers couldn't find it.

"Do you know what Ian told me about Ro this morning?" said Zach. "He helped her run away."

"What do you mean?"

"He helped her get away from my dad. Set up her escape to California, sent her money, helped cover her tracks. She swore to him she'd keep in touch and that she'd figure out a way for us all to be together again."

"Oh, my God," I said, realizing what he was saying. "Ian knew where she was all these years, and he let everyone believe she was dead?"

Zach shook his head. "For the first year, Ro kept

her promise. She stayed in touch with Ian, but then, she wrote to say she'd found someone who would help her leave the country. Duped some man into it, probably. She said she needed to cut herself off from her old life, all of it." He pounded his fist on his chest. "*Her old life.* She meant me! And Ian. We fucking loved her!"

"I'm sorry, Zach," I said.

"You're not sorry! You did the exact same thing." He stabbed his finger in my direction. "How do you think I will stand it? Knowing your life is going on away from me? Imagining you with other people when you were supposed to be with me?"

"Zach, please stop yelling at me. You're scaring me."

"Good!"

He didn't mean it. He was drunk, mad, hurt, and possibly mentally ill, but I knew the Zach who wanted to be good, who tried so hard, was still in there.

"Listen to me," I said. "This isn't you. Ian is the one who's full of hate and anger, and he wants you to be, too. That's why he told you this now, to feed your anger. Don't let him do that."

"Ian went all those years knowing that lying bitch was out there somewhere, living her life, being *happy.* She had no right to be happy. It killed Ian, ate him up." Zach ran his hand down his face. When he spoke again, his voice was quieter but scarier, flat and strange. "But you know what? Maybe she isn't. Maybe she isn't out there living like we never even existed. Maybe she's dead."

Zach took an unsteady step toward me, looming large, and I pressed back against the car, trapped. "God, I hope she's dead. If she died, that would balance things out. It would make things fair, don't you think?"

Suddenly, Dev was there, standing behind Zach, looking surprised, his hair still wet from the shower.

"I don't know what's happening here," he said in a low voice. "But it needs to end."

Zach whirled around so fast he almost fell. "You! Shut the hell up!" he shouted.

He turned back to me and took me roughly by the shoulders. "Him. Jesus Christ, it's always been him. You left me because of him."

"Let her go," said Dev.

"No," I said to Zach, and then, without planning to say it, I said, "and also yes."

Zach twitched backward, as if I'd struck him, snatching his hands off my shoulders. "*What?*"

I pulled myself up straighter. I would tell the truth. No more lies about Dev to myself or to anyone else. "It *has* always been him. But I didn't realize it; I didn't really, really know it, until today."

Zach pressed his hands to the sides of his head and said, "How can you say this to me?"

"I owe it to you not to lie to you. I need you to understand, once and for all. Dev isn't the reason I broke off our engagement. I didn't choose him over you. *We're* the reason I ended it. We don't belong together. I could never live my life with you. It would be wrong."

Zach stood, his head hanging down, and then, suddenly, with a guttural, animal snarl, he spun and charged Dev, knocked into him, his shoulder ramming Dev's chest, and Dev fell backward onto the grass. I thought he would leap on Dev then, and I got ready to pounce, to jump in and help, but then Zach was coming at me instead, wild-eyed, arms flailing, and I balled my fists, ready to hit him, energy surging through me, even though I had never hit anyone in my life. But he was reeling, off balance, and Dev was up and on him, grabbing him around the chest, holding him back, Zach twisting and turning, trying to free himself.

"You don't want to do this," said Dev, panting out the words.

"The hell I don't," sputtered Zach.

"You don't want to hurt Clare."

As if Dev's words were a bucket of cold water thrown over his head, Zach stopped struggling. He shook himself and stared at me, stunned, breathing hard. "Hurt Clare? I wouldn't. I wouldn't. I would never hurt her."

Dev loosened his grip, and Zach turned sideways and

crouched in the grass, where he rocked, his fists pressed against his eyes. "What am I doing? What am I doing?"

Dev and I stood watching him. It was as if a space had opened up in the jumble and noise of the night, a doomed, sad empty space with Zach right at the center of it. I thought I'd never seen someone so alone.

"Zach," I said, gently.

"I'm sorry." He stood up, his back to us, and began walking to his car, fumbling in his pocket for his keys. "I'll go. I'll go and I won't come back."

"You can't drive," I told him.

"No, I can. I'll be fine," said Zach. But when he got to the car, he just stood there with the keys in his hand. I walked up and opened his fingers and took them.

"Come on," said Dev. "Let's go inside. You look tired."

Slowly, Zach turned around. "I am tired," he said.

"We'll go inside and call Ian," I told him. "He'll come pick you up."

"Okay," said Zach, nodding wearily. "Okay, okay, okay, okay."

I took Zach's arm and together, with Dev a few steps behind us, keeping watch, we walked into Blue Sky House.

Chapter Twenty-Seven
Clare

The next morning, when Dev and I were in the car on our way to North Carolina, Zach called.

"I'm sorry about last night," he said.

"I'm sorry I hurt you in all the ways I did," I said.

"It's okay. Or maybe it's not totally okay, yet, but it will be. I know you didn't want to hurt me. You did what you had to do."

"That's true."

"You were right that I'm not like Ian. I can't let myself turn into a man like him, angry all the time. He let Ro's leaving wreck him. I think I wanted you to save me from being like him."

"I don't think I could have done that, no matter how much I would have wanted to."

"I don't know. Maybe not. Maybe I need to do it

myself. I know I need to get rid of all this bitterness. And after last night, I feel less mad, so there's that."

"That's a start," I said. "A *good* start."

"But I need to get rid of my hope, too. About us, I mean." He paused and took a breath. "So I'm asking once and for all: Is there any hope for us?"

I waited for the urge to reassure him, to say whatever would make him happy, but it didn't come. "No," I said.

I heard him exhale. "Ouch. But okay. I won't wait for you, then, not even in the back of my mind."

"I'm rooting for you, though," I said. "I always will be."

"Thanks." He gave a wry laugh. "Maybe one day, I'll be able to say the same about you."

"I'll understand if you can't," I said.

"Yeah, but I probably will."

"Knowing you," I said, smiling.

"Hey, you know what else?"

"What?"

"I feel less mad at Ro, too. I didn't really see that coming, but it's true."

"I'm glad."

"Who knows? I might even look for her."

"Good luck, Zach," I said.

"Good-bye, Clare," said Zach.

We couldn't see Edith's house from the curvy, pothole-pocked, wood-lined country road, so we parked the car near her mailbox, and I held Dev's hand, and we walked together down the long gravel driveway. The driveway was narrow, barely one car wide, and the trees stood so thick on both sides that we walked through a twilight dimness. As we got closer, I could see radiant glimpses of green lawn and the aluminum foil shine of the lake through the trees, and just before we got to the spot where the gravel gave way to grass and the world filled with light, Dev said, "It's always been you, too."

I smiled and pressed a kiss onto the smooth back of his hand, and we broke free from the trees and were standing in Edith's yard, dazzled by sun and by the glittering water, and by just being together and there. I might have stood all day with Dev, breathless, blinking in the light, prickles sparking along the insides of my arms, but a dog started barking, and Dev pointed toward the house and said, "Look."

The house was small and modern, all honey-colored wood and windows, with a stone chimney and a deck wrapping around. An old green Jeep Cherokee was parked on the grass behind it. The front of the house faced the water, but from where we stood, I could see what I thought must be the kitchen door, a screen door at which bounced and spun a white barking mop of dog. For one crazy second, I thought, *She's here. Edith is alive after all and she has a dog.*

"Someone's home," said Dev.

"I guess someone bought the house after Edith died. Of course, that would have happened," I said.

"Why don't we knock?" said Dev. "Maybe the people living here would let us take a look around."

We walked around the side of the house, climbed the deck steps, and knocked on the front door.

A man answered, elderly, tall and thin, with the kind of pure white hair you know used to be blond. He wore khaki pants, white sneakers, and a plaid shirt with the sleeves rolled up.

"Hello?" he said and before we could say anything else, the polite smile faded from his face, and, in a hushed voice, he uttered the most amazing thing: "You're Clare." Then, looking at Dev, he said, "And I'm betting you're Dev."

"You're right," I said, awestruck. "But how did you know?"

The man stepped out onto the deck and offered me his hand to shake.

"My name is John," he said.

"She wanted to come back to Antioch Beach so that she could visit me," he told us.

Dev and I sat on a leather sofa in John's house, the beamed ceiling soaring above us and the butter-yellow sunlight flooding in on three sides. Fitzy, the dog, sat at my feet.

"But even though by then the police had stopped looking for her, I worried that if she came back, they'd have no choice but to at least bring her in for questioning. She had her fresh start, hard won as it was, and I wanted her to keep it. But she wrote me every week for four years, and even though she wasn't with me, she *was*. Just knowing she was out there, waiting for me, made me less alone. When I got out of prison, I packed up everything I owned and came to find her."

He leaned back in his chair, looked around at the walls covered with beautiful black-and-white photographs, and sadness crossed his face like the shadow of clouds passing over water. He smiled. "We were married fifty-three years."

"I'm so sorry for your loss," I said.

"Me, too," said Dev.

"Thank you," said John. "We knew when she got diagnosed that she didn't have long, just six months or so, and she decided she wanted to find you before she died. We plotted and schemed, and then she found the engagement announcement with your wedding date in some online newspaper, and it all fell into place."

"Why do you think she didn't just tell Clare who she was?" asked Dev.

John cocked his head, thinking.

"I'm not so sure. She did promise Gareth she'd never get in touch with Martin, and not because Gareth made her promise. She wanted Martin to be happy, not to be torn between two sets of parents. She never stopped missing him, not for a single day, and she just kept up with him from afar as best she could. His death hit her hard. It was a dark day when we found out about that. Afterward, she kept up with you, Clare."

"I'm glad," I said. "I'm so glad."

"You know, even though she'd made that promise, she might have told you who she was the weekend of your wedding. She didn't go there with a plan, but she said she might tell you. So many years had gone by—decades—since she'd made that promise. But then she found you and talked to you and decided to leave you Blue Sky House instead."

Slowly, I nodded. "I think I understand that," I said.

"You broke off your engagement, I guess," said John, with a grin.

"I did. It was the right thing. Edith is the one who helped me see that."

"She thought you would."

"How did you know Dev was Dev?" I asked.

John's eyes twinkled. "Edith told me she met Dev and saw you two together. In my experience, Edith's faith is almost never misplaced, and she said she had faith that you'd find your way home."

We talked for hours, until all the windows went dark. John told us about Edith's job as a nurse at the camp in the summertime and about how, using just the initials E.H.W., she sold her photographs in galleries, sometimes for breathtaking sums of money. He told us how he'd trained to become an accountant in prison and how, after all that had happened, spending his days in the cool, abstract company of numbers was a relief. He had changed his last name to Smith when he left Antioch Beach and kept it even after he and Edith got married.

"But that was only on paper," he said. "In our private, everyday lives, we went by the same name."

Edith and John had spent the last nearly five and a half decades being John and Edith Waterland.

When we were leaving, he hugged me and kissed me on the temple and asked us to please keep in touch, to come back anytime. I told him that he was my grandfather, the only one I had ever had, and that I wasn't about to let go of him.

Afterward, when Dev and I were sitting in the car, just before we left Edith and John's house, Dev said, "You told John you thought you understood why Edith just gave you her house without telling you who she was. Do you think she knew what would happen?"

"I only know what I feel," I said. "I feel like she knew everything. Like she made everything happen, every single thing leading up to right now, this very moment."

"The two of us sitting in this car together in front of her house?"

"Yes."

"And what about the next moment and the one after that?" asked Dev, twining his fingers in my hair.

I recognized the excitement billowing in his voice, as if our future together would be the most fun in the world, one adventure after the next. Who was I to resist excitement like that?

Oh, this here and now, this particular snapshot fragment of forever. Dev talking to me, his face lighting up the darkness: one more thing to carry, to bring with me wherever I went.

"I think she would say the rest is up to us," I said.

Acknowledgments

My heartfelt thanks to the following:

Jennifer Carlson, my above-and-beyond agent, for her brilliance, friendship, and faith in my work (even when my own falters);

Jennifer Brehl, my lovely editor, for her dead-on instincts and uncanny ear for language;

all the extraordinary folks at William Morrow, especially Andrew DiCecco; Lynn Grady; Jennifer Hart; Kaitlyn Kennedy; Tavia Kowalchuk; Nate Lanman; Andy LeCount, Carla Parker, Mary Beth Thomas, and the entire sales team; Bonni Leon-Berman; Elsie Lyons; Laurie McGee; Julia Meltzer; and Liate Stehlik;

Carolyn Ring, who gave me invaluable help in researching 1950s life (and museums and laws and beach towns and hairstyles);

my friends, who rescue me with conversation over and over, especially Lynda Arai, Karen Ballotta Garman, Sherry Brilliant, Maureen Buzdygon, Mark Caughey, Susan Davis, Susie Davis, Susan Finizio, Linda Jaworski, Theresa Proud, and Karen Taormina;

Mary and Arturo de los Santos, for being a sanctuary all my life;

my dogs, Huxley and Finny, twelve pounds of pure sunshine;

Charles and Annabel, who crack me up, fill me with wonder, and are my blue sky every single second;

and, as always, David Teague, my best everything and the one who has looked like home to me from the very first day.